Totally Bound Publishing books by Deana Birch

Single Books
Love Repaired

The Covington Heights Crew
Escape

With Amelia Foster

Single Books
Luca's Lessons

I0680722

The Covington Heights Crew

ESCAPE

DEANA BIRCH

Escape

ISBN # 978-1-83943-911-7

©Copyright Deana Birch 2020

Cover Art by Louisa Maggio ©Copyright September 2020

Interior text design by Claire Siemaszkiewicz

Totally Bound Publishing

ESCAPE

Dedication

For Deana's Divas,
Let the Book Boyfriend games begin!

Chapter One

Fiona

The dark gray grime around the rim of the tub would not go away, no matter how hard I scrubbed. I flipped my long ponytail over my shoulder and sprayed the foaming cleaner into the corner where tile met porcelain. While my efforts would bear no fruit, I couldn't stop. If I could just make our dirty apartment shine, there might be hope for our lives.

The baby whimpered then wailed from her crib in the back bedroom, and I stored the worn-down green sponge and the bottle that promised gleaming effects on top of the medicine cabinet, rinsed my hands in the sink and went to tend to Violet.

Her sobs quickly morphed into coos once she was in my arms and I'd shushed her with an easy bounce and kiss on her sweaty head. Even though she could walk, I carried her to the kitchen, and I wasn't surprised to see that my mother had not left any milk. After a diaper change—at least we had those—I packed Violet into her wobbly stroller and rode the slow, rickety elevator down to the ground floor of our apartment building. The florescent light flickered over the beat-up metal mailboxes as we crossed the depressing lobby.

The sun shone bright and blinded me for a quick second. The weather had two gears, hot or storms. And while the storms were a relief from the heat, the wind and rain that came with them didn't make running errands easy. I navigated the stroller through the cracking cement of the courtyard, careful not to step on anything sharp or deadly with my flimsy sandals.

Predictably, the Covington Heights crew were huddled around their bench across from the run-down park—all in their signature black jeans, which must have been torture in the heat. In three months, their numbers had doubled and I was sure it could officially be considered a gang. I recognized a couple of them from their lives before they'd decided to become delinquents. I was even sure the tallest one had been a star basketball player in his day. And, while their matching pants unified them, the physical similarities stopped there. Blonds, shaven heads, dark hair in a man bun... They were all different in race and creed.

Internal groan. I was brewing a perfect stew of resentment, hate and disgust for those fuckers—and maybe just a pinch of lust. *Ripped asshats.* They were like a calendar spread for hot bad boys.

Their business was an endless supply of drugs that fed my mother's meth habit, and groupies drooled around them like they were rock stars. *Gross.*

But they were also an anomaly. As long as you called Covington Heights home, they kept you safe, client or not. And for that, I gave them my respect.

Maybe it had been my odd hours that had kept me off their radar—the sole benefit of working the night shift. Not to mention, the maid's smock and comfortable shoes I had to wear to work hadn't done much to make me stand out. Or perhaps I was just too old for their tastes. Their female hangers-on didn't exactly look over eighteen—not that it was any of my business. And not that I had been paying attention.

But the whispers I had heard about them weren't all horrible. Girls had sworn they were harmless, a notion I couldn't quite swallow, knowing their primary source of income.

Violet sucked her thumb in the stroller below me. I lowered my head and picked up my pace to pass by the group of drug-dealing male models.

"Hey, little mama," a dark-haired guy with a black tank top over his muscled chest called. "Where you been hiding?"

Great. I'd officially bleeped on their screen. *Fuck.*

I let out a slow breath before turning with a wry smile. "Been here all my life, big boy." And a big boy he was. He had almost a head on me. It was best to ignore his olive skin and dark inviting eyes below thick brows. I kept walking.

"Hey!" Black Tank Muscle Man stepped in front of the stroller and my breath hitched.

I met his gaze, and even though my spine was like an iron rod, I softened. "I'm just trying to get some milk. I don't want any trouble." And I certainly wasn't interested in being their customer. With my thumbs hooked on the handle and a hopeful smile, I opened the rest of my fingers in a small surrender then clasped the stroller again.

Black Tank's eyes traveled the length of my body and he licked his plump lips that looked like the softest thing on him. Jesus, he dripped danger and sex at the same time. *Those two ingredients should not be allowed to mix.*

He jutted his clean-shaven chin toward the stroller. "This your baby?"

I should have lied. Single moms were probably less appealing to someone like him, but for whatever reason — maybe fear of being caught by one of the crew that did know me — I told him the truth. "It's my sister. Please let us pass. She needs her milk."

He stood his ground, staring at me for a long beat. I couldn't tell if he was mind- or eye-fucking me, but there was nothing pure about the vibes he was sending, of that I was sure. A lump grew in my throat and I wouldn't allow myself to try to swallow past it. I was a girl who'd grown up in the projects. I knew damn well that if you gave an inch to a bully, they would take a whole damn mile.

After one more glance at my chest, which made me hate the boob fairy who'd given me D cups, he stepped to the side. The tension from my back released and I pushed Violet to the deli. There wasn't a doubt in my mind that those menacing dark eyes followed me the whole way.

On the return trip, his electric, wicked energy stalked me, haunted my every step. Yeah, I was officially on the radar and had no idea why or how to disappear from it. It was only once I'd closed the door to our apartment on the seventh floor, gotten Violet her milk and turned on her favorite program that I allowed myself to shudder in the corner of our tattered brown couch.

What was worse was that I couldn't make heads or tails of it. The hard truth was that I'd liked his attention, even though I was sure I hated him and all he stood for. At least I wasn't stupid enough to trust him. But, to be fair, I didn't trust anyone — an addict for a parent could do that to a girl — and, yeah, Black Tank certainly did not have take-you-out-to-dinner-and-buy-you-flowers ideas forming in his beautifully dark eyes.

I made Violet a peanut butter sandwich with our last two pieces of bread and cut an apple that we shared as I ate instant oatmeal. While the clock ticked closer and closer to when I needed to leave for work, it came — the instinctual awareness that my mom would be late coming home…again. And therefore *I* would be late for work…again.

I cleaned the small mess we'd made from eating — I didn't think what I'd done could qualify as cooking — and I sat with my uniform on, ready to bolt out of the door.

Over the years, it had been a sad and constant element of my life. When she was late, I usually knew why, and I was sure that this time would be no different. The door finally opened thirty minutes after I'd needed to leave and her skinny, fidgeting frame walked through. Every ounce of my being hated leaving Violet with my mom while she was high, but if I didn't work, we would be worse off than we already were, and I didn't want to imagine what that might look like.

My mom ignored me and went straight to the kitchen, where she took out a glass and filled it from the tap.

Fighting with her, high or sober, was a battle I'd surrendered to in high school, so I hid my sigh and stood.

In the calmest voice I could muster, I asked, "Can I have the phone, please? I need to let work know I'm running late."

She darted her bloodshot eyes around the room, looking anywhere but at me. As she twisted her lips, I understood that the phone was gone—either lost, stolen or sold. *Great.*

"Right," I said with a knowing nod. "I'll be back for breakfast."

Her guilty conscience must have been keeping her from both eye contact and speaking, because she turned her back to me and drank the rest of her water. I hurried out of the door and flew down the seven flights of stairs instead of waiting for the elevator. It was all I could do not to run through the courtyard and down the three streets to the subway station, where I was lucky enough to catch a train, my heart still thumping in my chest.

At the stop in Midtown that led to the hotel where I worked, I hurried up the stairs, retying my long hair into a tighter ponytail as I went. I entered the side door in the alley for employees and hauled ass down the stairs to the locker room where we kept our personal belongings.

The cold LED lighting was a bright contrast to the dark basement, and I had to blink several times to adjust my eyes. But once I'd focused, I saw my supervisor sitting on the bench in front of the row of mint green metal lockers.

Fuck.

"Fiona." He crossed his arms and frowned. Sweat puddled around his thinning blond hair. Carrying around his massive stomach must have been a lot of work.

"I know." I brought my hands together in a plea and slumped. "I'm so sorry. I'd love to say it won't happen again, but my mom—"

He held up his chubby hand that looked more like a ball of dough with five short, fat sausages sticking out of it. "You're fired."

My chest contracted at the loss of oxygen.

"No, no, no, no, no. *Please*." I needed to make him understand. Me losing that job wasn't just a paycheck. It was our livelihood. The government didn't hand out checks to addicts anymore. The only thing we had for security was the shitty apartment, because no one in their right mind would want to live in our neighborhood.

A neighborhood where the police rarely made an appearance... A neighborhood where criminals ruled with wicked eyes, iron fists and where they openly exploited the addictions of their own... Where girls gave up hope of leaving and settled into worshiping drug dealers because instant gratification was more attainable than a long-term plan...

No. I needed this job. I had a fucking dream to get the fuck out of Covington Heights. Roly Poly on the bench in front of me did not understand what he was doing to me and my sister.

"Mr. Hansen...please." There was no need to fake the tears streaming down my face and I hoped my trembling bottom lip would show him how desperate I was. I tapped my fingers on my cheeks as I searched his mole-like eyes for any hint of sympathy. There was none.

"I'm sorry, Fiona. If I can't keep my cleaners in line then it's me without a job. I've been warned about being too lenient. I can't stick my neck out on the line for you or anybody else. It's nothing personal."

For him, maybe. For me, it was everything—and definitely personal.

I clasped my hands together and begged. "I'll work overtime for free, I promise. I'll...I'll..." I would do what? The hope of convincing him slipped away as he shook his head.

He pushed into his tight gray slacks and stood. "No exceptions. I have to set an example. You show up late and you lose your job. It's not like this was the first time."

"I'm sorry, but I need this job more than anything. *Please*."

His keys jangled on his belt loop as he wobbled toward the door. "You can pick up your paycheck on the fifteenth."

"Wait. You don't even want me to do my shift?"

"'Fraid not. Gotta set the tone. The others will have to work harder without you here." His voice trailed off as he walked down the hall. I stood there, gazing at the empty doorway, my skin tingling and my head spinning, for what seemed like hours.

Somehow I left, found my way back to the subway and plopped down in an empty seat on the train. It was like walking in a hazy nightmare. I officially had nothing — no job, soon enough no money and no way out of Covington Heights. Hell, folding endless numbers of sheets and towels had been a nice escape from the projects.

The repetitive beat of the train drowned out the voice in my head telling me I was meant to fail, reminding me that change could never happen to a girl like me and that no matter how hard I clawed to get out of a hole, my filthy passage would never end.

I'd developed an ability to go deep, deep inside when I had been a little girl. I could drown out my setting by closing my eyes and repeating my favorite mantra. *Don't cry, Fiona.* So that was exactly what I did on the train ride home.

In my sacred quiet spot, I reminded myself of the bigger goal—not letting Violet have the same fate as me. I needed to give that little sweetheart a better life, despite our circumstances. I could do it if I just stayed focused. We would *not* end up like our mother.

The calm of my mind settled me. Sure, losing my job would be a setback, but it wasn't a death sentence. Maybe I could figure out a trade with the blonde girl I'd seen at the park a few times who watched other people's kids. Hell, maybe she needed some help.

With a new sense of purpose, I opened my eyes.

Shit.

I was officially two stops past my normal one. And it wasn't like I could just swipe my card and ride back down. Without a paycheck, each fare would be precious until I found a new source of income. I would have to walk the twenty blocks south, which wasn't a big deal. It wasn't like I had somewhere to be, except for *where* I had to get off the train. The neighborhood north of Covington was somehow worse than where I lived. *Shit.*

The train screeched to a halt and I wobbled a bit with my footing before the doors rattled open. I hitched my bag over my shoulder and climbed the urine-stenched stairs. On the street, Bradford Towers loomed over me. It was a funny thing about the projects. They were basically all the same—giant concrete buildings with a courtyard and a park.

They even had their own drug dealers. But instead of the black jeans that the hottie criminals in Covington Heights wore, the BTs were all bald and wore oversized white T-shirts. And they didn't exactly have the code of 'protect your own' that we enjoyed in Covington. The

BTs had a reputation for loving to be cruel, and I'd had a taste of it in high school when a guy who I'd thought was my boyfriend had really wanted to be my pimp. He'd played an evil game with my lonely heart and I considered myself lucky to have realized what he really wanted before he'd used my body like he'd warped my mind.

I avoided the congregation of BTs out of the corner of my eye. I'd already had my gang run-in for the day, thanks very much. I picked up my pace and swore at myself for being so stupid that I'd missed my stop. Worse, I'd risked my safety for the cost of a train ride, but there was no way I would head back underground, I would be trapped if they saw me. If *he* saw me.

"You lost, mama?" A taunting voice called out. I seemed to be on everyone's radar today. *Fuck.* If they figured out I was from Covington, I would be either raped or beaten. Of that, I was sure. And if Justin caught a glimpse of me? I would be both. I broke out in a sweat, half from my quick movements and half from my racing heart, which felt like it had transplanted to my throat. I sped up and glanced over my shoulder. Two of the BTs were headed in my direction with wicked, crooked grins on their ugly faces.

"Hey, J.D.! Isn't this your Fiona, all grown up?"
No, no, no!
Normally I was a fan of tattoos on men, but the ink on the guys from Bradford Towers screamed the worst kind of danger. One of them had a black, evil-looking something on his cheek and my stomach flipped in fear. With one block between us, my only hope was to run.

I pumped my legs at a pace I didn't know I was capable of, not wasting time or breath to apologize to pedestrians who wouldn't stop the BTs behind me. No one wanted trouble from them. The setting sun flashed between the tall buildings with each street I passed.

I didn't even feel guilty as I shoved an old woman out of the way ten blocks into my sprint. I was halfway home and I could see the Covington Heights roofs — a tiny glimmer of hope.

But the two bald fucks — and now fucking Justin — were gaining on me, and my one-block advantage was shrinking. My bag banged against my back with every step and my muscles burned with the overuse. But I had to keep going.

The tightness in my chest made it hard for oxygen to reach my lungs and I was sure I was panting. I crossed an intersection and barely missed getting hit by a car, a fate preferable to getting caught.

Five more blocks.

I whipped around a corner, giving me a clear view of the courtyard. The irony of wanting to be in Covington when all I'd ever wanted was to get away wouldn't slow me down.

The realization of where I was headed must have motivated the assholes behind me, because they'd narrowed my lead to a quarter of the block.

Each time my foot landed on the cracked concrete, pain shot up my leg. Buildings and people passed by like a blurred rainbow and I allowed myself to believe I might just make it.

I focused in on the crew. They were around their normal bench with a few girls hanging on — the sight of the previously loathed a bitter pill of relief. With sweat dripping down my back, my heart thumping and my adrenaline flowing full speed, I screamed, "Help!"

Black Tank Muscle Man from earlier in the day whipped around, clocked the BTs behind me, smacked the Male Model drug dealer to his left and relief washed over me as they bolted in my direction.

I didn't dare look over my shoulder, but when the two men in black jeans coming at me slowed to a jog, I knew I was safe.

Don't cry, Fiona.

As I huffed and willed air into my aching lungs, I bent over and pushed into my knees in hopes of not collapsing.

Black Tank crossed his arms, licked his plump lips and looked down at me. "How?" he asked and raised a thick eyebrow.

"I..." I let out some slow breaths, willing my heart rate to lower. I was safe. I'd made it. I swallowed and the moisture coated my dry throat. "I got off at the wrong stop."

The hottie with the amber eyes next to Black Tank laughed and said, "I'll allow you to explain it to her, Leo, but if it's cash, I get a cut. My bad ass scared off those pussies too." He gave me the once-over, winked and jogged back to his crew.

Leo narrowed his dark eyes and I wondered if they were more dangerous than the bald shits he'd just scared away. He cleared his throat. "I wasn't really interested in whatever foolish position you got yourself into to be chased down the streets by rapist human traffickers. You're welcome, by the way." A fake smile spread on his stupidly attractive face. "However, I *do* want to know how, exactly, you plan on repaying us for saving you."

Oh, he was a fucking asshole...and smug...and a total dick.

"I—"

Leo made a grand gesture of shaking his head. "Don't even try and sell me some stupid shit about how you didn't ask. You literally yelled out the word 'help'."

He had to be joking. I owed them something for running a block in my direction? *Fuck him.* Weren't they all about keeping their own safe? I snarled and he smiled, a real one. It had no business making him more attractive—and I was a fool for thinking so.

"Come on," he said and put his bare arm around my shoulder. He smelled like the kind of soap that only came from a bar. "You're lucky. The bossman's in town. You can negotiate our fee directly with him."

Chapter Two

Leo

The day was turning out to be a fucking beauty. Not only had Golden Boy figured out some online shit that was beyond my scope of understanding, but whatever he had hacked had already started generating money on the virtual black market. Then the hottie I'd been checking out since I'd gotten to Covington had run right toward me, screaming to be rescued.

Bonus of the day? Those Bradford Tower idiots had taken one look at me and Golden Boy and run in the other fucking direction. They knew who I was—or at least they'd heard what I was capable of. No one but the bossman actually knew *who* I was, which was A-fucking-okay by me.

The crew sent catcalls as I ushered the little brunette past them. There was only one way she could pay us back, and I'd bet they'd also seen through her boring-ass uniform and imagined the perfect curves awaiting underneath as many times as I had. The glimpse I'd gotten earlier in the day had my imagination running fucking wild.

It was pretty cute how she'd tried to push my arm off her shoulder and sworn at me under her breath. Did she know what she'd gotten herself into? *Probably not.* Did I give a flying fuck? *Nope.* Was that cold and cruel? Maybe, but I was born a criminal. My moral compass had been smashed into a million pieces before I'd had the pleasure of taking my first steps.

I opened the clanky glass door of Covington Heights Two and gave the little hottie a 'gentle' nudge to step inside. She stumbled a little and swatted my hand away. I smiled as I pressed the button to call the elevator. I was a sucker for feisty.

"Ever been to the third floor before?" I asked, more serious than I felt.

She glared at me and propped her hands on her gorgeous hips that were in harmonious proportion to her insanely perfect-sized tits. Fucking hell, angry suited the shit out of her. I could have licked that flush right off her pale cheeks.

She scrunched her nose in full disgust and I wondered if steam might blow out of her ears like in a cartoon. It was hard to hold back my laugh.

She ground out, "Why the fuck would I go to the third floor? My mom is a fucking junkie. The last place on earth you will find me is asking for any of your fucking product, you miserable prick."

Steaming hot—every last curve and hair on her pissed-off body. It really was a banner day.

But, in fairness, I *was* a prick. However, I was the farthest thing from miserable. And not just because the grumbling beauty in front of me was going to probably go ballistic when Anton explained the terms of our payment plan, but also because I had escaped a destiny that I did not want.

For the three months I'd been living in Covington, I'd made my own unattached money and become a part of something greater than just family. I'd made friends — real friends, casual friends, small-nod-on-the-street-as-a-sign-of-respect friends. And unlike those stupid fucks in Bradford, none of our crew used drugs. Sure, we'd kick back a beer at the end of a poker game we'd hosted or get a little drunk after one of our fights, but absolutely none of us were addicts.

We all worked out at least once a day, either with weights or sparring. We ate real fucking food and, yeah, we sold drugs and hosted back-door dice and card games — but we had some limits. No raping, for example. That was a big no-no for Anton. His mom had been the leader of their crime family for years, and not abusing women had been drilled into Anton for as long as I'd known him. It might have been our only virtue.

The elevator dinged and the little hottie's mouth fell open. Yeah, the third floor didn't look like any of the others. With sleek and polished concrete and the dark wooden doors to the suites, it resembled a luxury hotel instead of the projects.

"To the left." I thumbed the direction and watched that fine ass exit in front of me. I bet she didn't realize that she was half as gorgeous as she was. It wasn't like someone with her life could afford make-up or nice things. But with her long dark hair, smoking little body, perfectly thin nose and high cheek bones, she was a bona-fide beauty. I had to swallow down the fucking drool as she stomped down the hall.

In front of the last door on the left, I typed in the security code, and after the small buzz of the unlocking mechanism, I pushed through. Anton sat at the counter and his steel blue eyes scrutinized me, then her. He sat perfectly still, giving away nothing, which almost made me laugh, because I knew exactly what he was thinking.

The rebellious spark the brunette had boasted in the hallway flickered out with the bossman's silent power. Her shoulders fell and her eyes widened. Anton was thicker than me, just a little shorter and way fucking crueler than I was. She seemed to understand that in just the small twinkle of his light eyes.

She turned to me and chewed her bottom lip. Yeah, I was the safer option—which, when put into perspective, was downright hilarious. I walked over to Anton and slapped him on the back.

"Anton, meet... What's your name, anyway?" I licked my lips slowly.

A bit of her fight came back with a glare. "Fiona."

I continued, "Meet Fiona. She owes us for protection."

Without taking his eyes off Fiona, Anton said, "Well, isn't she lucky. BTs?"

"Chased her all the way home. But Goldie and I scared them off. Fucking pussies. I could have used a good fight."

Anton glanced at me, but in that fraction of a second, it spoke volumes. I always needed a good fight. The beast inside me was malnourished, starving for the real deal.

But Fiona would understand nothing of our exchange. He sat back on his bar stool and interlaced his fingers behind his head. "Let's go ahead and assume that since this is home, you can't pay us for our protection. And let me tell you something you probably haven't realized yet. You are now on the top of their list. The minute they catch you alone, they'll nab you."

"Let me tell you something *you* don't know," she grumbled. "I already *was* at the top of their list."

Say what?

Anton remained unfazed. "Explain."

Fiona shook her head, maybe disappointed in herself. "One of them…Justin… He…bullied me in high school. Tried to get me to work for him, if you know what I mean."

"How'd you get away?" I asked and Anton shot me a glance. Yes, he was supposed to be the one doing the questioning. I was forever forgetting my place as number two.

"I didn't. He went to jail, and by the time he got out, I wasn't in school anymore, and since I live here, he didn't have access to me."

"Then you really do need us." Anton's wicked grin spread easily across his face. *Too easily.*

A nicer group of people might have showed her some sympathy. But forgiveness and leniency weren't exactly traits of effective criminals. The smallest fraction of decency I had left in my heart empathized with her, but she'd known where she'd gotten off the train. She'd grown up on these streets. There was no mystery as to what was happening in Bradford Towers.

The problem was that those idiots were shortsighted. The more they raped and sold women, the fewer there were around—either by force or by fear—which meant fewer customers and less income. Bradford Towers was becoming a ghost town of single men, and their income depended on their cruelest of intentions, which was why they had started picking off girls who were out of their territory. And to show that we were stronger, we *had* to keep our ladies safe.

There was a silent pause where the new information had sunk into Fiona's being. For as much of a prick as I was, relishing in her spirit-breaking wasn't my thing. What Anton said next was proof that there was more ice in his veins than mine, that his brutality was more acute than my own.

He asked, "So, that begs the question, Fiona. How do you plan to pay for your protection?"

She fluttered those damn lovely eyes with hope that should have been murdered with her upbringing. "I can clean. That's what I was doing before I got fired. Laundry, ironing, you name it."

"You got fired from cleaning?" Anton crossed his arms and shrugged. "I'm not sure that gives you a glowing referral." His energy shifted to the spooky calm. I didn't even need to see his eyes to know the glaze was there. Slowly, he asked, "What can you give me that makes this arrangement beneficial to both of us?"

The desperation washed off her face and was replaced by total comprehension. Her little nostrils flared and her cheeks flushed a deep pink. Yeah, she was pissed again. I had to admit that it was fun to watch.

Fiona scoffed. "You expect me to fuck you for protection? Is that why you have all those other chicks fawning all over you?"

Anton shot me a look. He wasn't around as much as I was and it was true that some girls had started hanging out by the bench. It wouldn't be something he liked for business. I'd known I should have put the kibosh on it but hadn't wanted the headache of the bitching from Scooter and Jackson. Bossman wouldn't bring it up in front of Fiona, but I'd hear about it the minute we were alone.

Fiona, bless her angry beating heart, snarled at Anton. "How, exactly, is this different from rape? You're forcing me to have sex."

It was my turn to talk. Anton and I had a solid game of good criminal-bad criminal. He gladly passed me the download mic.

Trying to hide my smugness, I said, "Well, as it turns out, that's where you have a little bit of an advantage. You see, fucking is a lot more fun when all parties are interested. Normally, we don't have that problem, so you'll just have to solve that bit yourself."

Fiona's eyes scrutinized us both in an offsetting ping-pong. "Well, that's going to be a bit of a challenge, because I already hate you both," she said with such vigor that I had to fight my smirk.

Anton laughed and stood. "See her home and come back. I'm going upstate tonight." After a sardonic smile to Fiona, he walked down the hall to his room.

I fake-frowned. "I save your life and you hate me? I'd call that pretty fucking ungrateful."

Fiona turned and headed for the door. With her hand on the knob, she said, "You tricked me."

I stepped in and crowded her space, and I didn't imagine that she shivered. Even with no make-up and a sweat-stained face, she was beyond pretty. I tried to be gentle, though it wasn't in my nature. My soft side was a thorn bush for a normal person. "You asked for help. I gave it. You grew up here. You know that nothing in life is free."

"You're no better than those bald fucks. You prey on the weak to make yourself look strong."

I resisted the urge to touch what was sure to be satin skin. God, she was going to be the most interesting thing that had happened to me in Covington Heights. I welcomed the challenge more than she'd ever know.

Deana Birch

Because, while I liked the crew and the escape from my former life, I was bored. Tormenting Fiona was officially my new hobby.

With all the gentleness gone from my voice and gaze, I narrowed my eyes. "I can drop you off at their corner and you can see for yourself."

"Fuck you."

I leaned in and whispered in her ear. "That's the point, little mama."

Her chest rose and fell against mine, and if I cut through all her bravado, I was sure I'd find heat. And, for fuck's sake, her tits grazing my chest with her angry huffs was heaven. My dick even twitched to life.

But I had shit to do and orders to follow. I stepped back and painted a smug expression on my face. "Come on."

She opened the door and marched down the hall. Fiona jabbed the button to the elevator several times. When I caught up to her, she said, "I don't need an escort to go up four floors."

"Just doing what I'm told." I studied the little dark hairs on her nape. I bet she had a spot somewhere there that would make her squirm and melt.

The elevator clunked open and we boarded. I pressed the round button with the seven in the middle.

Fiona's eyes widened. "You know where I live. You're a stalker, too. Fantastic."

"You said four flights up. Four plus three is seven."

"Oh, great. A criminal genius. My lucky day." Her pouty grunt was somehow adorable and hot. She crossed her arms but it only boosted her tits.

"Eyes up, asshat."

I spent the rest of the ride trying not to laugh. When we got to her door, she unlocked it, stepped in, flipped me off and slammed it shut. I chuckled my way back down to the third floor until Anton ripped me a new asshole in our kitchen about girls hanging around the crew in public.

Once he'd let out his steam on that, he flung his overnight bag over his thick shoulder and said, "I'll be gone a couple of days. Don't let my shitty little empire burn."

I nodded. "What do you want me to do about Fiona? She might throw herself at one of the other guys just to piss us off."

Anton's steel gaze sized me up before a small, rare, true smile broke across his staunch face. "There is some fire behind those dark eyes."

I scratched my neck and stepped closer to the island. "If what she said is true, keeping her close is a big 'fuck you' to the BTs. She's not safe."

"What are you proposing?" Anton's energy had calmed. He was always better when we were talking about external issues.

Good question. What the hell am I getting at? Fiona was at risk generally, but more so now that we'd stood up for her. But why the hell did I care?

"I don't know. I wonder if word gets out that she's next up for you, the BTs will work extra hard to take her."

He grabbed his phone from the counter and shoved it into his back pocket. "Keep an eye on her, then." He shot me a glare. "An eye, Ricci. She's mine first."

"As she should be, bossman." That was the problem with my being second in line. I was second in line. It was like a splinter in the toe — a tiny truth that threw off everything else.

Anton and I walked out together and the lack of sun had taken off a bit of the heat's edge. I barked his orders to the crew as he walked to his black SUV. The three girls who had been at the bench when we got there scattered quickly.

As the bossman pulled away, the familiar baby-blue shine of my brother's pride and joy came into focus.

Fuck.

I jogged over and climbed into the passenger seat.

Frankie, dressed in a perfectly tailored navy suit, looked me up and down before a definitive frown of disgust formed on his clean-shaven face.

"You done playing drug dealer yet?"

I'd never really thought I'd escaped from my family. Me hiding in Covington Heights was a lie I told myself as I bought time away. Frankie had probably known I was there since day one.

I turned to face him. "We've been through this, big brother. The family business isn't for me."

"Leonardo, we *are* the family business."

He was right, but it didn't make me any more ready to face destiny. I decided to change the mood. "You miss me?"

"Hardly. But I have plenty of work for you." Frankie tilted his head. His eyes — the same deep brown as mine — almost pleaded.

"I can't." That was a lie. I could. I just didn't want to.

An airy grumble came from his throat. If anyone on the planet understood my refusal, it was my big brother. And for all the bickering and battles we'd had over the years, there was one thing I knew to be true. He would never force me to join him.

As if my thoughts were his own, he said, "Right. You need anything?"

"Nope." No way I would take help from him. Taking meant giving. Hell, I'd just lectured Fiona about the same lesson an hour prior. I reached for the handle and yanked.

Frankie called, "You know where to find me."

I walked back to the crew without watching Frankie pull away, because he was right. I knew exactly where to find him and I feared the day when I would.

Chapter Three

Fiona

With my mom passed out on the couch and the sun just peeking into our window, I scraped together enough money to buy a loaf of bread and two cans of tuna. Our assistance had dried up and we had four more days until my mom's benefits hit the bank. I would need to persuade her not to smoke away what came in. And I needed to get a damn job, so I'd have to convince her to take care of Violet, too.

Banging my way to safety? Not exactly my utmost priority.

I shoved the money in the pocket of my shorts and pulled on a beat-up hoodie to cut the morning chill. I slipped on my flip-flops and was out of the door like a quiet mouse, happy that the deli around the corner opened early and I wouldn't have to run into Anton, Leo or any of their crew. My plan was to stay inside and watch repetitive kid's TV all day while I tried to find a job. Lying low was my master plan. I would ignore those pricks until I figured out how to be rid of them. There was certainly no way I was having sex with one of their muscle-defined-drug-pushing asses.

Just to be sure I would avoid Anton's crew, instead of taking the main exit that led to the courtyard, I decided to take the alley to the deli. The alley would stink of trash, urine and vomit, but I would hold my noise and run. Anything would be better than seeing those manipulating shits again.

But I was stopped in my tracks the minute I stepped out of the broken emergency exit.

"Morning." Leo sipped coffee from a blue-and-white paper cup.

Fucking stalker.

"I'm just going to the deli. You don't need to call your boss." I rolled my eyes and plowed forward.

Leo took a cautious sip then quickened his pace to catch up. "I need your phone number."

Well, that was going to be easy. I smiled. "Don't have one." Finally, something my mother had done served me well.

"You're joking." He almost choked on his coffee. *Good.*

I kept walking—even though I was pretty sure I was stomping and not being subtle about it—and he followed me into the deli as the door chimed our entrance.

In a huff, I grabbed the bread and two cans of tuna and plopped them onto the counter, where the old man behind it asked if that was all.

"Just a minute," Leo said, addressing the clerk. Then to me, "Don't you usually buy apples or something fresh too?"

How long has that fucker been keeping tabs on me?

I turned back to the old man, "That's all. I don't need a bag."

He rung me up and I counted out the exact change. I swiped up Violet's and my meal for the next couple of days and was out of the shop before Leo had a chance to think he could be some kind of hero and pay our way.

He ditched his paper cup and said, "Hold up, Fi."

Ugh. A nickname? Gross. The thought that it might help me take orders from him was laughable and perhaps the funniest thing to happen to me in twenty-four hours.

Try again.

No longer needing to avoid Fuck-O, since he was taking wide strides next to me to match my hurried pace, I walked directly to the courtyard, through the doors of the building and—since my anger and shame had done a number on my blood pressure—I stormed up the seven flights of stairs.

I reached out to yank the door open to my floor and he slipped in front of me, blocking the threshold. *God, he's quick. Spooky fuck.*

Leo let out a small sigh and looked down at me. He opened his mouth to speak but I cut him off.

"Don't you fucking dare pity me." I shoved my shoulder into his side and ducked through the space I'd created.

"So… I sorta need to come in and spend the day with you."

Cleary delusional. I stared up at him and deadpanned. "Punished… I'm very obviously being punished."

Leo cleared his throat. "Bossman's orders."

I pushed the cans of tuna into his hands and dug into the pocket of my shorts for my keys. "And I care about that, why, exactly?"

"You're under our protection. It wasn't me who got off at the wrong stop," Leo complained with a small whine and a whole lot of accusation.

"You basically gave me no choice, which is bullshit. And you know what? Fuck you for saying I got myself into this mess. I missed my stop. That was it." My voice was a whispered scream.

"Okay, okay." Leo held up his hands, a can of tuna in each. "Just let me come in and we'll talk about some options."

It had to be a trick. I didn't believe for one second that he had the authority to make decisions about me. That had been made abundantly clear the night before.

"Please." He dipped his chin and his tone was actually sweet.

Well, color me shocked.

Leo had some damn manners. *Huh.* I held the key at the bottom lock. If I really thought about it, I was probably safer with Leo than any other man I'd met in my life. He followed his boss' orders like a dumb puppy behind a raw steak—if puppies had the perfect amount of morning stubble, beautiful olive skin and a smile that hid secret intentions.

"Fine." *Fine?* What the hell was wrong with me? I hated him. "But be quiet. The baby is hopefully still sleeping and my mom…"

"I get it."

The toilet flushed as we walked in and my mom muttered something about going back to bed—which was funny, because she'd slept on the couch. But at least Leo didn't have to witness her coming down off her high. I exhaled a long breath. I'd let the hot asshat inside. This was going to be bad…and annoying. He was probably like having herpes—no cure and frequent flame-ups. I would never get rid of him.

Leo set the tuna cans on the counter in the small kitchen and asked, "You have any coffee?"

"Nope." I made my way over to the couch and curled up, pulling my hoodie over my bare knees and letting my flip-flops fall to the scratched wooden floor.

Truth be told, it had been easy to get up early to go to the store. I hadn't slept much the night before. Between the anger and bitterness, the dark ceiling had been a more welcome view that the back of my eyelids. I yawned.

The need to avoid Leo—and the energy and drive that had pumped through my veins when I'd thought it a possibility—had shriveled away the second I'd decided to let him in. Defeat was exhausting, resistance invigorating.

As Leo approached the couch, he took out his phone and thumb-punched it. *Probably a status report to the other fuck-face.*

He sat down at the opposite end of our worn-out couch. Still looking at his phone, he said, "Go back to sleep, Fi."

I smacked my tongue against the roof of my mouth. Through heavy lids, I asked, "Why are you being so…bearable today?"

"Path of least resistance. I'm stuck with you—and vice versa." Leo placed his phone face-down on the table next to the couch. "Plus, with us officially protecting you? You just got a lot more interesting to the BTs."

With my eyes closed and my head on the armrest, I said, "I still hate you."

Leo let out a small laugh and stretched his entire body. He was too comfortable in my apartment. "Keep telling yourself that," he said, and I could sense the smile.

I was too tired to fight. "You're not so tough when you aren't in front of him."

"Neither are you."

I could have read his tone four hundred ways. Annoyance? Cocky? *Surely.* A hint of flirting? *No fucking way.* That had to be my lack of sleep. The fatigue got the best of me and I drifted off.

Too soon was Leo was nudging my shoulder.

"Hey," he said in a sort of urgent whisper.

I peeled open my eyes, the reminder of my confused and depressing life magnified by his dark eyes. I snarled but it had no effect on him.

"Your sister is babbling from the back room. Do you need to get her?"

After a small moan, I scrubbed my face and stretched, brushing my calf against his leg then recoiling at the thought of contact. "What time is it?"

Leo pressed a button on his phone and it lit up. "Eight-thirty."

Then yes, I had to get Violet. I stood, Leo watching me the whole time with skeptical eyes. "Simmer down. I'm not making a break for it." I shook my head down the short hall to the back bedroom. The curtains were drawn and only a sliver of bright sun hit the end of the disheveled bed. My mom, with her thinning dark hair in a rat's nest, lay stomach down with her head tilted to the side. Her mouth was open and light snores came from her throat.

I brought my finger to my lips and smiled to Violet, who lifted her arms above her head. With quiet steps around the bed, I picked up my little sister, swiping a clean diaper, onesie and the wipes. Once the door was closed, I nuzzled into her warm neck and she giggled all the way to the living room.

Unfortunately, Leo was still there. With his legs spread wide on the couch, he'd officially found his throne. *Ass.* He glanced up from his phone as I knelt down and placed Violet on her back.

After her diaper change, I flipped on the TV and went to the kitchen for milk. Leo followed—as I was learning he was prone to do—and if I'd eaten any breakfast, it would have soured in my stomach.

When I went to close the fridge, he caught the door and opened it wide. "Fi."

He really needs to stop calling me that. We weren't buddy-buddy. I didn't want a nickname from him.

"There is nothing to eat in here."

I lifted a shoulder in a half-shrug. "I wasn't expecting a guest...or an intruder. I'm not sure you've reached guest status."

Leo closed the fridge. He grumbled and frantically punched his thumbs into his phone on the way back to his spot on the couch.

I handed Violet her milk and she stared at the TV. A hand puppet was somehow planting a garden and I let the simplicity of the children's program numb my mind.

When the end credits rolled for her episode, a knock at the door startled me back to life. We didn't get many visitors. Leo stood, opened it, took some bags then dumped them on the table.

I closed the door on a dark-skinned guy with a lip ring without asking for his name and followed Leo's path. He wore a white wife-beater and it fit him like a second skin—even his back had definition. If I hadn't been so busy hating him, I would have admired Leo's toned frame and pretty dark eyes that hid behind curled lashes.

Leo unpacked carrots, celery, onions, three huge cans of peeled tomatoes and some ground turkey. Behind the thin white plastic sack, three packages of pasta remained.

"I need a knife and cutting board. You can peel the carrots." With as grumpy a look as I could muster, I collected the necessary items from the kitchen. "Oh, and olive oil and your biggest pot."

I stared at him. Was he really stupid enough to think I had either of those things?

Leo raised his eyebrows, like the gesture would make the items magically appear. I decided to let him figure it out for himself. *Fuck him.* After a mini stand-off of wills, he dropped his bushy but groomed brows. He grumbled, wiped his hands down the front of his jeans, then pulled out his phone. Leo pressed a couple of times and said into it, "Bring up two big pots and a bottle of olive oil." He narrowed an eye at me then spoke into the phone again. "Plus salt, pepper, chicken stock and oregano." Leo sat the phone back down on the table and shook his head.

By the time the knock came again, Leo had cubed the carrots and celery and chopped the onions. He was sitting at the table and motioned with a quick tilt of his head for me to answer. I rolled my eyes but, for some reason, obeyed.

"I didn't get a chance to introduce myself before. I'm Scooter," the same guy said as he handed me the loot.

"Congratulations." A tight, fake grin was my offered thanks to Scooter, and I kicked the door shut.

"What's that?" Violet toddled over to Leo, although her question sounded more like, 'Was dat?'.

"You wanna help me cook, little bug?" Leo asked in a voice that I wouldn't have thought him capable of.

My little sister nodded her head and gave him a timid smile, which he returned. *Christ*, he was practically endearing.

"Violet," I said as I put everything on the table. "Her name is Violet."

"I bet you are going to be fantastic at stirring, Violet." Leo's sweet tone was enough to make me vomit cotton candy.

I couldn't stand to witness any more. I left them to it, hating Leo even more because it was all an act. He was a criminal, and after one thing that had nothing to do with being nice and helping my broken family. That huge specimen of a man might have thought I'd been fooled by kindness, but I'd learned my lesson. He'd said it himself. Nothing in life was free — especially in Covington Heights.

From my little corner of the couch, I pretended to watch TV and not care, to be oblivious to the fact that Violet was probably having the first genuine exchange in her life with a man. It being fake only seemed to bother me. I ignored her giggles and little hand claps of a job well done for the following hour.

As Leo's spaghetti sauce simmered on our dingy stove in one of the pots Scooter had dropped off, Leo and Violet played on the floor next to the couch.

"Hop on my back, little bug," Leo said as he got into a plank position on all fours. "I can use the extra weight."

Sure enough, she jumped right on and sat below his ripped shoulders as he did push-ups. I reminded myself that it was not ridiculously cute.

The problem was that Violet smacking Leo's side and saying 'more' over and over gnawed at a deeper issue. She — much like myself — had never known her father. If my mom had boyfriends, they weren't concerned about teaching us how to throw a ball or ride a bike—or even our well-being. Attention from a man was new for Violet, and she was eating it up and licking the spoon clean. I was almost jealous—especially of the way Violet got him to do what she said, until I remembered to hate that sexy fucker again. *Wait.* He wasn't sexy. He was pompous.

Violet's chuckle turned into a full laugh that I'd rarely heard her use. I frowned hard so I wouldn't smile at her having fun. And the wide grin on Leo's face? It could jump out of the window and keep going all the way to hell.

"Who the fuck are you?" My mom propped her hands on her hips and peered down at Leo, who was now on his back pretending that Violet had broken him.

He batted his eyes, a move that had probably gotten him into a lot of panties over the years. With Violet on her own two feet, Leo stood and dusted off his hands before stretching out the right one.

"Leo Ricci... Nice to meet you."

My mother stared at his hand for a beat then cut her eyes to me. She lifted her nose and sniffed. "Why does it smell like...*food* in here?"

The flavored vapors rolling off Leo's sauce were not only enticing, they were completely foreign to our apartment.

I stood to explain, but Leo answered before I could. "It's my nanna's secret recipe. Although, I'm pretty sure I just gave all the secrets to this little monkey." He swept up Violet and propped her on his hip and the little one babbled her delight as Leo oversold his charm.

"This one, on the other hand?" With his free arm, he hooked around my shoulders and brought me close. *Gross. Definitely gross.* I absolutely hated the way he

40

smelled. "She just sat on that gorgeous ass of hers and watched us work. Fi, go start the water for the pasta and set the table. Violet and I need a break." He winked at me. *Fucking winked*. It was all I could do not to explode with laughter.

Vicki Thompson was many things—several of which should have gotten her kids taken away from her because they were so vile—but she was not blind or stupid. I could only imagine her sizing Leo up as I walked away.

She shimmied up to me and whispered, "When did you decide to date a dealer? Weren't you under the impression you were too good for them?"

"I'm not dating that idiot." I recoiled.

"Then what the hell is he doing in our apartment?" She raised a thin eyebrow and cocked her head.

"It's complicated." I grabbed our mismatched plates and took them to the table, all under the watchful, assessing eyes of my mother.

"Fiona," she said, my name somehow a warning.

Since middle school, I'd played the role of friend or sister to my mother. She had been sixteen when I was born. I'd thought we'd stayed with her parents for a while but I had no memory of them. We'd always been more of a duo than parent and child. So for her to step toward me with concern and a sense of parental duty was like wearing a dress that was six sizes too small—suffocating, exposing and filling me with need for her to avert her gaze.

"It's fine," I lied. *Time for a subject change*. "Oh, I'm sorry, but I got fired again, so I need you to stay home tomorrow so I can try and find a new job."

"Why did you get fired? We need that money." And just like that, the glimpse of a mother disappeared into the much stronger hold of her disease. It hurt every bit as much then as it did the first time I'd recognized it for what it was. Because with recognition came deep understanding that it was stronger than us.

So instead of fighting or blaming or fucking screaming, I apologized again while I filled the second pot with water.

It was already past mid-day when the four of us were seated at the small wooden table and having lunch.

In another surprising act of parenthood, perhaps a show for Leo, my mom helped Violet eat. That was, if 'helped Violet eat' meant cut up the spaghetti and let the two-year-old shove fistfuls into her face, occasionally making it to her mouth.

After lunch, my mom showered as I did the dishes and tidied up the kitchen. I had no idea what to do with the rest of the sauce, so I just put the cover back on and let it sit on the stove. Once I'd finished, my mom had too, and we all met near the couch, where Violet's head was doing slow bobs as she fought the beginnings of her afternoon nap next to Leo.

"Fiona, since you're going out tomorrow, I'll take advantage of today." There it was, the angle had officially been worked.

"Leo, I'm so sorry to ask, but I don't get my check for a couple more days. Can I borrow twenty bucks until then? With Fiona losing her job *again*, times are tight."

Five years prior, I might have been shocked or even embarrassed. But the moment she'd seen Leo, even with her little warning to me, I'd known she'd hit him up for money.

Leo lifted a butt cheek off the couch and pulled out a wallet from his back pocket. He took out a hundred-dollar bill. Of all the things I'd thought of Leo, I'd never once imagined him a fool. He knew what she was. He knew what she'd do with the money. And that much? I sure as shit would not see her the next day.

Thanks, Asshole. Just one more reason to hate you.

My mom gushed her gratitude and my stomach churned our lunch a little harder. I went over to the couch and picked up Violet to take her to her crib in the back bedroom. The amount of money he'd given my mother was downright dangerous. The greedy disease in her would use it all. Once Violet had settled in, my anger rose to a boil. I fumed all the way back to Leo, who was still on the couch, but alone.

I pointed to the door. "Get out."

Chapter Four

Leo

I had no idea how Fiona made gritted teeth sexy, but her little body hovering over me and her arm extended to complement her hilarious order was scrumptious.

"Not happening." I interlaced my fingers behind my neck and sprawled out.

"I hate you." Fiona gave a little head movement with the second word like she was adding bite.

Did that sting?

I closed an eye. "Let me get this straight. I saved you from certain rape, possible human trafficking, made you my nanna's secret sauce, played all morning with your baby sister while you sat on the couch pouting and *you* hate *me*?"

Fiona shot me daggers with her eyes. "Do you know what she'll do with all that money? Are you hoping to kill her? I'm not going to see her for days now. I needed her here for Violet."

Okay, so yeah. That had been the wrong move. Fiona's mom had asked for twenty and I'd given her way too much. It was entirely possible that I'd been showing off. I did that sometimes. *Shit.* But saying sorry? Not really my strong suit.

"Where do you need to go tomorrow, anyway?"

"To the corner of None-of-your-fucking-business and Go-to-hell." Fiona crossed her arms and frowned. "I want you to leave."

"Do you think I like spending my day in this shitty apartment babysitting your annoying, grumpy ass?" I kinda did, but I would never tell her that.

The grin that spread over Fiona's face was that of an insane person. She waved her arm in a grand gesture. "The door awaits, asshole."

I shrugged. "Already told you. Not happening."

Fiona dropped her head back and groaned dramatically. Then she locked her eyes with mine and said, "You really are the biggest prick I've ever met."

"Possibly." *Childish retort with innuendo? Absolutely.* But dammit if I wasn't having the time of my life watching her blow up at me.

Fiona studied me as she walked around and sat in her spot at the other end of the couch. With each step her anger dissipated and was replaced by something else that I couldn't put my finger on.

"Nah," she said. "Guys like you, all pretty and buff… You usually have nothing to back it up. You lift weights and get ripped because you have a small penis complex."

I shook my head and ignored her. Besides, she was totally off base.

"Hmm-m…" Fiona examined her hands. "I wonder which one of my fingers is most like your baby dick."

She was baiting me, reeling me in. But she was talking about my dick and her fingers were fucking tiny. I said, "You may want to move up your arm. It's more like that." I tapped the crook in my elbow.

"Doubt it. It's probably more like my thumb, short and stubby." Her eyes lit up in the worst possible way while she examined her shortest digit. "Oh my God. I'm a genius. You just got your own nickname. Stubby." She popped up and the crazy-ass grin on her face was frightening. "I'm going to take a bath. See you later, Stubby."

She skipped into the bathroom and closed the door behind her. I didn't hear a lock, just some muffled humming like she was happier than Mary Poppins, cleaning up a mess with snaps and songs. For the record, my dick was not small. It certainly wasn't fucking 'stubby'.

The more she hummed, the more I needed to prove her wrong and get back the upper hand. For fuck's sake, I'd cooked for her and gotten into a tickle war with a toddler. Being around Fiona was not just bad for my persona. It was also murder for my ego.

There was only one thing to do — prove that little pixie wrong. I stood, knowing I was being a brute but giving zero shits, went to the bathroom and swung the door open. As a complete and total perk, I stole a glance of her soapy naked body before whipping out my dick above the toilet.

"Nice tits. I need to piss." I tried to make the last bit sound like an apology.

"You're going to pee? Right in front of me?" There was a bit of shock in her voice and I dared to think she was staring at my very un-stubby dick.

"Better than the kitchen sink, right? Shitty timing," I lied.

"Wow," she quipped. "A real-life dick pic. You're a girl's wet dream."

I finished and washed my hands as she mumbled more insults under her breath, none of which had to do with my dick.

I took one more quick look at naked Fiona. With her hair up in a messy bun on the top of her head and a few wet strands clinging to her pale, flushed skin, she was the most naturally beautiful woman I'd ever seen — and I'd just whipped out my dick like a Neanderthal douchebag. My nanna was rolling over in her grave.

An apology was in order for sure, yet again, but I was more addicted to our fighting and now quite possibly her body. So instead of being the good boy I thought I might have been deep down inside, I let the gangster win and said nothing.

"Get out, asshole. You proved your stupid point."

I left and went back to my spot on her beat-up sofa. A half hour later she joined me, smelling fresh and her hair still wet. Fiona wore little pajama shorts and a tank top without a bra. She was trying to kill me. *Death by sex kitten.*

She tucked a foot under her ass and sat down. "Can I ask you some questions about my — uh — payment?" Her voice was calm, smooth, soft.

Holy shit. She'd gained the upper hand yet again. Maybe talking business would put me back in control. I avoided looking at her any longer, instead staring at the blank TV. "Shoot."

"So if I sleep with one of you, my debt is paid?"

As much as I relished that she'd included me in that option, she needed to know how things worked.

"Not exactly. His turf, his payment."

Fiona hummed. "Let me get this straight. I have to sleep with *him* to pay off my debt for *you* saving me. But I have to *want* to do it."

"Pretty much." It was true that she would probably need ongoing protection and the 'cost' of that would only go up. But, honest to God, we'd never had a girl who didn't want to 'pay' us.

After a small sigh, she turned and stared out of the window. I didn't need to see her face to understand that the gears were grinding in her head. After a few minutes she asked, "How does he expect me to want him if I don't know anything about him?"

An excellent question and, again, something we'd never come across — or at least I hadn't in my short time in Covington. The whole 'payment by sex' thing had come up more as a joke than a proper plan. And it hadn't been until Bradford Towers had started eying girls in our territory that we'd needed to figure out a way to make that an advantage for us somehow. Because that was what criminals did… We worked the angles and exploited people's fears.

"Maybe Anton figures I'll drive you so insane that fucking him will be a relief." I winked at her.

"Well, in that case," she said with big eyes, "it's totally working. You know you can't just show your dick to girls. We actually don't appreciate that. Some might even call it sexual harassment." She enunciated the last two words like they were foreign to me. "And don't give my mom any more money."

My soft side needed a vacation. Besides, Fiona wouldn't be falling into my bed until the bossman had had his fill. I said, "There's always Bradford."

Any joking that she'd offered vanished. "Don't do that. Don't throw that shit in my face. Your choice is a fabrication." Fiona stood, an uncomfortable resolve on her face. "You can go. Violet and I will stay in. I promise."

It wasn't that I didn't believe her. It was that I couldn't trust her. I pulled my phone out of my back pocket and sent Scooter a text. Fiona had disappeared into the bedroom, so when the knock came an hour later, I answered the door.

Rafa — aka Golden Boy — handed me a phone and its charger. "All the bells and tracking whistles — linked to you, Anton and me."

I slid the sleek metal and cord into my back pocket and stepped into the hallway. "How's business?"

"Meh. The boys are pissed about the 'no ladies' rule. But it's the fucking projects." He lifted a shoulder. "Drugs keep selling. You gonna stay up here all damn day? Everybody's wondering what so special about Fiona. Plus, I wanted to spar and Jackson's wingspan kills me every time."

"I'll be down in a bit. Get the peons to secure the doors and borders. I'll meet you in the gym before I have to leave for the dice game downtown." The idea of leaving Fiona didn't appeal to me, but I needed to make our money. With Anton gone, I was in charge. And enforcing rules was hard to do while I made sauce and traded insults with the brown-haired firecracker. I hadn't needed to stay with her the whole day. It had just kinda happened like that.

When I went back in, she was on the couch with a book. "I had hoped you were gone." Her drab tone made me smile.

I reached for the phone and charger and handed it to her. "There's a whole list of contacts in there, but the only one you need is mine. If you need or want to leave, text me first. If you run out of diapers or milk, just text and someone will bring them up."

She shook her head. "Don't you think you're being a little dramatic? What is this? House arrest?"

"You are officially the most valuable item in Covington Heights and everyone knows it, because I spent my entire day up here. We're not nice Boy Scouts who play by the rules. We have enemies...plural. It might not be tonight, but until something changes to make you less important, they're coming for you. Keep your door locked."

Her fallen face was a sobering goodbye.

I jogged down the four flights of stairs and changed into my workout gear in Anton's and my apartment before heading to our private gym across the hall, where the elite crew members refined their bodies. Jackson, the former basketball star, was bench pressing in the corner, his loud exhales blasting out of his mouth with every repetition. Scooter, who was by far the weakest and hated all physical activity, was biking with headphones on. But in the center, on the huge dark blue mat, Golden Boy waited with a smug grin.

Sometimes I liked to warm up before fighting, jump a little rope or do twenty minutes on the treadmill. But as I stalked my way to Rafa, two things were clear. One, I was ready. Two, I was in no mood to play nice. I pulled off my shirt—the eventual sweat would work in my favor for slippery punches—and popped in my mouth guard. After a crack of my neck and a twist of my spine, I narrowed my eyes and Rafa must have seen the switch in my mood.

"Not the face." He held up a finger before securing his own mouth guard.

I signaled for him to come at me, and when he did, I easily weaved out of his way. Usually, I let the boys blow out a little bit of their steam before I attacked. It gave them the illusion that they had a chance. But I was tired of hiding my skills — annoyed with being second in line, second son, second in charge. *Fuck that.* So when Rafa's balance was off because he hadn't landed his blow, instead of letting him get his footing back, I grabbed his wrist, twisted his arm behind his back and jabbed him twice in the gut. Hard.

He groaned and blinked several times as I let him go. *Yeah, sorry, Goldie.* I was a kiss on the cranky side. But bless him, he came at me right away, trying to swipe my legs for a takedown. I hopped and could have landed a perfect palm to his nose, but he'd asked me to save his face. It was a pity he found himself so precious. Once I landed, I immediately brought my knee back up then whacked his side with my shin.

Out of the corner of my eye, I could see that Jackson had taken interest in our fight and was standing on the side with a towel draped over his lean shoulders. I slid away from all of Rafa's advances and he peered at me, his amber eyes filled with determination. The problem wasn't that they were shitty fighters. The problem was that I'd been sparring with Frankie under the critical eye of our father since I'd been three. Two years his junior and still a baby when our lessons had begun, I'd learned that defense wasn't half of the fight. It was all of it. Twenty-seven years later, only Frankie could land a punch on me, and that was because he knew me as well as he knew himself.

Defense, as artful as it was, wasn't going to work out my frustration. I went on the attack. My assault was quick. I flipped Rafa and had my knee in his back and his wrists bound before he could even imagine what was coming. He strained for breath beneath me, his cheek squished into the mat. I released him with a huff and stood.

Scooter, who was now standing next to Jackson, gaped at me.

Rafa scrambled to his feet and shook his head with a little wiggle. I took out my mouth guard and met Jackson's stare.

He said, "You've been holding out on us."

I looked over to Rafa, who added, "I seriously don't even know what just happened."

Scooter, who had finally closed his mouth, studied me before saying, "You're like a lethal weapon."

Yeah. Yeah, I was exactly that. But instead of confirming, I nodded to Jackson. "Leave in twenty?"

"I'll meet you at the bench. Gotta say goodnight to J.J. He's at Lisa's."

I had to admit that Jackson was a good dad. He always put his son first. How he balanced that with selling drugs was something I recognized from my own criminal father. The difference, though? I didn't think Jackson wanted the same life for his son.

We met at the bench, drove downtown and ran our dice game. The big burly Scot won all the Asians' money for once, and even though he was in the mood to celebrate, I just wanted to get back to Covington Heights and my lie of a life.

Chapter Five

Fiona

The storms had kept Violet and me inside for two days. We'd lived off leftover spaghetti and the tuna I'd bought that first day with Leo. When the sun finally poked through the window, I packed Violet into her stroller and headed to the park.

We weren't the only ones who had gone stir-crazy. The rusted jungle gym and metal swings were crawling with kids. As I bent down and unbuckled Violet, I didn't need two guesses as to the shadow hovering over me.

Violet toddled over to the swings—her favorite—and waited for me in her little yellow dress. I sighed more dramatically than I needed to and pushed into my bare knees as I rose. Sure enough, Leo stood with his arms crossed over his skintight black tank. Damn, he was ripped. His pecs were a solid double mass of muscle cleavage and his angry fists pushed his biceps to the point that they looked like they would burst out of his olive skin.

"Text. You just have to send a simple fucking text, Fiona."

He was being utterly ridiculous. I'd had two full days to think of his stupid warnings. Anton and his crew brewed fear. They were just trying to spook me into bed. It wasn't going to work. There was no way I was going to have sex with any of them. Their plan was flawed. If I didn't want them, they didn't want me. *Guess what, asshats?* I had zero desire to throw myself at those drug-dealing calendar boys. *Nope.* Not even sexy Satan himself standing before me.

I met his cranky gaze. "I like to keep you on your toes. It's all part of my master plan to never see your dick again." I wiggled my fingers and settled on the middle one as I walked away and found Violet.

A swing had opened up and I secured Violet before stepping behind her and pushing. Leo leveled his eyes at me then frowned and walked away. The blonde girl who took care of kids led a group of them inside the gate of the park. Her little pack spread out instantly and I watched as she seemed to have tabs on all of them at the same time. It didn't look like she needed any help, but it was the one prospect of a job I'd had, so I took Violet over and introduced myself.

"Hi, I'm Fiona and this is Violet. I've seen you around."

"I'm Lisa." She held out a hand and I switched Violet to my other hip so I could shake her hand. "And she is gorgeous. She looks just like you."

I smiled down to Violet and kissed the top of her head. "She's my sister. My mom is —"

"Probably the same as my mom."

A little boy ran up to Lisa and she squatted down to listen to him. She pulled two toys out of her bag.

"Bunny!" Violet pointed at one.

"*Boing! Boing! Boing!*" The boy made the stuffed rabbit hop in the air and Violet giggled.

She squirmed to get down and her yellow dress slid up and revealed her diaper.

"Wanna play?" The boy handed her the bunny and they toddled off to the slide, where the bunny and his dinosaur proceeded to have a wonderful, apparently hilarious adventure.

Lisa and I looked on until she said, "Don't tell anyone, but J.J. is my favorite." She grinned at the little boy playing with my sister. "I might have just the tiniest crush on his dad too." She measured out the size of her crush with her thumb and index finger.

I followed her gaze over to the bench, where the Covington Heights crew was in full-on-asshat-drug-dealing mode.

"Ugh. I hate those guys, especially Leo. He's by far the worst."

Lisa twisted her face and looked at me as if I had just asked her to serve Jell-O to the Pope. "First of all, Leo is hotter than Hades. Not my type, but he's gorgeous. So if by 'worst' you mean panty-melting masturbation fuel, then yes."

I couldn't help but smile at her assessment. It wasn't like she was wrong, but I had to stand my ground. "Well, he's annoying."

"I have no idea. I've never talked to him. He sticks to himself. Anyway, they're not all that bad. I mean, they pay me to watch their kids or siblings. My rent is free and there is always food on my table."

"You run the drug-dealer daycare," I said with a smile.

Lisa laughed and shrugged. "I guess I do."

It was there, in that moment, when I had to ask for help. I hated the tight pride squeezing in my chest, but times were tough and I needed a job. How else would I get Violet out of this hellhole? I let out a breath and asked, "I don't suppose you need any help? My mom, well…" I started again with more resolve, "I need a job."

Lisa gave me a tight smile. "I wish I could say yes, but technically I work for Anton. All jobs go through him. Sorry."

"Right. Thanks, anyway." I rubbed my upper arms and looked at Leo out of the corner of my eye. If they were going to keep tabs on me, they would probably ruin any chance I had of working—unless I worked for them. I closed my eyes. Maybe I had to get into Covington before I could get out of it.

"Will you watch her for a second?" I asked Lisa, who nodded.

I set my shoulders and walked over to the bench. In all the months since the dealers had claimed their space, I had never once imagined that I would approach it or them. Asking criminals for help was something I'd sworn never to do. But I was officially out of options.

The crew parted as if they knew exactly who I was there for. Leo sat, legs open wide and arms draped over the bench. I swallowed over the lump in my throat.

"Can I talk to you? Privately?"

Leo licked his plump lips and grinned. I hated that grin. It was a victory lap around my pride. He stretched his arms overhead and the black tank he wore slid up his torso just enough to reveal the hint of a sinful happy trail. Lisa was right. He was wickedly divine.

"Sure," he finally said, and I was certain I'd been caught checking him out. "Be right back, boys."

Leo stood and draped an arm around me. I wanted to bat it away, but I was eating a shit sandwich, so I might as well let his physical contact be a side of crap chips to go along with it.

He led us over to the thin alley where the buildings met and the hose was stored. I turned to face him, and his arm dropped with the movement. Being so close to him was unsettling in the best and worst kind of way. He smelled nice. His skin was flawless and his eyelashes were abnormally long.

I took a step back. I hated the idea of being under his sex spell. Surely noticing my unease, he crowded my space and framed my body with both of those stupidly muscular arms.

"I…" What did I need? I couldn't remember. Worse, my pulse was racing and I had actually let the thought of kissing him enter my brain…in a good way. *What the hell is happening?* I loathed every fiber of his live dick-pic being. *Shit. Now I'm thinking about his dick.*

Leo nestled into my neck. I didn't think he was supposed to be doing that and I sure as hell shouldn't have whimpered when he did. *No, no, no.* This was all wrong. He was toying with me. *Asshole.*

I pushed him away right in his solid-as-a-rock chest. "Get off, creep. Eww."

Leo smirked and jutted his chin. "What did you want, anyway?"

Asking for more help. *Ugh.* I let out a little huff. "I need a job. I need you to ask Anton to give me a job."

Leo studied me then said, "Say please."

"Fuck you." That wasn't a very good 'please', but it tasted so nice rolling off my tongue.

"Is that on the table?" He faked surprise. Leo was a horrible actor. He should have stuck with male modeling for Women's Drug Dealing Weekly.

"Shut up, asshat. I'm serious. You have me on lockdown and I need money. The only solution is you asking Anton to give me a job."

Leo narrowed his dark eyes and stepped back. "Ask him yourself. He's coming home tonight." He walked backward as his eyes trailed the length of my body and back up before turning on his heel and getting lost in the sea of black jeans.

I went back to the park and fetched Violet, whose eyes were beginning to droop. We said goodbye to Lisa and headed upstairs.

While Violet had her afternoon nap, I took a long bath. I couldn't figure out why I was nervous to see Anton again. I just needed to treat him the same way as I did Leo. It wasn't like I was in any danger. They were protecting me, whatever that meant.

The water turned cold and I wrapped the towel around my chest after I dried off. I hated that I was going to make an effort to be pretty, but I had to use every asset I had. I found a simple black sundress in the back of my mom's closet and I took time to blow out my hair. My make-up was old, but a little mascara and light gloss was really all I knew how to do anyway.

Just as I had settled Violet in front of the TV and given her a peanut butter sandwich for a snack, my mom stumbled through the door. Her cheeks were hollow, her skin dirty and, as she passed by, I got a whiff of her stench — body odor mixed with what I'd always likened to burnt Styrofoam. It was not a pleasant smell.

"I'm sorry," she said, just like she had so many times before.

"I know."

My mom slipped down the hall and into the bathroom. A quote from my high school counselor came to mind. After I had cried my eyes out and confided that my mom was pregnant for the third time in two years and planning to give the baby away again, the plump, middle-aged woman behind her desk had said, *'Fiona, you can't change people. You can only change the way you react to them.'*

It had been a turning point for me. I'd realized my mother's addiction, her disease, was stronger than the bond I was sure a mother and daughter must have deep down. I'd fooled myself for years, thinking that she would choose me one day, that I would come before drugs. But with the counselor's words, I'd known that my only power was me. So when Violet came along and my mom had decided to keep her, I'd promised myself I would give her a chance. I would never touch drugs. I would be stable.

Once I could prove that I had a steady income and a safe place to live, I could get custody of Violet. As bitter a truth pill as it was, my mother was a lost cause.

Thirty minutes later, in clean clothes and with wet hair, she joined me on the couch. After a greeting to Violet, she said, "You look pretty. Do you have a date with Leo?"

Two points to Vicki Thompson for remembering his name.

"No. I'm not dating him or any of those dealers. I'm going to go try and get another job." I offered just enough truth to get me by. The overwhelming urge to get out of the apartment and get away from my shitty life rose. I assessed my mother's state and settled on her being sober enough that I could leave Violet with her. Hell, it wasn't like I was going on a romantic weekend getaway with the man of my dreams. I was going down four floors to beg for a job of some sort.

I gathered my little backpack where the phone and charger were hidden and said that I would be back in a bit. But it was early and I didn't want to sit and be glared at by Leo until his boss decided to grace Covington Heights with his presence.

The stairwell offered a cool relief and much-needed retreat. I sat down on the step next to the entrance to the fifth floor and dug out the phone that Leo had given me. There were, indeed, plenty of contacts listed, none of which had the name Anton attached to them. *So I'm good enough to offer up my body, but I can't have his number? Jesus, they really think highly of themselves.*

I downloaded a free game and played until I was bored stiff. Then I watched videos of guys getting hit in the nuts by children and pictured Violet 'accidentally' taking a swing at Leo's jewels — not that I was thinking about his dick. Because watching him pee? That was grosser than gross. Although, he did prove that my attempt at a nickname for him had been very, very wrong.

A message popped up and I paused, right before an overweight dad was going to take it in the nuts with a kid running around with a bucket on his head. It was from Leo.

You can stop hiding on the fifth floor. He's here.

I stared at the message. He knew exactly where I was and he wasn't even shy about it. *Stalker.* And damn that phone— I had just started liking it. Now I would have to stomp it into the ground and bash it into a million pieces. Leave it to Leo to ruin a good thing. *Add that to my growing list of reasons to despise him.*

With my soon-to-be demolished phone in my bag, I walked down to the third floor and pushed through the door. It was hard to believe I was in the same building. When I'd first seen the modern, clean hall that lead to the crew's apartments, I'd been shocked—even more so when I'd entered Anton and Leo's place with its massive open kitchen, sectional and flatscreen. We were living in opposite worlds and I'd been completely oblivious. It was probably yet another reason why girls threw themselves at the crew. The promise of money could go a long way. But that wouldn't be me. I would work for my paycheck, even if it meant shoveling drugs into tiny packets in a back room somewhere. Whatever it took to get Violet and me out...

I rolled my shoulders back and dug deep for my strength. Violet's sweet face came to mind as I knocked on the door. Leo opened it and that arrogant prick was shirtless. There was no way I could let myself be distracted by his...

Holy Hell.

The man didn't just have a chiseled six pack. He also had one of those perfect V's that led all the way down to...

Mother of God.

He was only wearing gym shorts, and they were barely hanging on his trim hips and tighter-than-should-be-allowed ass.

"Eyes up, Fi."

His smirk could go directly to hell.

Leo opened the door wider and Anton's spooky-ass eyes pierced a hole in my chest. With just one look, all the confidence drained out of my body. I took a cautious step forward, no longer sure about what I was getting myself into.

Chapter Six

Leo

She'd worn a dress, and it fit her better than a damn glove. Fiona's tits were pushed up and her cleavage could have made a man go off the grid indefinitely. It was like the potential that I'd always known was there had reached up and smacked me in the face. She was gorgeous. And from the small narrowing of Anton's eyes, he'd also been bitch-slapped with her hotness.

The bossman taking her in shouldn't have pissed me off. Hell, I'd been the one to offer her up. But heat spread up my spine as I closed the door, and I was feeling just a wee bit possessive. At least she'd checked me out. Was it a coincidence that I'd answered the door half naked when she was coming to ask my employer for a job? *No.* I'd wanted to throw her off and maybe show her what she was missing. Petty and childish? *Absolutely.* But I wasn't a criminal because of a sophisticated palate and impeccable manners at the dinner table.

And damn it if she didn't go all wobbly in front of him. Where was her spit? Her vinegar?

"Hi," she said to Anton with an innocent smile.

Not that. Not the bashful beauty bit. Good God, he would tear her apart. At least it would be entertaining. I brushed past Fiona, who seemed to be dead in the water, and went to the kitchen to make dinner.

The bossman stayed silent, his hold on the room steady. Fiona's chest rose and fell slowly. I noticed because I was checking out her tits again. Days... I could have gotten lost for days and months in those heavenly lady lumps. I pretended to be focused on the broccoli but flipped on my acute hearing.

Fiona nodded to herself — *probably an internal pep talk going on* — then cornered around our huge couch. She plopped right down next to Anton and her boldness almost got him to crack a smile. Almost. Either that or he'd had a muscle spasm in his cheeks.

"I want a job — one that I can't get fired from if my mom fucks up. And if you are going to insist that I want you, well... I'm going to have to get to know you."

Wait, wait, wait. What was she saying?

She continued, "I have to at least see you. I can't just turn on a button and want to have sex with you."

Uh? She'd come down to ask for a job, not some fucking quality time with a drug dealing asshole. Anton glanced over at me. Maybe he was as confused as I was. He sat back and I didn't imagine his eyes raking over Fiona.

Anton rubbed his sharp jaw and asked, "Can you make drinks?"

"Absolutely." Fiona's answer was too quick. Was I the only one catching all the fucking lies on the other side of the room?

"Then you can bartend at Leo's poker and dice games. You can keep whatever you make in tips."

"She's gonna do what now?" *Oh shit.* Those words had actually come out of my mouth.

Anton turned to me. "It's perfect. You can keep an eye on her that way."

Before I could object—which I definitely was going to do on grounds of my games my rules and one-hundred-percent-stubborn ass—she said, "Oh God. Anything else. I have literally never met anyone I've loathed more in my life."

I raised my eyebrows. Her little shiver earlier in the day had said otherwise.

"You showed me your dick, sicko, and drooled all over my boobs while I was naked in the tub."

That got a questioning glare from Anton, but she'd come in here to ask for a job, not to nanny-nanny-boo-boo tattle on me for my bad behavior. And now she was going to get in on my hustle? *Fuck that.*

"No way." I chucked the knife down and wiped my hands on the towel I'd flung over my shoulder. "I am *not* taking her to the games with me. I guarantee she couldn't even make a vodka on the rocks."

Anton stood and walked over to the island. In a low whisper he said, "You got a better idea? Cuz I seem to remember something about your dick."

The threat woven into his voice wasn't about him kicking my ass. We both knew that couldn't happen. It was more about me staying where I was and continuing to avoid my brother.

"She's worthless," I said, loud enough for her to hear and instantly regretting it.

"Not to me." Anton turned and walked to his bedroom. "Fiona, you're staying to eat."

Fiona lifted a shoulder and shot me a smug grin.

I crossed the room and went to mine. I found my favorite jersey and pulled it over my head. *No more eye candy for that traitor.*

"Catch a chill?" she taunted as I walked back to the kitchen. I sautéed the chicken breast and ignored how she'd taken off her shoes and bent her legs so that the hem of her dress hit at mid-thigh. She wasn't sexy at all. She was an evil trickster. Whatever her plan had been, it had worked like a charm and Anton was officially intrigued by her. She'd upped her stock and was going to eat into my money at the same time.

I set out the plates and utensils around the island. Anton came out of his room freshly showered and in black training pants and a white tank top. His light hair was still damp and the water seemed to have washed off his mood from before.

With a scowl at Fiona, I served up dinner. If she was expecting small talk, she was sadly mistaken. Plus, Anton would never discuss business in front of an outsider. But one detail of his plan had been eating at me since he'd decided it.

My father had trained me to assess immediate threats, and they came to me almost like premonitions. A face had popped into my head and wouldn't go away. The red-headed slimy fuck Anton let gamble at our games... He was a former rival of Anton's father who had slithered his way back onto the scene after a lengthy jail sentence.

Neither of us trusted Mac, but we had no problem taking his money. His sister, who happened to be our go-to private doctor for all things broken or split open, had proven her loyalty over the years and had vouched for him. But that didn't stop his ugly mug from lurking in my thoughts.

"Leo!" Anton shoved my arm. "Jesus. When did you start daydreaming?"

I blinked and straightened.

Anton continued, "Fiona needs new clothes. She can't bartend in a hoodie and cut offs. She needs —"

"Oh no." I said slowly and shook my head once. "I am not going fucking shopping with her. I have some limits."

Anton pursed his lips, but I held my ground.

"Scooter can drive her, watch her go in and come out. I have way better shit to do than sit in a corner while she tries on tight jeans and tanks."

Shit. I'd fueled his damn fire with a visual, not that it mattered. It didn't fucking matter. She was a self-righteous narc. And, damn it, she would look fantastic in tight jeans and heels. Now *I* had the damn visual.

I shot her the evil eye.

Anton's gaze bounced between Fiona and me through the meal, trying to size up our mutual disgust. When we'd finished, he said, "I need to talk to Rafa about a thing. Walk her home."

"Oh, come on." I dropped my head back in protest. "She can hit a button and ride a damn elevator."

"I can absolutely do that without this tool's help." Fiona pointed her thumb at me.

I scoffed. "I'm not a tool."

"You're *his* tool."

The breathy hum coming from Anton was not a good sign. He wasn't very good at patience or bickering. Silence, calm and money — not necessarily in that order — were more his speed. I didn't want to piss him off further than I already had, so I rolled my eyes and stood. "Fine. Let's go, Fi." I grabbed her elbow and she shook me off.

Once we were in the elevator, I said, "Nice game. Coming down here smelling all lusty and putting your best assets in his face. That line about spending time with him nearly broke my heart."

Fiona stalked forward and cornered me. The heat between us rose, causing me to break a sweat. "Let's get something straight, errand boy. Call me 'worthless' again and I'll pull your fucking nuts off with my bare hands."

She'd said something, and it had sounded a hell of a lot like a threat. But it had also sounded a lot like her hands on my junk. And okay, I'd insulted her a little bit, but she'd been rapid-firing at me all the damn night.

Her pissed-off gaze brought a little smile to my face. I was impressed that she'd gotten Anton to give her a job. Apart from Lisa and the doctor, there weren't a lot of ladies working for us.

Fiona shoved my shoulder. "Don't do that. Don't give me those bedroom eyes when I hate you."

I pushed her back against the wall. In her ear, I said in a low, airy voice, "I'll give you whatever the fuck eyes I want, whenever I want." I may have even pressed a little too much on her chest, because it was just too tempting not to.

After a fluttering of those made-up eyelashes, Fiona stepped back. "I don't think your boss would approve."

That was where Fiona was wrong. Jealousy wasn't an emotion that ran through the bossman of steel. Chances were, if I found something to benefit him, he'd give me the green light with Fiona. But she could hedge her bets on him giving a fuck about her. That was fine by me.

The doors opened and I followed her down the hall. "Scooter will drive you downtown at ten." I dug into my pants and pulled out some money. "Oh, and send me pictures of your clothes. If I'm buying it, I get final say. They're my games, after all."

Fiona snatched the cash from my hand. "You just want pics of me to whack off to."

An excellent idea all around. "Maybe." I grinned, and the middle finger she showed me as she entered her apartment lacked just a little more conviction than her previous ones.

The elevator was busy so I jogged down the stairs. At our place, I left the dishes — someone would be around to do that shit for us — and got lost in a basketball game on TV. When Anton came back at half-time, he muted the sound and sat down next to me.

"Rafa said you kicked the shit out of him. I thought we'd talked about that." Anton raised his eyebrows. I was well on my way to being on his shit list. He crossed his arms and offered a rare smile. "She is up in your shit, hard."

There was no point in lying. He'd seen enough. Plus, if I couldn't be brutally honest with him, what was the point of being in Covington?

"Pfff…" I rubbed my neck. "I may have been just a tad frustrated."

"I can't let you fuck her before me. I gotta keep up appearances. And there is no fucking way I'd fight you for her." The illusion of not being equals was part of my cover.

Give him something he wants more than her.

"I'll work with the Golden Boy and make him stronger, quicker."

The joint in Anton's jaw popped to one side as he considered. "For what?"

There was no way he'd just let me have her. Besides, it was her call anyway. I needed to tread lightly and not overplay the crappy hand I had. "If she makes a move on me, I don't have to step off."

Anton laughed. "She seems pretty sure she hates you."

The game started back up on the screen behind Anton. "If you really believed that, we wouldn't be having this conversation."

I un-muted the sound and we watched the rest of the game without talking. There was no doubt in my mind that he would pull something to try to out-maneuver me. But I was already three steps ahead of him.

Chapter Seven

Fiona

I grazed through the racks and racks of clothes, completely lost. The thought of spending the money in my bag on just one outfit was beyond comprehension. Two beautifully put-together girls giggled opposite me. Their straight hair shone, the rips in their jeans looked masterfully intentional and their makeup was flawless. My cut-offs, hoodie and knock-off designer bag were a sad comparison. Hell, I hadn't even worn mascara.

A middle-aged woman in a black suit and name tag around her neck approached me with the look – the one that said she thought I was there to shoplift.

"Can I help you find something in particular?" she asked as she tilted her head with doubt.

I sighed. I was lost, out of place and worried that I'd choose the wrong thing and Leo would find a way to hurt my feelings again. Because that 'worthless' comment? That had stung more than I'd wanted to admit.

Fuck it. "I have nine hundred dollars and I need to look like a classy whore. Black jeans and a tank top—not dressy, just not cheap."

The clerk sized me up then her brown eyes glimmered. "I can work with that."

I let out a long breath and gave her a shy smile. Asking for help wasn't something I was good at, but in that moment it was my best option for getting in and out of the store as quick as possible.

"I'm Karen. Follow me." She waved over her shoulder and I fell in line. Her energy had changed. She seemed to enjoy the mission—or perhaps it was a challenge.

Karen stopped in her tracks and spun around. She bit her lip and closed an eye. "I don't mean this to be rude. I just want to find your comfort zone. Is this"—she pointed to me and did a little loop with her finger—"what you normally wear?"

I swallowed and shifted my weight from side to side. "Pretty much."

"Okay. Jeans it is."

As if I had a choice... I was now an official part of the crew and the thought had my stomach flipping. Karen headed over to a wall of shelves with folded denim from floor to ceiling and propped her hands on her hips once she was in front of it.

"Black," I repeated.

"Good idea." Karen pulled out three pairs and handed them to me in a pile. "These are all under three hundred, which will leave you the same amount for heels and tops. Let's start a room."

With the absurd-costing pants in hand, I once again trailed her like a mindless robot. She opened the dressing room door with a key from a clear springy bracelet around her wrist.

"Um…" I winced. "Is there any way you can just bring everything here? Like the shoes and the shirts?"

Her tight smile read more understanding than pity and I relaxed a little. "Sure thing, sweetheart. Shoes size seven and a half?"

"Please." *She must know what she's doing if she can guess right at my shoe size.*

I stacked the jeans on the little stool in the corner, slipped off my bag and unzipped my thin hoodie. I was sure Karen would leave but she entered the tight space with me, staring at my chest.

"You're gonna need a better bra, dear."

By the end of an hour, I had an outfit and had received a lesson in how to walk in heels without falling on my face. Apparently, small steps were just as important as heel-to-toe. My fairy godmother in the black suit took a step back to admire her work.

I did the same, the reflection staring back at me so foreign that I had to squint. The jeans were tight, tighter than I'd ever worn, and they gave my hips curves that I hadn't even known I had. The razor-back tank didn't leave much to the imagination either and the woman had been right about my bra. My boobs were now smashed and high. They barely looked real.

"Holy crap," I whispered.

"Yeah. You're hot. Your boyfriend's gonna be happy." Karen nodded her head in approval then replaced the unwanted shoes back in their boxes and secured their cardboard lids.

Right. Fucking Leo. I had to show him. The dread I'd felt walking into the store crept back up my spine. I wobbled over to my bag, I would need to practice in heels — I was still far from being a pro — and dug out the phone. I snapped a pic and sent it to him.

Within seconds, the bubble next to his name popped up with the dots that he was typing.

Show me your ass.

Fucker. God, he was a horrible excuse for a man. But I turned around, took another picture — complete with me flipping him off — and sent it anyway. I looked over to Karen, who had curiosity in her dark eyes, but her lips remained sealed. A part of me wanted to explain that I needed approval, but the other side screamed that it would make me look like more of a whore than I already did.

The phone dinged with an emoji of a thumbs-up. I guessed a compliment was beyond Leo's scope. *Douchebag.* And now he had his jerk-off ammo.

"I'll take it all," I said to Karen.

She perked up and grinned. "Do you want to wear it out of here? I can cut off the tags."

Did I? Could I fully commit to the transformation? It would mean I'd surrendered, but hadn't I already? Maybe the consolation prize of me being sexy, for what was probably the first time in my life, could get me through to the end of the day.

"Yeah, that would be nice. But maybe a bag for the shoes."

"No problem. Let's ring you up. The scissors are at the desk."

I didn't take offense when Karen scrutinized the hundred-dollar bills. It was her job and a different girl from my same background might have tried something a little bolder. I thanked her for all her help, she gave me a big enough paper bag to add my old clothes inside and, wearing my flip-flops, I headed out of the department store.

The warm summer air tasted like a freedom I didn't think I'd be getting for a while. There was a little coffee shop down the street that promised homemade gelato. I'd heard of the Italian dessert before but had never tried it. If I could lie to myself for fifteen minutes and imagine that I belonged in this higher-class world of downtown, that and the ice cream would be a selfish treat I'd rarely known. I tapped on the window and told Scooter I was going to get a bottle of water for the way back.

Lie told, I proceeded to walk down the block pretending to be a confident woman who was perfectly at ease. I set the bag next to my feet and plucked the laminated menu from the metal holder while I sat at the wire table on the sidewalk. The variety of complicated flavors batted away my fake persona with an unsettling ease. Passion fruit, pistachio, almond butter and honey… Where was chocolate chip? My palms turned clammy. Even the vanilla had a fancy name.

The waiter, a skinny but gorgeous man with hair gelled to perfection and spotless skin, came over with a small tablet.

"What can I get you, honey?" he asked with a warm smile.

"What's your favorite flavor of the gelato?" *When in doubt, ask.* It really was bizarre of me—asking people for help twice in one day. Who knew I was capable?

"Oh, I don't eat that. Way too much sugar."

Crap. My flavor probe was dead on arrival. And if I was going to spend five dollars of my dwindling money, I really needed to choose wisely.

"I..." I stared at the colorful menu with its round colorful balls of ice cream. "I'll just have chocolate."

The waiter studied me. "We don't have chocolate."

Fucking hell. I'd just wanted a sweet treat. Why was this so impossible? I rubbed my temples.

But it seemed to be a day of saviors, because the waiter added, "You want to try a couple before you commit?" The casual shrug after the question was so endearing that it made me forget that nothing in life was free. It lured me over to the counter and let me indulge with tiny colorful plastic spoons on flavors I'd never known existed. His simple kindness plastered a real, true smile on my face. When I tasted the *stracciatella* and realized that it was just chocolate chip, I ordered a scoop and floated back to the table. The blast of sugar spiked my blood and made me lighter than air.

But when I pulled out the metal chair to sit, my chest tightened and my head shifted from blissful buoyancy to a typhoon spinning out of control.

Stale air. That was what had replaced the big paper bag with my old clothes and new, beautiful heels.

My fingers and toes tingled as I frantically searched the street. Each pedestrian walked with calm purpose. There was no bag in sight.

Fuck. Leo would be pissed. Two hundred and eighty-five dollars gone in a poof. And I'd sorta fallen in love with those heels. My only saving grace was that I'd kept my mini backpack on and I still had my phone and money. The embarrassment of screwing up a simple shopping trip pecked away at the confidence I'd found an hour prior. Leo's insult of me being worthless stung in my memory.

When the waiter brought over my glass dessert bowl and long silver spoon, I faked my calm and thanked him with a tight smile. I had no idea how I would get the creamy goodness past the massive lump of panic and stupidity in my throat.

Each small bite was a struggle, the joy having been sucked out of the air with the disappearance of my belongings. My celebratory scoop transformed into a pity party, the sweetness of the gelato lost in my sour stomach.

I paid the waiter, left him a bigger tip than I could afford and slogged down the street. Defeated, I climbed into the back of the SUV, only to be met with fierce blue eyes.

Crap, maybe it was *his* money I'd lost being so careless.

"What's wrong with you? I thought chicks liked shopping," Anton asked.

How, after just a glance at me, could he know something wasn't right?

I crossed my arms. "What are you doing here?" Maybe it was wrong to go on the defensive, but old habits died hard and I needed a change of subject.

"I had an opening." Anton shifted in the seat so that he faced me. "Listen… You said you wanted to see more of me." He held up both hands in surrender. "Here I am."

I stared out of the tinted window, wondering how I would be asked to pay back the money I'd spent on the shoes. Had I just added to my nonsensical debt? Also, I'd grabbed that money out of Leo's hand without even a thought that I would owe him something in return. The Covington Heights crew was turning me into an idiot.

"Fucking hell, Fiona. You seriously know how to send mixed signals. Unless you were just using me for a job..." He grabbed for the handle and before he yanked, he said, "You look amazing, by the way."

Maybe it was the anger in his tone that shook me loose from my melancholy. Maybe it was just the compliment that stroked my ego. But before he got his foot out of the car, I said, "Someone stole my shoes."

Anton froze. Slowly, he turned back, glanced at my feet that still had my flip-flops and asked, "What?"

"While I was tasting gelato, someone stole my bag."

He closed the door and sat silent for a moment. Maybe, if I was a part of his crew, he would think they'd also stolen from him. Then he turned to me and his blue eyes burned me in a whole new way that was equal parts thrilling and scary. The hint of a smile played at his lips and his eyelids were only half open. Just above a whisper and with a blend of lust and hope he asked, "Are you asking me for new shoes?"

Nothing in life is free, Fiona.

My heart pounded. I could either roll the dice with Anton or Leo—and I fucking hated Leo. He would be smug, call me an idiot and belittle me. I was nothing to him. But Anton? Well, I *knew* I had something he wanted. I hated to be calculated, but what other choice did I have?

And the seductive steam rolling off of him was not only unexpected, it was seeping into my skin, intoxicating my better judgment while stroking that one little part of my ego that liked the fact that *he*, the boss, wanted *me*, the nobody. It was the same spot that had leaped for joy at just having a little attention. And as those crystal eyes stared back at me, I feared the lesion was growing like a tumor — infesting me, poisoning who I was, changing my chemical make-up.

"Yes." It was a cautious response — a confession, risk and dare.

After a slow blink that offered me a second of reprise from his strong hold, he said, "Then let me taste the ice cream."

The air between us had grown thick, making it hard to think, to breathe. It was difficult to know exactly which moment I'd officially lost my way. Maybe me trying to bribe men with cleavage had set off the chain reaction to my demise, though in truth it didn't matter. I'd been headed down the horrible path the second they'd noticed me. I'd just never expected to want to be on it.

With the hope of being different and staying strong suffocated by Anton's powerful fog, I climbed into his lap and looked directly into his lust-filled eyes. And, God help me, I quite possibly returned the same hunger. His torso was thick, solid and I pressed my palms into his chest. I could hear my heart beating in my brain and wondered briefly if I'd been drugged. I brought my mouth to his, but he didn't move.

I almost asked if it was a joke until I remembered his rules. My throaty whisper was the voice of a girl I didn't recognize. "I want you to taste it."

Anton's lips were way softer than they should have been, than I wanted them to be. And his embrace was just as gentle, perhaps to hold me hostage in the confusing haze. Figuring out what had flipped in my brain and how the son of a bitch below me had voodoo-mind-fucked me into actually wanting to kiss him would have to wait. I hushed my doubts, fears and better judgement and opened my mouth wide enough to allow his tongue to slip inside.

He let out a barely audible groan and, heaven help me, I rubbed my tits into his iron chest and draped my arms over his thick shoulders. His docile manner left me craving more, needing him to show me the rough side behind those ice-blue eyes. He pulled back ever so slightly and brushed the tip of his nose against mine. Then his warm, wet lips claimed another sinful kiss.

"Harder," I said between breaths, my body making all the decisions and my brain choosing not to witness my transgressions.

Anton snaked an arm up my back and the opposite hand grabbed a hold of my hips. He spun us around so my back was on the seat and the kiss intensified. We teased each other with our tongues as we mimicked the same wicked tangle of lust with our bodies.

I could have wept at how fucking true and raw my desire had become. Anton kissed and nibbled my neck, then he hit a spot that made me shiver. Hell, I didn't even care that Scooter was still in the car. I was lost. The voices in my head had been silenced by an unfiltered craving for the one man who I'd been sure, days prior, that I could never want anything from.

But the worst part? The absolute fucking horror of it all? He fucking knew it. How could he not? I was panting below his massive brick of a body, grinding my crotch into his, ready to strip off my clothes and beg him kiss me everywhere. Jesus help me, I'd even whimpered when he'd dug his fingers into the flesh of my ass.

And just when I was on the brink of begging for more, to confirm that I wanted him, he stopped. He sat up, wiped his mouth with the back of his ink-lined forearm and smirked.

"Well worth a pair of shoes," he said and winked.

It made perfect sense that I had no idea if that was a compliment or an insult. I gave my head a tiny shake, half hoping Anton and I would never acknowledge the last five minutes had ever happened. I righted myself in the back seat and pulled down the hem of my tank top where it had risen with all the bodily friction.

Anton reached for the handle of the door then turned to me with a devilish grin. "It's in the back, by the way."

Maybe it was the kiss-fog or maybe I was just slow on the uptake, but he really had me at a loss. "What's in the back?"

"Your bag." He opened the door and was on the other side of the street before I could question him further.

He couldn't have. My jaw fell open as I spun around and let the burn of being used sear my soul with the proof of my foolishness. Sure enough, my bag was in the back of the SUV. *Jesus Christ, he calculated the entire thing.*

That motherfucker had stolen my shit to make me desperate. He had mind-fucked me and I'd fallen right into his trap. *Fucking every layer of hell...* I'd wanted him. He'd toyed with me, played me like a child and he'd won. I sat there, stunned, humiliated and sure I was a fool until Scooter cleared his throat.

As we drove uptown, I spread ChapStick over my kiss-swollen lips. Anton might have won the battle, but he'd shown me something too. He wanted me. There was something that brought him to me. A tiny thread connected us — and I was going to tie that motherfucker into a million knots.

When we pulled up to the courtyard, I had to stop myself from doing a happy dance. As predicted, Anton and his crew were on and around their bench — black jeans, tanks and a few with black baseball hats. In my new outfit, I looked as much the part as any one of them.

Leo clocked me and narrowed his eyes when I smiled from ear to ear. If Anton wanted to play games, we were going to play a great one called Public Display of Affection.

Not taking my eyes off Leo — who looked like he knew exactly what I was doing — I swayed my hips all the way up to him. I dropped my bag at his feet, threw my arms around his neck and hopped up so he was forced to hold me.

"Thank you for my clothes and shoes," I said before going in for a sloppy, overly dramatic kiss.

Leo was a sly fucker — and maybe it was all in my head — but I was pretty sure he was enjoying himself, because he was copping all kinds of feels. His hands were on my ass and with his lips still pressed into mine, he said, "See you later, guys."

Without letting me go in any way — he was kissing the shit out of me and I was giving it right back, his stubble burning my skin — Leo knelt down and picked up the bag. He carried me all the way into the building, our spectacle no longer within view of Anton and his crew. But Anton hadn't objected.

I was sure Leo would drop me flat on my ass, but he pinned me against the wall next to the rusting mailboxes and let the bag fall to the ground. I should probably not have squirmed, not dug my nails into his neck just below the soft baby hairs that were tickling my fingers.

I shouldn't have been enjoying it, especially after I'd kissed his boss less than an hour earlier. Nor should I have liked the pain in my back against the cool concrete wall or the fire in my belly lit by the idea that Leo had kept kissing me when he wasn't supposed to.

I should have hated his free hand cupping my breast, squeezing it savagely. Wrapping my legs around him tighter was wrong, too. All of it... All of it was wrong. And it was fucking invigorating, liberating. They say revenge is best served cold, but I wasn't so sure. What Leo and I were doing was hot as fuck and spiked with retribution.

Why he hadn't stopped was a mystery, one I didn't care to unravel.

A fake cough came from the doorway.

Leo finished his heartless assault on my mouth and I loosened my grasp. He licked from my collar bone up to my ear and took the lobe between his teeth. His delicious stubble scraped my cheek and he whispered, "You're playing a dangerous game, Fi."

"You started it," I said for only him to hear.

"Don't make me finish it." It was a challenge, a dare—one I shouldn't have wanted to take. But if those drug-dealing shits were going to use me, I would use them right back.

Another cough.

"What is it, Scooter?" Leo asked through gritted teeth and a little too loud next to my ear.

"The boss wants you back. You need to go on a run." *Maybe I struck a chord with the almighty Anton after all.*

Chapter Eight

Leo

"You have to get to the point where your instinct tells you what they're going to do next but your head knows what you're going to do after that. It's like pool. You have to see the path of the ball before you hit it." I offered Rafa my hand and pulled him back up to stand in the middle of the navy-blue training mat.

The gym was empty. Me working with Rafa was a three-way secret. Anton had agreed to my Fiona terms and we'd told Rafa that I'd studied under a one-on-one combat guru, which wasn't exactly a lie. He rolled his neck and a drop of sweat fell from his hair to his bronze shoulder. With his darker skin tone and jet-black hair, we could have been brothers, except his amber eyes that came from his Brazilian heritage. Mine were a deep brown and they hid all the dark secrets of my father and brother.

"I suck at pool." Rafa shot me a scowl, but there was a grateful twinkle in his eyes. I'd already corrected his footing and his punch had packed more heat, despite his fatigue.

"All right. Let's make it relevant to you then. Hacking... When you're breaking into a server, are you thinking about the person's password or what you're going to get?"

Rafa rolled his eyes and reached for his water bottle. "I have a program for the passwords. It's automatic."

I walked over to the bench where I'd thrown my shirt and pulled it on. "Right. So your defense has to get to the point where it's automatic and your offense is calculated."

After a drink, he dumped the rest of the bottle over his head. "And how, pray tell, does one do that?"

Fight every day since you could walk.

"Practice." I headed for the door. "I'll see you tomorrow, but not too early. Jackson and I have the poker game downtown."

"Right...with your new bartender." The small taunt in Rafa's voice wasn't worth the rebuttal, so I let it roll off my back. Besides, I could make him pay for it the next day. *Idiot.*

With my uniform of black jeans, black tank and black hoodie on and my hair still a little damp from my quick shower, I knocked on Fiona's door.

Holy hell.

She hadn't worn the heels the day before, and as sexy as she'd been when she'd hopped up onto my dick, those shoes? They were the cherry on top of the Fiona sundae.

I swallowed down my lust and asked, "You ready?"

Fiona hiked a little black backpack over her shoulder. A curious glance twinkled in her pretty brown eyes. I bet she thought I was going to lead with a line about the kiss, but that would have been too obvious.

She shook off whatever she had been wondering and said, "Are you kidding? Getting out of Covington is my life goal, even if it is just for a few hours."

When the elevator doors closed, the heated, undeniable tension between us blanketed our space like an iron cloth. *Good.* It could hang in the air and suffocate her. She might have started that kiss to piss off Anton after whatever it had been that he'd so conveniently needed to do while she had been shopping, but it had ended as something completely different. She'd touched danger and she'd fucking loved it.

But when I saw through our fog of proven mutual lust, her comment about getting out of Covington picked at my side. *Funny...* My goal was to stay there and hide for as long as I could. Not that I was really hiding... Frankie knew where I was. *Avoiding...* That was a better way of putting it.

The doors cranked open and Fiona stumbled on her heels a little bit. She muttered something about baby steps, set her shoulders and strutted all the way to the waiting SUV. I reached for the handle of the back seat but stopped short of opening the door.

"Fi"—I looked down at her with a tight smile— "there's going to be a guy there with short, red hair. He's going to know something is up because he's been coming to games for a long time and there has never been a woman who has worked for the crew."

"Because you are misogynists."

Her spunk made me roll my eyes, but I liked that it had returned.

"He has a…history. He'll know you're special for just being there. It's best not to mention Anton." I yanked on the handle and had to stop my other hand from smacking her on her ass. Those jeans were toying with my overly active imagination. I hopped into the front passenger seat and gave the universal man-nod to Jackson, who was behind the wheel.

"Fiona, this is Jackson. Jackson, meet Fiona."

Jackson sent Fiona the peace sign and she said, "I actually know you. You went to my high school."

"You must be younger. I would have remembered you." Jackson winked and he and Fiona trotted down memory lane all the way downtown. The more they jabbered and laughed, the more I couldn't shake the feeling that bringing Fi was a mistake—and not because Fiona had just admitted to having a massive crush on Jackson when she had been fifteen or that she was ooo-ing and aww-ing over his little kid.

Because of my damn instincts, I shot a text to Anton. Mac's real beef wasn't with me. If I said Fiona was mine, not the crew's, Mac might just be less interested. Instead of writing back, my phone lit up with a call.

Anton, not one for flowery greetings, got right to the point. "Sounds more like a ploy on your end."

"It kills his motivation and makes her less of a target." I twisted in my seat in hopes that the other two passengers wouldn't hear me, and I lowered my voice. "I was taught to always look for the biggest risk. He's it. I know it."

Anton sighed on the other end. "He's old with zero resources. You and Jackson could take him out just by blinking. So either you're fucking with me or fucking with her."

I let out that slow breath, the one that meant I was serious, the one that went through my nose but heated the back of my throat like a grumble and the one that told Anton that while it was his crew and his call, my judgement when it came to enemies was a fine-tuned machine that hummed with certainty.

He understood that breath. He'd heard it when we had been fifteen and cornered in an alley by four dudes double our size and pissed off that we'd taken all their money shooting dice. He'd also seen the carnage after one of them had dared to take a swing at a skinny young Italian kid. I'd broken one guy's nose with a single, quick jab.

After a long pause, Anton muttered out, "Fine," and I broke the connection. His timing had been perfect, because we'd pulled into the underground parking garage and Jackson had stopped chatting with Fiona to take a ticket.

I swiveled around to her. "Change of plans... As far as the outside world is concerned, you are my new girlfriend."

Fiona laughed. "How am I supposed to act like your girlfriend when I hate you?"

Jackson whipped into a spot, threw the car into park and, with raised eyebrows, looked over his shoulder. "Was that what happened yesterday? Cuz you could have won an award for that performance, sis."

Fiona opened and closed her mouth a few times.

Mm-m-hmm-m. What he said. I tried not to gloat as we exited the garage, weaved around people and tables in the dingy bar, through a back hall that reeked of every bodily excretion known to man and down the stairs to the room we rented for poker nights.

Jackson unlocked the door and flipped on the dim lighting. The round felt table in the center of the room was in its usual pristine condition and the bar glimmered with cleanliness. Fiona circled around and opened and closed small fridges, inspecting her supplies. Trapped and with nowhere to go was exactly where I wanted her, so I stalked over, because apparently she'd turned me into some stupid animal. I crowded her space.

She'd worn perfume, a sweet citrus smell that I couldn't identify, and if I thought her jeans were a snug fit, the tank top was making her perfect chest even more inviting—which I'd already been sure was impossible.

Behind her, with all kinds of wonderfully dirty images bombarding my thoughts and for her ears only, I said, "You wanna talk about what happened yesterday or shall we just try again real quick?"

Little goosebumps flushed over her pale skin and her breath stuttered on the way out. But she flipped around and leveled me with her beautiful eyes. In her heels, she'd gained some height, and in my stalking, I'd lost some, so we were almost face-to-face.

"It was a momentary lapse of reason brought on by an extra case of douchebaggery by your fucked-up boss." She held the gaze, maybe hoping I couldn't smell her lie. And while her words rang true—certainly the douchebag part about Anton, who had no doubt overplayed his hand—the little blinks she couldn't control told another story. It was a story where her heart might just have been going *pitter patter* a little faster when I was around—one that was daring me to do it all over again…and more.

I leaned in and brushed my stubble on her smooth cheek. In a low voice I said, "Keep telling yourself how much you hated it, how much you hate me. It doesn't matter. I see everything about you, Fiona Marie Thompson."

She pushed into my chest and I stepped back with my smirk firmly in place.

"Get off, asshole."

"Interesting choice of words." My tone was lighter, teasing, and I lifted my eyebrows to match the reference.

"Oh my God! You really are a piece of shit. Can you stop thinking about me and my tits for longer than thirty seconds? Gross."

Probably not.

I cleared my throat. "In all seriousness, Fi, don't fall for Mac's tricks. And if he doesn't believe you're mine, well…"

"Well, what? The big, bad bald wolves will come and rape me?" Fiona wiggled her fingers and her tone was taunting. It wasn't the first time she'd hinted that we were overreacting. But she didn't understand the mind of criminals, because she wasn't one.

Once a person had broken the law, they had an enemy. The better someone got at crime, the more the other law breakers hated them. Anton was doing well in Covington. His supply of drugs was never an issue, due to his family connections. Not only had the guys from Bradford Towers tried to invade our territory, but there had also been minor threats from Jefferson Manors to the east.

But Mac? That was a dormant grudge against Anton and his family for ruining his business decades prior. When someone made it personal, they lost perspective — or at least that was what my dad always said.

Three quick knocks came from the door and I glanced at Jackson and nodded. To Fiona, I said, "Trust me."

She rolled her eyes and turned her back. Maybe it was asking too much, but she would see soon enough. Mac had a slithery way about him that could make a person's skin crawl.

Two young businessmen wearing dark, tailored suits came in and Jackson frisked them. I walked around the bar and met them once they'd been patted down and cleared for entry.

"Gentlemen. I believe you know the drill. Ten thousand each." They each pulled out rolls of cash and handed them over. I tossed one to Fi, who caught it with a start. "Count."

The Wall Street shithead with the blond, slicked-back hair asked, "While you verify, we're going to fuel up." He pulled out a little baggie with cocaine and dumped a small pile of the white powder on the bar.

I didn't give two shits what those pricks put in their bodies, but out of the corner of my eye I could see that Fiona had lost track of her total and had started her pile of hundreds again. *Maybe I should have warned her about the drugs.*

Five little white lines were perfectly parallel on the black bar. The businessman wet his finger and rubbed it on the credit card he'd used to separate the coke. He spread the residual powder on his gums then stored the card back in his wallet.

With a rolled-up bill, they took turns snorting the lines until only one remained. When I'd first taken over the games, they'd asked me a few weeks in a row if I wanted a line. I'd always said no, so eventually they stopped asking.

The blond twisted his wrist so the bill was in Fiona's direction. "You're up, sweetheart."

The color drained from Fiona's face. "I —"

With a quick sidestep, I was between the blond banker and the bar. "You think I'd let my girlfriend do blow with two strangers?" The threat hiding behind my light tone was enough for him to put his hands up and step back.

"Just trying to share." He looked at his buddy. "Split it?"

As I walked around the bar, they finished their drugs. Fiona handed me the stack of money. "Ten thousand. I counted it three times." Her voice was steady, but I didn't imagine that extra-long exhale as I stepped closer.

Under the bar, I found our little black envelope-like bag where we kept the money next to our stash of chips. I unzipped it, found the rubber bands, wrapped them around the two stacks and stored the money. I tilted my head to Fiona and hoped my silent message of her actually doing her job would do the trick.

It worked. She leaned into the bar, and blondie on the other side dropped his gaze to her chest.

"Eyes up," I said with a glare.

Fiona ignored me and asked him, "What can I get you guys to drink?"

"Jack and Cokes."

Fiona nodded and rubbed her palms together as she surveyed the stash behind her. I decided not to be a hovering prick and let her work that shit out. It wasn't nuclear science, for fuck's sake. I took out the chips and recounted them. Fiona managed the drinks and the two babbling bankers made their way to the table.

Another knock came from the door and our high-roller, Roland, walked in with his high-class hooker. He always brought arm candy, sometimes the same one. But the platinum blonde in her tight, hot-pink dress and overly plumped lips was new to me.

Jackson checked them out and found a barstool for the blonde, who ordered champagne, then dug out her phone and got lost in a game involving unicorns and candy. Roland was dressed in his usual light jacket and white open-collared shirt. The handkerchief in his pocket was a light blue silk that popped the color in his fading eyes. He handed me his money in a nice, clean pile and I didn't bother counting it, out of respect. Besides, his stack was always what I took home, and it had never been off once.

"Can I get you a drink?" Fiona asked with a simple smile.

"Roland only drinks water," I said as I brushed by Fiona a little too close. What could I say? I was an opportunist. "Keep it fresh for him."

I carried the three stacks of chips over to the table and distributed them to the players. Roland studied the bankers while they continued the diarrhea of the mouth that came from sniffing a stimulant.

When the final knock came, the hairs on the back of my neck stood at attention. I made my way over to Fiona, picked her up and sat her next to the sink. With a nudge from my knee, she opened her legs and I leaned in. "Put your arms around me."

"You're being —"

"*Now*, Fiona." My sharp tone got her attention and her eyes fluttered but she obeyed. I drew her nearer and kissed up her soft neck until I found it. The spot that made her giggle like her adorable little sister.

She shifted to try to get away, and with a true smile on her face, she said, "That tickles, you shit."

Jackson greeted Mac from behind us and I pulled back so we were nose-to-nose.

"Good," I said then gave her a quick peck on the lips. I moved to step away but she'd locked her hands around my neck.

Something had settled in her bright eyes and I couldn't put my finger on it. *Lust? Mischief?* Maybe it was trust.

"One more."

If she was acting, we would be just fine. I shifted my gaze to her lovely lips then back to her eyes before closing my own and leaning in. In any other setting I would have said 'fuck gentle' and replayed the day before in the lobby. Our lips met and I held the kiss. I cupped her cheek with one hand and wrapped my other arm around her waist. Her breath hitched, and I didn't know up from down.

Jackson coughed, and with regret, I stepped away and turned to face Mac, who was scrutinizing me from behind his dark glasses.

"Who's this?" he asked without motioning to Fiona, and he handed me his money.

"Scooter got promoted." I focused on counting. If anyone would be short, it would be him.

"That's not what I asked." Mac tapped the bar.

"Well, that's the answer you're getting."

The money was all there, and I stored it with the rest. Our games were winner takes all, minus our cut for keeping it safe and fair. Walk in with ten thousand, walk out with thirty. There were only four players allowed, so the chances of making money were pretty damn good if a person knew how to play. Getting high and wasted hadn't proved to be an effective strategy, but the bankers seemed to enjoy mixing with darker characters more than winning. They probably bragged about their secret nights to interns and other equally douchey dicks.

"Can I get you a drink?" Fiona asked, and just the thought of her interacting with Mac made my skin crawl.

"Vodka on the rocks with a lemon twist. Sorry... I didn't catch your name."

"Fiona," she said and I instantly hated him knowing.

Mac smirked like he'd won some sort of prize. "You can bring it to me, Fiona. Such a pretty name for such a pretty face." He walked to the table and shook hands with everybody.

I couldn't show that I was pissed at her for being stupid. Couldn't let out the anger bubbling beneath my skin that, in two seconds flat, Mac had picked up on her presence meaning more than it should. *Damn it.* I'd warned Anton. My only hope was to sell the lie of her being mine.

Chapter Nine

Fiona

I added the three ice cubes to the vodka and walked it over. Since Mac had come in, I'd understood a little slice of what Leo had warned me about. I fought off a shiver. The red-headed man with the dark glasses reeked of slime. I slipped his drink into the little cubby hole next to him, and just when I thought I would get away, he laid his hand on my bare forearm and I froze. He gripped my flesh and let out a small moan. "You that soft everywhere, gorgeous?"

It was everything I could do not to puke in my mouth.

"Hands off my fucking girl, Mac."

One sinister finger at a time, he let go of my arm, and I backed away and returned to behind the bar. Jackson had positioned his bar stool to watch the game and he shot me a brief look of compassion.

I refilled the blonde's champagne and wiped down the bar countless times. About two hours in, when one of the bankers was about to lose everything, he won a huge hand, taking half of Mac's remaining money. Leo called for a break and the guys took turns going to the bathroom and refilling their bodies with drugs and drinks.

Of all the years my mom had used drugs, she'd never done them in front of me. I guessed it was her one saving grace. I'd seen her high or coming down to a hard crash, but I'd never seen her—or anyone, actually—put the toxic chemicals into their bodies. So as the two bankers sniffed the white chalky powder from right there on the bar in front of me, I turned my back and rewashed some glasses, an uncomfortable heat crawling up my spine.

They ordered two more Jack and Cokes and I served them with a clipped smile.

Mac, who had been chatting with the man named Roland, bellied up to the bar, ignoring the bankers and their white lines. "So, has Leo fucked you in your tight ass yet?"

I swallowed hard, trying to buy time to find an answer or just ignore him. I decided not to respond and was about to turn around when Leo slid in behind me and roped an arm around my stomach. He copped a feel of one of my breasts, dragged his lower lip from my collarbone to my ear, and said, "I've written my name all over her fine body. But this one doesn't kiss and tell, so you can stop asking."

I entered a space I'd never known existed—saf*er*. I was by no means safe and was pretty sure I hadn't given Leo any kind of permission to touch my breasts, but his marking me as his was keeping me safer than letting me fend for myself. It was odd to be grateful, and yet I was.

"It's unlike you to be so possessive, Leo. It makes a fellow wonder why," Mac said and downed the rest of his drink.

Leo tugged me closer and brought his other arm around my waist. He scratched my neck with his rough stubble and rested his chin on my shoulder. "What can I say? I finally found one I like having around outside of my bed."

Any other time I would have groaned or scoffed. Instead, I dropped my head back into Leo's shoulder and closed my eyes. For a fraction of a second, I allowed myself to bathe in the sense of security. I let myself believe the lie, because being held was nice. And nice was not something I'd had a lot of.

I spun around slowly and smiled up to Leo. "I have a drink to make."

Leo snaked his hands down my lower spine and took a proper hold of my ass. His dark eyes glimmered with desire. Maybe I was just as much his forbidden fruit as he was mine — or maybe he was just fantastic at faking. And that simmering energy pulsating out of my chest was just my nerves, because we were putting on a show.

Leo squeezed a final time and winked — which made me want to laugh, because him being playful didn't seem like something in his realm of normal — then let me go. They all reclaimed their seats, the two businessmen peppier and more jittery than before. I made Mac's vodka, and when I moved to take it to the table, Leo reached for it instead.

"I got this."

Roland was the first one to lose. His escort hadn't left her seat or phone the entire three hours they'd been there, but as soon as he approached and told her they were leaving, she stored her phone in her tiny sparkly bag and plastered a smile across her overly made-up face. She followed him to the door where Jackson stood and let them out.

The dark-haired businessman went all in on a bluff and Mac claimed his chips without even cracking a smile. The suit stayed at the table to support his friend, who was chewing on a piece of gum so fast that I thought his jaw might overheat.

Mac folded a couple of times, then found a hand he wanted to play and he raised. The fidgety mess across from him looked confident but Mac stayed cool, like the reptile I was sure he was. It was probably the drugs that made the banker dude go all in — stupid, fucked-up fool with his white-powder ego. He was going to lose. I didn't even need to see the cards.

The pile of chips in the center of the table went to Mac, whose bemused smile wasn't full. Instead, his gaze came to me, obvious even behind his dark glasses.

"Looks like your girl is my good luck charm." He stacked the chips he'd just won while the bankers swore at their loss and left.

Leo circled around the bar and took out the money. He walked over and gave three stacks to Mac, who thumbed through the bills with his pale, spotted fingers. Satisfied that he hadn't been cheated, Mac stood and meandered over to the bar where I was finishing the last of the glasses. He laid out two hundred-dollar bills and tapped them.

"Thanks for the drinks, Fiona. It was a true pleasure making your acquaintance." Mac hovered for a final second, his eerie energy wafting over and causing me to hold my breath. "Leo... Jackson..." Mac nodded to both men and, once he was out of the door, I let out a long exhale.

I stared at the money he'd left. Roland had tipped me a twenty and the bankers each fifty. In less than four hours I'd made over three hundred dollars, but the bulk of it in front of me, I didn't even want to touch.

Jackson leaned over the bar. "It's all dirty money, sis. Don't get wrapped up in the levels of the grime or you'll never get by." His softer tone matched his warm, dark eyes and I understood what Lisa liked in him. Jackson didn't have the edge that Anton and Leo had. He was just as built, and his chocolate skin was equally handsome, but Jackson seemed like a genuine nice guy.

"Right." I pocketed the bills but washed my hands for good measure.

Leo slipped behind me and stored the chips. "You done?" There more than just a hint of cranky in Leo's question.

"Are you mad at me?" I yanked back and gave him the once-over.

Leo let out that throaty grumble he did when he was annoyed. It was equal parts stupid and adorable. "You shouldn't have told him your name."

Not this again. "Listen... I get it. If I searched 'creepiest fucker alive', Mac's face would come up. And while your...protectiveness is appreciated, it's also a kiss overboard and short-sided. If I hadn't told him, it would have meant we had something to hide."

Jackson glanced between us and stretched up his long arms overhead. "She's got a point, Number Two. Come on. I still need to get J.J. from Lisa's." He went to the door and held it open.

The small glare coming from Leo said volumes. Not only did he not like Jackson taking my side, but he also didn't like being second in command. *Interesting.*

I followed Leo out and we drove back up to Covington in silence. The highway next to the river was deserted, due to the late hour, and without traffic to slow us down, the ride was quick. When we pulled up across the courtyard, I realized that the illusion of being a part of something was a feeling I wasn't ready to let go of.

When we got to the elevator, I asked with a tentative smile, "Leo?"

He seemed to be over his small tantrum. His energy was almost normal, whatever that was. But it somehow gave me permission and courage to continue.

"I'm not quite ready to go home. Can I come over for a beer or something?"

The glimmer came back to his eyes—the 'or something' had obviously set his imagination aflame. And while I was pretty sure I'd confirmed his desire for me the day before, a hot and heavy make out session with him wasn't what I'd meant. The real reason was that I didn't want to go home.

"Suit yourself."

Oh, his 'tough guy doesn't care' act in front of Jackson was laughable, and I wanted to call him out on it, but not as bad as I needed a bit of company. We said goodbye to Jackson on the third floor and I followed Leo into his apartment.

The small light over the cooktop was on and Leo found two beers in the fridge then motioned for the couch. I kicked off my heels, tucked my foot under my ass and sat in a corner. Leo handed me the cold, brown bottle before he sat in the middle of the sectional with his legs sprawled.

I took a cautious sip, and while I wasn't a huge fan of the bitter liquid, I swallowed it down. "I don't usually drink," I said in a small voice.

"Oh, yeah?" Leo turned his head in my direction and lifted his thick brows. "To what do I owe this pleasure, then?"

It was odd, having a real conversation with the man next to me. I was sure I hated him, knew I lusted after him, but was beginning to wonder if I needed him. Frustrating and insulting him was a fun sport and I was sure I would never give it up, but in that moment, I needed a friend. I could only hope he wouldn't use it against me.

"It threw me, the drugs." I fiddled with the label on the beer. Looking into his eyes would have meant confirming the vulnerable side of myself that I was so desperately trying to keep hidden from the world. "My biggest fear is turning into her."

"Sorry about that. I should have warned you."

My heart pounded, and when I finally dared to meet his gaze, the sincerity I found blanketed me and held me safe, not unlike he'd done at the poker game. It was horrifying and beautiful. "Why are you so protective of me?"

Leo worked his jaw but never blinked.

After what seemed like forever, he asked, so soft and yet so serious, "Why did you kiss me yesterday?"

Either he wanted an answer or he was giving me one. When I didn't offer my own, he got up and dumped the rest of his beer in the sink.

Before disappearing down a hall that must have led to his room he said, "You can stay here if you want.

And, Fiona, if the only reason you kissed me was to get back at him, don't ever fucking do it again."

I sat frozen and staring at the dead air that Leo had occupied for a long time. He'd been right. I was playing a dangerous game — one where there were rules that made no sense, one where there was more at risk than I could understand and one I wanted to keep playing.

The remainder of my beer followed Leo's down the drain, and I spotted a fuzzy throw blanket next to the couch and cuddled up. I probably should have checked on my sister, but I hadn't been selfish in so long. I decided that going home just to see everybody sleeping was silly.

* * * *

I woke up the next morning to the door closing, and as I blinked to focus, I realized that I wasn't alone. Anton stood shirtless over the stove, a blue-and-white striped kitchen towel over his shoulder and a baseball cap on backward. *Drug dealers... They're just like us.*

But his casual manner couldn't stop the fact that I was still pissed at him for manipulating me. I rose quietly and folded the blanket.

"Did you miss me?" he asked over his shoulder but without making eye contact.

"Hardly. What you did the other day was fucked up." I sat down on a bar stool and wondered how I'd become so at home in their apartment.

"Newsflash..." Anton stirred eggs with a wooden spoon as he turned toward the island. "Everything I do is fucked up."

"You really know how to charm a girl."

He piled the fluffy white and yellow mix onto a plate, grabbed a fork out of a drawer then sat next to me—no offer to share his eggs in sight. After a few bites, he said, "You should know that I'm not the jealous type. Jumping on one of my crew isn't going to piss me off. So, you can stop doing that."

What if I don't want to stop doing that? And, my God, Anton was going to choke on those eggs. He was piling them in at an alarming rate.

"Huh... I was sure you wouldn't want to share your toys." *Why am I poking the beast? Why?*

Anton scraped the plate and made one final pile before eating it. He wiped his mouth with the towel and said, "Call me crazy, but I like to take the new ones out of the box and play with them for a while first. But after that, I'm happy to share."

The steam seeping out of his gaze reminded me that I had actually liked kissing him, that he'd been damn good at it and that we'd had more chemistry than I cared to admit.

I cleared my mind of his sultry confusion and said, "I want to take my little sister out to lunch. Does that require a chaperone?"

"It does—but I don't do kids. You can ask Leo when you leave." Anton stood and dumped his dishes into the sink without giving them a second thought. "He's across the hall."

Hearing an obvious invitation to leave, I went back to the couch and slipped on my heels. I grabbed my bag from the floor and repeated my walking mantra in my head. No need to fumble in front of the wall of muscle. Anton held the door open and I easily slipped under his arm. Two doors down and on the opposite side of the hall, he punched in a security code. After a small click, we were on the other side in a state-of-the-art private gym. Leo and the one they called 'Golden Boy' were in the center of a huge mat, shirtless, sweaty and in the middle of a fight.

Holy hot criminals, Batman.

Leo tripped Golden Boy, punched him in the chest on the way down to the mat then was on top of him faster than a flying monkey.

"Better," Leo said. "But you're still thinking too much."

Anton left my side and went over to the large hanging bag in the corner. "Ricci, you're on babysitting duty again." He put in his wireless headphones, swiped a few times on his phone and pounded the bag to a rhythm only he could hear.

Leo got up, offered a hand to Golden Boy then came over to me. *Okay, so sweaty, shiny, naked-torso Leo is a force to be reckoned with.* Lisa was right. He was an instant panty-melter who fueled the best kind of dirty thoughts I'd had in a while.

"Eyes up, Fi."

"Whatever. Put a shirt on. Listen… I wanted to take Violet to one of those pizza places where she can make her own pie. There's one on the East side, and ass-face says I can't go alone, which is stupid because it's nowhere near Bradford."

"Must we do this every time?" His level, bored stare couldn't hide the humor in his brown eyes.

I smiled. "Can I buy you lunch while Violet has some fun?"

"Send me the address and I'll pick you up around noon."

Chapter Ten

Leo

The pizza restaurant was on the edge of Jefferson Manors, another rival neighborhood, but one that tended to be less violent than the bald shitheads north of us. I didn't want to cause trouble, especially with Violet, so I ditched the black jeans for some khaki pants and pulled on a navy-blue T-shirt.

The problem was that I looked like a preppy prick. The crew was going to eat me alive. Sealing the deal were the dark loafers on my feet. I ran my fingers through my hair and the man staring back at me in the mirror was the spitting image of my former self.

Fuck it. Their safety trumped my pride. I walked down the hall, shaking my head, and when I got to the open shared space of our apartment, Anton and Rafa looked up from the laptop in front of them and busted out laughing.

"Oh, Mr. Ricci, would you like a cup of tea? Or maybe a savory Merlot with your lunch?" Rafa mocked then continued laughing as he tapped his stomach.

Anton sauntered up to me, faking interest and batting his eyes. "You're the prettiest thing I've ever seen." He made kissy sounds that were so out of character for him that I cracked a smile.

"You can both fuck off. And Rafa" — I leveled him with my eyes and wiped the grin off my face — "every word out of your mouth is a lesson I teach you tomorrow."

That shut him up and he went back to banging his fingers on the computer.

Anton smacked me on the back and put an arm over my shoulder as he led me to the door. "Seriously, though. It was a good idea. The BTs are enough of a headache right now. Scooter caught two lurking a little too close to home last night. I'm going with Jackson upstate for supplies and will be back tomorrow night. Bring Fiona back here after your dice game."

One of the qualities that Anton and I shared was our competitive nature. The little sparkle in his light eyes was a dead giveaway that he had a feeling he was losing his footing with her — and the small hint was motivation.

"No problem, boss. Happy drug smuggling." I winked at him, my sign that the game was on. We had a deal, after all. If Fiona made advances, I didn't have to reject her. I just had to find a way to get her to want me enough to do so.

And by the wide eyes that greeted me when she opened her door, I was one step closer.

"Oh my God! You look so un-drug-dealer-y. Say something asshole-ish so I know you're not an imposter." Fiona opened the door and welcomed me in. "My mom went to pick up her check. Speaking of which, can we add that to our list? Why are you dressed like that, anyway? If you put on cologne and think this is a date, I'll cut you."

She was talking fast. Maybe she was just in shock. After she'd seen me in black jeans, tanks and work boots for weeks, I couldn't blame her. Even I had been shocked when I'd seen my reflection earlier.

Violet walked over from the couch and gave me a bashful smile. I squatted down to her eye level. "Hello, gorgeous girl. You ready for some pizza?" She nodded and might have even blushed a little bit. I'd never considered myself charming, but I pondered the idea that she might.

Fiona had on cut-offs with a baggy gray T-shirt tucked into them. Her legs shimmered and she smelled like citrus fruit. There was a sad excuse for a bun on top of her head and the stray strands of her dark hair that had escaped made her somehow prettier. She picked up Violet and secured her in the stroller.

In the elevator she wasn't shy about checking me out again. "I don't think I can call you Leo when you look like that. You need a name like Thad or Finn." She tapped her chin with her index finger. "No, worse... Skip. I'm totally calling you Skip today."

"It beats Stubby. Anyway, I'm trying not to draw attention to us. The Covington uniform would work against us today." We walked through the lobby and I held the door open as she pushed Violet across the threshold. The stares came and it was possible Scooter's eyes bugged out of his head when we passed the crew. *Christ, it's just a pair of pants and a different color T-shirt. You'd think I was in drag.*

108

"We're gonna walk, right? It not unbearably hot today and I love Violet seeing bits of the city." Fiona jabbed the button to cross the street several times.

"Are you nervous about something?"

"No." Her answer was so quick that it made me chuckle. "You're just…" Fiona made an expression like she'd just tasted something foul and couldn't spit it out. "You're very unsettling like that. Why does it suit you? Were you a socialite in a former life? Did you go to, like, parties on boats and shit?"

Hardly. "I didn't grow up poor, if that's what you mean."

We crossed the street and headed east. After twenty minutes, we were at the restaurant and we parked the stroller next to a booth by the window. I hadn't noticed any guys from Jefferson or their distinctive blue button-down work shirts. Why did all the crews have to look the same? If I thought about it, the sensation of blending in was like a warm bath. In black jeans, I was always labeled — always a marked man, which was the opposite of what I wanted.

As Fiona took Violet over to the make-your-own pizza stand, I considered the possibility of leaving Covington, maybe getting into a car, driving to the middle of the country and working at some kind of stupid job that I would hate.

Fiona slipped onto the red leather bench across from me with a smile. Damn, it lit up her face. "I told her to make one for us, too. She seemed pretty excited about the idea of getting you to eat, and I quote, 'fuzzy fish'."

I leaned back in the booth and crossed my arms. "No worries there. My nanna was the queen of stinky pizza. I've been eating anchovies since I could chew solid food."

Fiona looked out of the window then back to me, her face more serious. "You talk about your nanna a lot. Did she raise you?"

My past was not something I liked sharing, but I decided to give Fiona a tiny slice. "Sort of. My mom left when I was two. We spent a lot of time at my nanna's when my dad worked."

The waitress brought over a pitcher of water and three glasses. After she set them down on the fake shiny wood table, she said, "You guys... Your daughter is adorable. She has the cutest giggle. I hope her daddy likes his pizza spicy." She spun around and the strings of her red apron brushed the corner of the table.

"You don't have to eat it. I just wanted her to enjoy herself and get a change of scenery. After seeing how much fun she had with you in the kitchen, I knew she'd love this. And Lord knows my best dish is a tuna sandwich."

Violet's infectious laugh caught our attention. Behind the counter, her hands were covered in tomato sauce and there was flour in her dark hair. The waitress said something to her and she nodded eagerly. It was safe to say that Fiona's mission had been accomplished.

Once the pizza was cooked, Fiona settled her little sister into the highchair at the end of the booth and I proceeded to eat the spiciest, stinkiest pizza of my life. I actually broke out in a sweat, but my over-the-top reactions even had Fiona laughing. Although, a part of me wondered if she wasn't just taking pleasure in my suffering.

Fiona insisted on paying, which was stupid, because she had way less money than I did. But I let her have her way, understanding the pride that went along with the gesture. We thanked the staff and were out of the restaurant without incident.

In the subway station, I carried the stroller down the steps and watched as the juggling of the train lulled Violet to sleep. She was pretty damn cute with her little thumb in her mouth. I lugged her back up at the stop for Fiona's old employer and we walked a few blocks until we were in front of a chain hotel in Midtown.

"Why don't you run in and I'll stay here with Violet."

"Skip, you know your alter ego Leo likes to have eyes on me at all times? Are you sure he won't fire you for slacking on your duties?"

I couldn't figure out why — my instincts hadn't come with a decoder ring — but I'd felt safer with every step we'd taken away from Covington. And I had to admit, the little peek of a 'normal' life we'd had that day beat the shit out of selling drugs to strung-out junkies.

"Make it quick, so he doesn't find out." I winked. Jesus, I *was* turning into Skip.

Fiona glanced down to her sleeping sister and back to me as she chewed her lip.

"Go" — I shooed her away — "before Leo shows up and changes his mind." I bugged out my eyes for a final push.

"I'll only be a minute. I promise. Just keep moving the stroller back and forth and she won't wake up."

Fiona disappeared behind the circular doors of the hotel and I practically laughed at myself for doing as she suggested. Me, Leo Ricci, pushing a stroller… My brother would have died with laughter.

Across the street from the hotel was a biker bar with beautiful motorcycles lined up in a perfect row right in front. A group of bearded men came out in their bandanas and leather and saddled up. It hit me right before the sound. I was toast.

The backfire from the mufflers exploded in rapid succession and the chug of the idling bikes barely covered the wail coming from the stroller below me. I whipped around, unbuckled Violet as fast as I could, picked her up and covered her ears as I pressed her tight into my chest. Her little head was sweaty and hot and I didn't even realize I had kissed it until my lips were moist and warm. I bobbed up and down like I'd seen Fiona do a couple of times until all the bikers had ridden off and the sounds of the city went back to car horns and random insults.

Fiona came out of the hotel holding a white envelope and stopped in her tracks. Her face fell before a devilish grin took hold. "Dude... Skip, you are killing me." She walked over to the stroller and stored her check in her bag that hung off the handles.

A girl in ripped jeans and a flowy top came up to Fiona and said, "Girl, your baby-daddy just made my ovaries explode. Go, you."

"You have no idea." Fiona's answer came with a fake smile and the stranger walked away after giving me a once-over.

Fi circled the stroller and reached out for Violet. "Don't you dare gloat about that. My threat of cutting you remains."

Violet squirmed away from Fiona and cuddled deeper into my chest.

"Oooh, somebody else likes Skip. Come on, beautiful." I hoisted Violet over my shoulders and let her settle in. With her tiny feet in my hands, I walked.

Fiona shot me a fake sneer. "We need to stop and buy a sharp knife."

I let her joke fall between us, and as we waited for the light, I asked, "Would you rather take our time and just walk home? It's far, but we have the stroller and I'm happy to carry her for a bit."

She narrowed her eyes. "Who are you? But yes. That sounds — God, I hate to admit this — nice."

As we walked home, pausing to point small things out to Violet or her pointing to a toy duck in a window, I couldn't help but notice that I liked being Skip. The hard edge I'd been groomed to present had always rung false to the true me. Perhaps it was part of the reason I'd exiled myself to Covington. But Anton and the crew hadn't done anything to peel it away. In fact, they'd only sharpened it.

But what choice did I have? My skill set was...specific and my work experience non-existent. So yeah, the charade of my day could keep going as long as Fi would let it. I didn't even care about the crew's judgmental eyes as we crossed the courtyard at sunset with a stroller full of groceries and a tiny princess on my shoulders. I'd thought my goal was to stay in Covington, but after the taste of a different life, there was a growing chance that I wouldn't be staying much longer.

I made a simple pasta for dinner. Fiona's mom hadn't come home with her check, so the meal just seemed like a natural extension of our day. Fi gave Violet a bath and put her to bed while I cleaned their small, run-down kitchen.

I sat down on the couch and closed my eyes, still struggling with past, present and future.

"You still here, Skip?" Fiona had let her hair down and it spilled on both sides of her shoulders. She had changed into little green shorts and a tank top that didn't leave much to the imagination. "I got splashed. Stop staring at my tits. That's a Leo move."

I grinned. "That's a man move."

Fiona twisted her lips back and forth and studied me for a minute before she came and sat at the other end of the couch. "I have a problem I was hoping Skip could shed some light on."

"Oh, yeah? What's that?"

She pinned me with a playful, yet warm stare. "You see, I'd really like to kiss that Leo guy again, but I'm not sure if I'm some part of a game or just a passing challenge or... I don't know."

"I see your problem. You two have given each other a lot of mixed signals." I didn't fight the small smile offered with my words.

"What does Skip think?"

I loved that she'd asked, that she wanted some clarity, because quite frankly, I could have used some too. "Skip thinks you should kiss *him*. You know, to compare."

Fiona dropped her head back and faked awe. "Man, Skip, you are a genius."

That lovely haze settled between us and I toggled my finger in a come-hither motion. Eyes locked, Fiona moved slowly over and into my lap. She ran her fingers through my hair and said, "I don't know what any of this means. I just know that I had one of the best days of my life and it deserves to end with me kissing you."

I closed my eyes just as she brushed her soft lips against mine. It was completely different in speed and mood from our previous embrace, and she led me down a blurry path of desire and unrushed pleasure. We moved slowly, allowing each other time to appreciate all the aspects of our devotion, savoring the moment.

The savage in me stayed dormant, my hands remaining on her hips and barely encouraging her gentle grind. She played with the hair at the base of my neck, seducing me further into her heady cloud.

After three wet pecks that seemed like a cry for more rather than the sad ending that they were, she pressed her forehead into mind and whispered, "You should go before I do something I will regret."

I wet my lips, hungry for more of her sweet taste but I nodded. She climbed off me and I couldn't allow myself to look back as I left. It would have been the death of me and my somehow-under-control manners.

The last thing I said was, "Lock the door, please."

And I could hear the smile in her voice when she replied, "Goodnight, Leo."

Chapter Eleven

Fiona

Confusing. That was how I was going to describe the day I'd spent with Leo aka Skip — and pretty much my entire mental state since I'd met him. So when I saw him at the bench in his black jeans and skintight tank, I was oddly relieved. Notably missing were Anton and Jackson. Leo seemed to be in charge, sending minions here and there. The only muscles moving were behind his eyes as his gaze followed me and Violet into the park directly opposite him.

Lisa was at the swings with a little girl younger than Violet, and I offered the free swing to my sister. But she clocked J.J. and ran over to him. They climbed on opposite ends of a rusty seesaw that had a large metal coil in the middle to control the height.

"Hey." I gave a friendly smile.

"Hey, yourself." Lisa continued pushing the little blonde girl. "You have everybody talking about you, wondering what is so special about you that you get twenty-four-hour bodyguards." She winked, maybe to lighten the gossip jab, maybe to pretend she didn't care.

I couldn't blame her for fishing, though. Hell, I'd wondered the same thing. I shrugged a shoulder. "I guess I made myself a target. And it's not around-the-clock. They let me sleep in my own bed."

Lisa grinned. "I can't figure out if that's good or bad."

Tell me about it.

Violet ran around the play equipment, chasing J.J. My heart went *pitter patter* at the joy in her giggles. It wasn't that I'd never taken Violet to the park before, but now that she was a little older and my days weren't spent sleeping to recover from the nightshift, I saw firsthand how good it was for her to play with other children.

But then she tripped and fell. She cried out, and it was a fricking shrill sound. I jogged over and picked her up. Her knees were scraped, and I remembered from my own childhood how much a cement burn stung.

I bounced her over to the stroller, her crocodile tears a moist warmth on my T-shirt. And even though I wasn't looking in his direction, Leo was on his way. Twice, the day before, someone had mistaken him for her daddy. Twice he had said nothing. And more than a few times he'd made her smile. But where would it lead?

"What happened?" The accusation in Leo's tone blended with the resentment building in me and made a perfect cocktail of 'do whatever it takes to keep him at arm's length or you will get burned'. Because while all of his attention and doting were instantly gratifying,

I wasn't blinded by his charm. Leo Ricci was not the kind of guy who a girl could build a stable future with. He sold drugs and ran illegal gambling games. I was pretty sure those things didn't come with a retirement plan.

"She's a kid. She fell. Shit happens." I tucked her into her seat in the stroller and blew on her knees. Violet popped her thumb into her mouth and sucked as she watched me.

With a first-aid kit in hand, Lisa walked over and handed me a small bottle with a pump. "Non-sting disinfectant. I never leave home without it."

"Thanks." I took the little bottle and squirted. Foam bubbles pooled on Violet's little knees and I blew again. A long drip of the liquid streaked down her leg but she didn't cry. I buckled her in and stood.

"There's a dice game tonight. You should go nap." Leo frowned at me, and I didn't think I was imagining that he was being just a wee bit too judgmental about my kid sister skinning her knees.

Only adding to my annoyance was the fact that there hadn't been a sign of my mom since she'd left to pick up her check, which meant she'd gotten the money and used some of it to get wasted — which also meant that I needed to work that game.

I handed the bottle back to Lisa and asked, "How much would it cost for you to watch Violet for the night?"

She shrugged quickly. "If you're working for Anton, nothing. It's part of my salary." Lisa smiled and stored the disinfectant in her red pouch. "What time?"

"I'll bring her down after dinner, to make sure she's okay."

Lisa gave me the thumbs-up, shot a quick and cautious glance at Leo and went back to the little blonde girl.

I flipped off the brake of the stroller with my right foot and pivoted away from Leo.

"Be ready by nine."

"Anything else?" My ability to not be snarky had disappeared. I was pissed off that Violet got hurt, pissed off that my mom had a disease that put her addiction before her kids, pissed off that everything always fell on me and pissed off that he would be here today and gone tomorrow—not just for Violet but for me too. There was no point in taking anything further with him.

Leo's gaze tightened in on me, assessing my mood.

I'd made a mistake, kissing him for the second time. It had been his kindness and the day out of the confines of Covington. But we weren't those people, starting with the deceitful man next to me. The glimmer of hope that had flickered the day before had been a mirage. I needed to extinguish it from my imagination, put my eyes back on the prize and do what I needed to do to get out of this hell hole. No more momentary lapses in reasoning.

"See you later." I could tell by the wrinkles around his eyes that he still couldn't get a read on me, but that was the least of my worries. It had to be.

During dinner I explained to Violet that she was having a sleepover at Lisa's house. I'd thought she might be nervous, but as soon as I told her that J.J. would be there, her eyes lit up.

Dropping her off was hard—for me. There was the guilt of leaving her with a woman I didn't know much about, the sting that Violet had no trouble saying goodbye to me and the real possibility that my mother would come home to an empty apartment and go ballistic. She had a way of caring at all the wrong moments.

I could have left her a note, could have stated the truth. But then she would know I had a job—and, therefore, money. A lie would have been just as easy, but the darker part of me—the side that lurked in the shadows—wanted her to worry. It was childish and petty, but I was tired of playing by the rules. Thus far it had gotten me exactly nowhere.

All that simmered below my skin in a thick soup of resentment. I wasn't normally one to throw myself a pity party, but I was still human. So my resting bitch face stayed intact as Rafa drove us to the Lower East Side. He and Leo had talked about fighting the entire ride and I vaguely wondered what made Shithead such an expert.

The dice setup was similar to the poker game—a bar on one side and a table in the center of a cool, dimly lit room. But this time the only chair was a bar stool by the door, where Rafa and his pretty eyes took up residence. I opened and closed the metal doors of the mini-fridges to check my stock and Leo brushed against me before pulling out the gambling chips.

I hated that fucking spark, the wild energy that hung in the air between us. It was distracting, useless.

"You're still cranky," he said without looking at me. If he brought up some sort of 'Aunt Flow coming for a visit' reference, he would die. I would strangle his thick neck. I thought about it for a second and realized I did have PMS, which brought more irritation.

"You're still an ass." I slammed shut the door of the last fridge and crossed my arms. God help me, I was pouting. *Fucking hormones.*

Leo set four stacks of chips on the bar and stalked over to me, his eyes just slits. In my ear and with a warm breath that gave me a lust-filled shiver, he said, "I don't know what this little tantrum is about, but it's hot as fuck. So unless you plan on following up on what you're doing to me, I suggest you paste a smile on your pissed-off face and stop."

No, no, no. He couldn't just waltz over to me, say something sexy and get his way. And making *him* all hot and bothered? *Bonus.* Because I wasn't going to do anything about it, no matter how hard my body was screaming to jump him. *Nope.*

I tilted my head, meeting his challenge. "In that case, fuck off."

Leo laughed and stepped back, giving me the freedom to continue my pissy huff, which he watched with a bemused smile. But soon enough the patrons filtered in, and while the backdrop was similar to the card game, the energy of the men playing dice was completely different.

Mostly due to a man they referred to as 'The Scot'. He was more giant than a man, and when he ordered his not one, but two beers, his accent brought out a genuine smile.

"Yer cute." He tipped the beer in my direction then drank it down in one go. He set the empty bottle on the bar. "Whatcha doon in this shithole?"

"Just trying to make a buck like everybody else." I tossed the bottle in the trash and it clanked against the other ones below it.

"All right, everybody's here. Let's get rollin'," Rafa called from the table and Leo perched on the stool next to the door.

I'd never witnessed a dice game before, so I hadn't expected the shouting that went along with it. And it was confusing as fuck. The number seven was both lucky and unlucky, and I couldn't for the life of me figure out why. There were tons of side bets and Rafa managed to know all of them while keeping a relentless pace to the game.

When the money was exchanged, the Scot or someone would ask for drinks, but mostly I was a spectator to a baffling game. The one thing that seemed to be pretty clear was that the Asians at the end of the table were making bank.

After a particularly large bet that he lost, the giant Scot spouted out a string of curses and called for two more beers. I took them over and he grabbed my arm as I was about to walk away with his previous two.

"You ever play Craps?" He rolled the R and studied me.

"Nope." I looked at his hand on my forearm, over to Leo, and back to him.

His gray-blue eyes lit up and he turned back to the table, bending his knees and exaggerating the movement. "Oh, gentlemen, we have a virgin."

My mouth went dry and my heart pounded.

Leo stepped between me and the Scot, freeing his grasp. "Sorry, Reed. You know the rules. You can only roll if you have money in the game."

Reed frowned. "Ah, come on. They've taken almost everything. I'll give her the rest of what I have, and if she wins, I'll give her a cut."

"Who cares if she rolls?" Rafa asked the group.

The Asian men chattered between themselves then gave the thumbs up. They were probably banking on my inexperience and obvious ignorance.

I searched Leo's eyes. "I have no idea what to do. I'm going to lose all his money."

"He was going to lose it anyway." Rafa grabbed my hips and shoved me toward the table.

Reed clapped his hands and hollered his delight. He nudged next to me and handed me a stack of chips. "Do you know anything about Craps?"

"No. This is a terrible idea."

Reed furrowed his brow as if I'd insulted him. "It's a fuckin' fantastic idea. Trust me."

I checked over my shoulder at Leo, who silently encouraged me. *Are they all out of their minds?*

"So," Reed continued, "just take it one roll at a time. First things first... Roll a seven or an eleven and we win."

"Come on, Fiona." Rafa set a stack of dice in front of me. "Choose two and roll. You're holding up the game."

With my pulse racing, I selected the top and the bottom one. I scanned the table, unsure of my next move.

"You need to bet on yourself." Rafa took back the remaining dice and stored them next to a little mirror in the side of the table.

"Bet all of it." Reed whispered in my ear and his warm breath that was laced with assurance made the hair on the back of my neck stand up. A chill swept over me. I was going to lose his money in one go.

A seven or an eleven. That was all I needed. The seven had been so confusing to me that I focused on the eleven. *A six on one and a five on the other. Easy...not.*

I brought the dice up to my mouth and my stuttered exhale warmed my hand. I was sure I'd seen something like that in a movie. I closed my eyes and pictured the six and the five again.

With a shaking hand, I pushed the stack away from me and Rafa snatched it up then separated it into three piles. "Two-fifty. Two-fifty and three hundred."

The men in the shiny suits at the end of the table each matched a pile and Rafa nodded to me once he'd counted it. "Now you roll."

The younger guys on the opposite side of the table placed their own bet between themselves and I waited for a final nod from Rafa.

Six and five. A five and a six.

The chatter from around the table revved up and I blocked it from getting any further than the entry to my ears. I gave one last fleeting look to Reed, who was shouting about my virginity. Time slowed down and the chants morphed into slurs, the clapping and jumping into lethargic blurry lines of movement.

My own head was swimming in a murky soup. I forced one clear thought to rise to the surface.

Six and five. A five and a six.

I closed my eyes.

Six and five. A five and a six.

At the same time, I opened them back up, and with a light snap of my wrist, I threw the dice to the other side of the table. They tumbled on their sides and corners — one even took a little hop before it landed, resting perfectly aligned with its partner. A five on one and a six on the other.

"Yo! Eleven!" Rafa hollered out.

Reed screamed like a sheep in heat and one of the younger dudes pumped his fist in the air.

Adrenaline pulsed through my veins and the slow-motion moment switched gears to high speed. Over the course of the following half-hour, I won every last bit of money on the table. As the other players filed out and Rafa counted out their cut of Reed's winnings, I went behind the bar and pulled out three beers. I set two on the counter for Reed and opened the third for me. Reed took his cash and stashed it in various pockets. I twisted off the caps of his beers, we clanked the necks and he slammed his while I took a sip. The cool and bitter liquid washed through me, taking the stress of the night with it.

I leaned my ass against the counter and crossed my ankles. Just as I was settling into a relaxing lull, Rafa shouted at me for a drink. Leo and Reed chatted about the dates of future games and I walked the beer over to Rafa.

"Nothing like popping your cherry, huh?" He smirked and took a swig.

"I suppose not." I left him alone at the table went back to the bar.

"All right." Reed's glorious accent was still as charming as the minute he'd opened his mouth. "I'll see you fellas next week." He finished his second beer and pushed off the bar. Leo halted him with a hand in the air.

"I think you're forgetting her cut, good man."

After a little chuckle, Reed said, "Right. My mistake, lads." Then to me, "Thanks for the roll." He took a wad out of his front pocket, counted out five hundred and left it on the bar. Leo stood down, and after Reed was out, he relocked the door.

Leo checked his phone then punched out a text with his thumbs. Once he'd finished, he jutted his chin to Rafa. "You good?"

"Yeah. Let's roll."

Maybe it was me not being pissed off anymore, but something in Leo had changed. He stared out of the passenger window, far, far away. It was a quiet side of him that was somehow darker than his normal brutish ways. I didn't like it.

But when we got back to Covington and were walking toward the courtyard, I might have understood it.

"You've been summoned," Leo said then worked his jaw.

I swallowed hard and followed him to his place. *Shit.* It wasn't like I'd thought Anton would forget about my stupid so-called debt, but I'd kinda hoped he would. Once inside, Leo nodded his hello to Anton, who sat at the island with a beer and a stack of money, his steel eyes assessing my every inch.

"See you tomorrow." Leo disappeared down his hall, leaving me in heavy silence.

My bladder pushed against my jeans that had been made tighter by bloating and cramps and reminded me that I hadn't taken a break the whole night. "Can I use your bathroom?"

"Down the hall and through my room." Anton pointed with his beer.

I walked down the dark hallway. At the end, a massive, unmade bed sat in the middle of a sparsely decorated room. There was a long wooden dresser, a walk-in closet and, at the opposite end, another door. I flicked the switch and my heart stopped. The most beautiful sunken bathtub lined an entire wall. Opposite it were double sinks and an open shower. The actual toilet was its own small room and the floors were covered in light gray square tiles.

Heaven. It was fucking heaven. I kicked off my heels and the cool floor gave my feet instant relief. Once I'd handled my business, I washed my hands and the huge tub mocked me from the mirror.

I was a girl who loved a bath. The simple escape had offered me much solace over the years. I dried my hands on a fluffy white towel and decided I needed to just sit in the tub for ten seconds. I didn't even need bubbles or water. The act alone would offer reprieve and soothe my body and mind. I was sure of it.

With a cautious step, I climbed in. The gleaming porcelain was more spacious and welcoming than I'd imagined. I closed my eyes and relaxed. Ten seconds was not enough, and I stopped counting. Fictional water warmed over me and I got further lost in my lies.

The week's events washed away. The stress of facing my mother whenever she showed up disappeared. And the stupid mess of Anton and Leo evaporated. It was just me, in that calm moment.

"Technically, I think you're supposed to do that naked and with water."

My eyes flew open and my cheeks flushed. Anton leaned against the doorway with his eyebrows raised.

"Shit. Sorry. How long have I been here?"

He crossed his arms. "Well, after ten minutes I started to worry." There was something soft that passed over his face and it didn't suit him. "Then, after five minutes of watching you, I had to convince myself you hadn't eaten my cabinet of pills and were still alive."

Pity was worse than deception, of that I was sure. I straightened my posture. "Sorry. I'll go."

Anton approached the side of the bath, and sat on the edge. "You could stay. Have your bath, then sleep wherever you want." His eyes raced over mine. "There's no point in you going home. Violet's with Lisa, right?"

His soft tone and invitation lured me in, further proof of the imposter life I wanted to lead. He offered his hand. I took it, because I was a fool.

Anton whispered in my ear, "Take a bath then come to bed. You're safe."

His slithering words were the perfect counterpart to all the falsehoods already brewing in my brain. Someone should have shaken me, woken me from the spell and reminded me that it wasn't real.

I chewed my bottom lip. He'd gone from 'sleep whereever you want' to 'come to bed' within seconds. The fight in me was gone, extinguished by fatigue and confusion. Anton pushed on his knees and stood. "Nothing happens unless you say. You know that."

He'd proved to be a fan of consent with his kiss, but it didn't mean I was on board to sleep in the same bed. But fucking hell, I wanted a bath. Giving myself permission to be selfish wasn't easy, but in the quiet of the night, behind closed doors, maybe no one would see.

"Could I have a T-shirt to sleep in?"

Anton nodded and left the bathroom. I started the water in the tub and piled my hair on top of my head.

"You're not going to fall asleep in there, are you?" Anton handed me a plain white V-neck.

I shook my head and he left me alone, leaving the door ajar. It was silly to be bashful—he wasn't watching—but I stripped quickly and sank into the hot water before the bath was full. My muscles relaxed and I went back to the muted place in my head where I allowed myself to exist without judgment or emotion. I simply was.

The water cooled too quickly and I dried myself with a thick white towel. I brushed my teeth with my finger and some toothpaste then slipped on the crisp cotton T-shirt. It hit mid-thigh, the perfect pajama. I couldn't bear to look at my reflection. I was still lingering in a state without conviction.

At the doorway I hit the light to the bathroom and padded over to the bed, where Anton lay on his back with one arm behind his head. I was grateful that his eyes were closed. Their probing assessment would have been too much.

Chapter Twelve

Leo

I'd tossed, turned, groaned and twisted in my sheets all night. Fiona had been pissed at me for something, but it was me who was fuming — and I knew exactly why.

I didn't want her with him. But worse, this jealousy, this *possessiveness* was waking up a side of me that I'd been trying to escape from. It allowed dark thoughts to seep in like a lingering foul odor. It had me imagining ways to hurt Anton — creative ways, pleasurable ways…long, drawn-out, painful ways.

And it was ridiculous. It wasn't like I was in love with her, for Christ's sake. Yeah, I liked her, but the rest was surely just lust. There weren't butterflies in my belly flittering around with just the sight of her.

The desire to keep her safe and make her mine was foolish. My lust and attraction were distracting me from my main goal — to stay put and not turn into my father. The front door finally shut and I took it as the all-clear of her being gone. I'd stayed in bed longer than normal to avoid them both and to try to tame my runaway thoughts.

After my shower, I found Anton exactly where I'd left him the night before. He sat at the island alone, but instead of the bottle of beer he'd been drinking , he had a liter of water. He wiped his chin with the bottom of his inked-up forearm, shot me a look and chuckled.

"Stop eying me like you've decided to slit my throat while I sleep."

"I—"

Anton raised his eyebrows, daring me to deny it.

"You—" he said, drawing out the word, "have a problem, which means that *I* have a problem. I don't much care for problems, Leo. This you know."

He was right. And we'd known each other too long to pretend otherwise. But it didn't make me happy about confronting the shit I'd already spent half the day torturing myself with.

I went to the fridge, pulled out the carton of eggs and started making my lunch. Breakfast had been long abandoned.

"So here's how I see it. Someone has to back down. And, considering that I'm the leader of this crew, it ain't gonna be me."

If I'd have looked at him, my eyes would have probably cut him deeper than any knife. Well, maybe not. There was a survival knife we'd used on camping trips when I was a kid that my dad had deemed 'the sharpest knife in the world'. With the right thrust and angle, that baby would have gutted my so-called friend in a second.

I hummed at the idea.

"All right. Simmer down."

"I haven't said a fucking thing." I beat the eggs a little harder and frowned.

"No. But you did that throat thing you do when you're about ready to go into robot, ass-kicking mode."

Had I? I shook it off with a shiver.

Anton continued with a little smirk. "Nothing happened. Jesus and two Marys... She slept on the couch and was gone when I woke up."

"But I just heard the door..."

"Scooter." Anton pointed to a grease-stained paper bag. "My lunch."

I let out a long breath and some of the ice that had been running through my veins thawed.

"She took, like, the longest bath in the world and I fell asleep. She never got in bed with me. I would have woken up with the movement."

I poured my egg mixture into the frying pan and it sizzled with the contact. I stirred around the yellow liquid as it fluffed to life.

"So what do you want me to do?" I finally asked as I plated my food.

"I want you to stop thinking about beating my ass and make me some money. I agreed to let you live here and you knew the rules."

I cut off a steamy bite with the edge of my fork, still standing over the cooktop. I did know the rules. Anton and I both understood that I was innately more dangerous than he was, and that was saying something. But in order for my so-called safehouse to work, none of his crew could know that. I'd already slipped up the day I'd been too hard on Golden Boy.

If I didn't yield to Anton on Fiona, I would have to go. He'd cut me a pass for the fighting because I was toughening up his number three guy. He didn't care if I was physical with Fiona, as long as he had first taste. There was no jealousy in him for women. He'd never been in the position of needing it.

After a long, silent stare, he got up and went to the door. "I'm sparring with Jackson. Figure out how to solve my problems instead of being one."

I decided to share a cut of my money from the night before. It would give me some of the leverage I was missing. The plate landed in the sink with a clank and I was out of the door to sell drugs in no time.

At the bench, Scooter stood as I approached. I greeted the lower-ranking members of the crew with clasped hands and back taps then found my seat, confirming my rank. *Second in charge. Second in line for Fiona. Second son.*

A familiar and adorable giggle caught my ear and I strained to find Fiona in the park. The fact that she hadn't thrown herself at Anton had to be some kind of sign—or maybe she was just being stubborn. It was definitely in her character. I probably shouldn't flatter myself. It would only add to my undeniably over-active imagination.

Still with no sight of her, I stood and put my hands on my hips. Violet played on the slide with J.J., their soft toys taking rides instead of them. I pulled out my phone from my back pocket and called Fiona's. When she didn't answer, I tracked it. It placed her upstairs in her apartment. But then why was Violet in the park?

I had to stop obsessing. Ever since she'd come running at me, I'd invented threats to her safety. Mac was just a spook. The BTs wouldn't touch her now that they'd seen her with us. I was losing my mind. And I really needed to assess why and how Fiona had become the cause. Maybe she'd just needed a nap or was making lunch to bring it down.

Believing those theories would have been much easier if my gut wasn't aching that something was off — that Fiona and her phone were not in the same place. My instincts chipped away at me and the only sound I could hear was my blood throbbing between my ears.

Scooter said something about his girlfriend not answering his texts, but I swatted him away like an annoying fly. I scanned the courtyard on my way over to the sad excuse for a park.

"Leo!" Violet smiled at me and reached her arms overhead.

I scooped her up and kissed her head. When had I started doing that? "Hey, munchkin."

As I tickled Violet under her arms and reminded myself I was overreacting, I walked over to Lisa. "Hey."

She startled and stood straighter. "Hi." Lisa avoided my gaze. It didn't look like she was breathing.

"Why do you have Violet?"

Still no eye contact.

I gave Violet one last tickle then set her down slowly. I waited for her to go back to the slide. With a shocking amount of calm in my voice, I asked, "Lisa, where is Fiona?"

My tone finally snapped her eyes up. "I...I don't know."

Standing still was the easiest and hardest thing I'd done in my life. "Go on."

Lisa rubbed her upper arm and her posture rounded. "She got Violet pretty early this morning, then was back about two hours ago. She had obviously been crying and said she'd had a fight with her mom. She asked if I could watch Violet while she got some air. Apparently her mom had crashed and Violet was restless. I'm sorry, but that's all I know. I didn't think she would be gone this long."

I spun around and started marching toward the entrance to our building. There was no need to question Lisa any further. I had all the information that I needed. Maybe Fiona was just hiding in the stairwell, had gone back to sit on the couch while her mom slept it off — or was taking another bath somewhere, hopefully not on the other side of my apartment.

"Leo!" Scooter ran up to me with a bleak and painful expression etched on his face. "They took her," he huffed out. "The BTs have Callie." On the screen of his phone, Scooter showed me a picture of his girlfriend from a side angle. Her wrists were bound behind her with a white plastic tie and her head hung down. Her light pink hair framed her face, making it impossible to see if they'd hit her.

A second froze then passed as I remembered that Callie lived on the north-most block of our territory. It would have been easy for Bradford to watch her, know she was Scooter's and that this would be a blow to one of our top members. Scooter waited for me to say something and searched my face with his anxious blue eyes.

Right. I was meant to be in charge of shit like this.

"Come on." I grabbed him by the shoulders and squeezed a few times. "Let's go upstairs and make a plan."

"We need to get her *now*!"

"I know." I hoped my level voice would bring him some calm. "But we need a plan."

And I needed to locate the woman who was most likely next on their list. I called Rafa and told him to meet us at our place. Jackson and Anton were still in the gym, so I filled them in and they followed us across the hall.

Once in the apartment, Scooter paced in front of the flatscreen, muttering curse words and whimpering pleas. He wasn't going to be any help.

Rafa had a laptop and brought up a satellite map of Bradford Towers. Anton sat next to him and Jackson and I looked over their shoulders.

Our Golden Boy hacker began, "So we know that Bradford's setup is the same as ours." He zoomed in the screen. "They mostly live in building four. The others are either full of junkies or rats."

Jackson shivered and I cocked a brow at him.

"I fucking hate rats."

I rolled my eyes. A confession like that would have earned an insult from my father, followed by a fear-facing exercise where rats were the least of my problems. Lucky for Jackson, his dad had taught him how to play ball instead.

Rafa continued, "They don't have anywhere else to take her and they are correct in assuming that we are coming for her, so, I guarantee she's in that building."

Scooter had stopped his frantic pacing and peeked over my shoulder. His skin was covered in sweat and he pounded his fist into the opposite palm. "Let's go then. We get the whole crew, a bunch of bats and we storm the place."

Anton turned around and glared at Scooter. "You... Go sit on the couch and shut the fuck up. This isn't *West Side Story*." Then he looked at me. "We go, we get her, we come back—least amount of casualties, maximum amount of power. It sends the message that we're smarter and leaner."

Rafa began frantically typing, and code ran up and down his screen. "Give me five minutes."

"I'll shower." Anton, who was still in his workout clothes, stood and headed down the hall.

"He can't be serious," Scooter complained. "Callie is probably getting raped this very second and he's going to fucking shower?"

This time it was Jackson who scolded him. "We get it, Scoot. But this is the kind of shit that only Anton has experience with. You have to trust him."

Rafa kept banging on his keyboard, occasionally encouraging it in a sweet voice. It was almost like he was trying to seduce it. He spoke in Portuguese, which only made it more entertaining. Perhaps it was wrong to enjoy his hacking during such a tense time, but I had no emotional attachment to Callie. It was why Anton and I were going in alone.

Jackson was a teddy bear, and if push came to shove—which it just might—he would flinch and think about his son. Rafa would drive. He knew the streets better than any of us, and Jackson, with his imposing frame, would stay home and keep the minions calm.

There was only one problem. Once the spray of the shower stopped, I walked back to Anton's room. He sat on his bed, threading his legs into black jeans.

"Fiona's missing."

Anton finished getting dressed, his silence code for more of an explanation.

"Lisa said she had a fight with her mom and took off," I explained.

"And?"

I closed my eyes and worked through the logic that Anton had managed in only seconds. They didn't have her. We would have known immediately if they did.

The BTs were braggy fucks—case in point, Callie's photo sent to Scooter. If they had Fiona, they would have been flaunting her like a flag on Independence Day.

"Listen… The cops usually let us eat our own up here, but they will step in if we pile up dead bodies. Try not to kill anyone."

Isn't that the whole point of me being in Covington?

I shook my head and said, "Quick jabs to the arteries in the neck. Remember… Most of them are stoned half the time. It should be easy."

Anton grinned, it was devilish, inappropriate, sinful and matched my own. "Might be fun."

We walked into the kitchen as Rafa was proclaiming his undying love to his computer.

"I have eyes on the streets." He slid the laptop toward us and a live feed from the traffic lights around Bradford Towers appeared in four grainy squares on the screen. The twinkle in Rafa's golden eyes matched the happy nerves twitching in my body. I hadn't gone full throttle on anyone in months.

Anton went over to Scooter and took him by the shoulders at arm's length. "We're going to walk in there, get your girl and walk out. You're going to stay here and wait. When we walk back through the door, all this whimpering will cease. You will be her rock."

I went over to Jackson. "If you see Fiona, bring her here. They're not going to like what we're about to do and she's on their list."

Anton joined us. "Jackson, get on that bench and keep everyone in check."

Jackson blinked his understanding and left before us. Rafa explained his theory on the best way to get in and we were driving north within fifteen minutes. He dropped us off next to a narrow back street and we hopped a few fences until we were behind Bradford Four.

As we pushed our backs against the filthy wall, I whispered, "I'm dying to hit someone. Mind if I go first?"

The metal handle of the door made a loud click from the other side and I moved on the lone scout before he'd even realized we were there. I put him in a cross choke and his eyes bugged out with fright. The smile that pulled at my cheeks was both evil and genuine.

"Which floor?" Anton asked as I squeezed tighter.

Realization flushed up his face and he said the word, 'five' just before I cut off all the blood to his bald, tattooed head. I gave him an unneeded headbutt and let him fall to the ground with a light thud. *Fucking bliss.*

Anton snickered and we slipped inside the building. I led the way up the steps, and once we'd climbed four flights, we paused to listen.

Two voices chatted, one of which had a nervous cadence. "How big do you think their crew is, anyway?"

"I don't know, but I would feel better if we had more guns. A girl I used to fuck from Covington told me that that Anton dude is like a brick fucking wall. He looks like he could bench press a truck."

The compliment did nothing to Anton's expression. We hadn't come into their territory to get flattered. A shrieking scream echoed through the stairwell and the distraction was a perfect moment for us to move. We raced up the stairs and the two skinny excuses for security barely put up a fight.

Anton's movements mirrored my own, quick alternating jabs with the edge of our hands at their necks and they were down. It was almost funny how unfair the matchup was.

With a look of pity and disgust at the two passed-out bodies below us, Anton said, "Jesus, don't they even train?"

I pointed to the guy on the left, the one whose bloodshot eyes had filled with terror the second he'd seen us. "That one was high. Who puts a methhead on security?"

We listened at the door before cracking it open an inch. Down the long hallway, there were three more men, one with a handgun.

I signed what I saw to Anton, signaling that I would take the guy with the gun and he would take the two with bats. He pointed to his chest and made the universal sign for gun with his thumb and index.

No. It had to be me. I was quicker. I shook my head and stared into his light eyes. I silently transmitted something that he didn't want to hear. I was better. Under any other circumstances — and certainly if there had been an audience — he would have objected again. Instead, he blinked his acceptance and we waited for our moment.

Maybe Callie knew she was about to be saved because, once again, her blood-curdling scream acted as the perfect match to the inferno of hurt we were about to lay on the three BTs guarding the door.

I shot down the hall, Anton at my heels. The bald fuck with the gun fired and missed, and the realization of his error spread on his hollowed-out cheeks. But it also sounded an alarm and our fight got a lot more crowded and seriously more dangerous.

Three more BTs, all carrying guns, poured out into the hallway. A perfect calm spread in my veins and all my years of repetitive training took over my body. As the first gunman lifted his weapon to my head, I grabbed the firearm with my left hand and held it tight in my palm at the same time as I hit his wrist and held it in a sloth grip so I didn't break my thumb.

The element of surprise was still in our favor and Anton had the two other original guards already passed out on the floor. I spun my guy around and used him as a human shield, holding his nasty body tight to mine. It was circumstances like this where I understood my father's insistence on being able to shoot a gun with both hands. Anton hid for cover behind me and I shot all three remaining rivals in their kneecaps. They fell to the ground as quickly as I'd shot them, and I whacked the carotid artery of the guy I'd been restraining. The only thing that was counter-intuitive was me not snapping his neck and shooting to kill.

Callie was naked on a mattress in the corner of the room. Anton swore under his breath before scooping her up fireman style and running out.

On the way down the stairs, I got a better look at the damage they'd done to Callie. Her eyes were swollen and her nose had been broken. She was mumbling something but seemed to know she'd been rescued. I called Rafa, who told me to take the front exit then switched the phone for the gun and took the lead.

We stopped at the entrance and slowed our breaths, the adrenaline pumping hard in both our bodies. Anton nodded and we busted out through their courtyard. At the sight of the gun, there weren't any brave heroes, and the small crowd parted.

Our black SUV screeched to a halt and I opened the back door for Anton, who threw Callie in while I climbed into the passenger side. My heart thumped hard and my mind went fuzzy. Somehow, I pulled off my shirt and handed it to Callie.

Chapter Thirteen

Fiona

I would have to deal with Leo's bullshit when I got back to Covington. His overprotective ass was going to be pissed that I'd snuck away. I didn't doubt that he'd find out about it and part of me hoped he was pissed. It had stung the way he'd left me to Anton, like I didn't matter.

So when I'd found my mom at home that morning and she'd screamed at me and accused me of kidnapping Violet, I'd had to get out. I'd waited for her to crash, taken my sister down to Lisa and decided to spend a little bit of the money I'd earned on myself.

Plus, I'd headed downtown where no one gave a shit about Covington or Bradford. I'd eaten an overpriced sandwich on a sliver of a park bench not covered in pigeon shit and bought myself some bath bombs. *Big splurge.*

But as I rode the train back north, the suffocating energy that was Covington Heights filled my lungs. I had to get out, and after my tiny moment of self-indulgence, I wondered if my love for Violet might have been holding me back. I wanted a better life for her, but would it cost me my own?

I exited the train and trudged up the stairs past a homeless man and his gray dog. My freedom adventure had long lost its glory with the realization that — just like the amazing day with Leo — it had to come to an end. At the crosswalk, I noticed that the park was empty and Jackson was on the bench. From what I could tell from the crew, he was fourth in line, so that meant Rafa, Leo and Anton were away.

Jackson's gaze met mine and he popped up. Flanked by two minions, he rushed over and met me at the curb once I'd crossed the street.

"Damn, sis, it's good to see you," he said with a tilt of his head. His phone buzzed from the back pocket of his baggy black jeans. Jackson reached for it, read a message, and turned to his left. "They're going through the alley. Go meet them." Then to me, "You... Anton's, *now.*"

Normally Jackson's brown eyes were soft and gentle, something I suspected Lisa found irresistible. But, in that moment, they issued a warning. I hurried through the courtyard and ignored that I needed to take Violet home. I would deal with her once I found out what was going on. Maybe she was safer with Lisa.

I knocked on Leo and Anton's door and Scooter opened it. But it wasn't Scooter. It was a version of him that made my stomach tie into a tight knot and turn to stone. His skin was pale and clammy and his eyes were bloodshot. If I didn't know any better, I would have thought he was strung-out.

He held the door open for me, and I studied him silently and moved to the couch. I placed my backpack on the floor and sat. The tension in the air was heavy, and while I was curious as to why, Scooter didn't look like he was ready to play twenty questions.

The door swung open with a bang and my heart stopped. Anton cradled a broken woman in his arms. Her curly hair was a ratted mess and her face was covered in dried crimson blood and black streaks of makeup. She wore only a T-shirt and red marks on her otherwise-pink legs screamed of future bruises.

"Jesus," Scooter said under his breath.

Anton locked eyes with Scooter and signaled to the left, barely glancing in my direction as he continued his path back to his bedroom. Rafa came in and said he'd call the doctor, then he moved to the island.

Last in was Leo, whose dark eyes leveled me as his bare chest rose and fell. He stared at me, through me — his message painfully, shockingly clear.

That could have been you.

Leo let out that steamy grumble he did when he was particularly annoyed. He frowned and it gave 'resting bitch face' a run for its money. After a long blink, he stalked down the hall to his room and slammed the door.

But I got it. A selfish flood of relief washed over me and I started to shake and twitch. I bit my thumbnail and my teeth chattered.

Rafa finished his call and disappeared down the hall, maybe to give news to Scooter and Anton about the doctor. The walls of the living room somehow expanded and the emptiness of being alone was a bellow to my fire of fear.

Don't cry, Fiona.

All the times I'd thought Leo had been overreacting and I'd slipped away in a tantrum anyway. Maybe it was all for the crew, but it wasn't Anton who'd worried. It was Leo. I stood and walked slowly down his hall. The shower stream came to an abrupt halt and I waited a minute before giving his door a light tap.

Leo opened and a whoosh of air washed over me. His hair was still wet, and he wore navy training pants that bunched at the ankles and hung on his hips, exposing skin below his navel that was sure to be illegally sinful.

"I'm sorry," I said in a soft voice.

The coldness in his eyes left in a blink. "Don't *ever* fucking do that again."

"I won't." I let out a stuttered breath. "I need to get Violet. She can't stay with Lisa forever and my mom has already accused me of kidnapping."

"I'll take you, but if your mom is high, I'm not leaving your sister there." Leo turned and went to open a drawer. He pulled out a white T-shirt and put on a pair of tennis shoes. It was the second time I'd seen him out of black jeans, and he was so much softer that it made him beautiful.

Rafa was back at the island and Leo told him we'd be back in a bit. Violet was happy to see us and I carried her and her bunny all the way up the elevator, realizing that holding her was more for me than her.

I unlocked the door to find that my mom was awake and watching a cooking show. She glared at me, still bitter about our fight. But I was pretty sure she wouldn't air our dirty laundry in front of Leo. In fact, she went the opposite route.

A devious grin formed on her tired face, and in a sugary voice she said, "Glad you guys are back. I'm going to take Violet to the zoo."

One thing about my mother was that she had a cycle. It was as predictable and as reliable as the sun rising in the morning. She was in the part where she was going to replace drugs with a man. She'd seen Leo taking care of me, been reminded of how nice it was and gotten jealous. The man would eventually leave, then she would go back to drugs to comfort herself.

Rinse, wash, repeat.

But finding a man required getting out of the neighborhood and making an effort. Thus, the zoo. I slid Violet down my side and she went to change the channel to something she liked.

"I'm happy you're feeling better." I smiled and turned to Leo. "Let's go."

He hesitated, but I nodded that it would be okay. I appreciated that he trusted my instincts. I reached for his hand and took it. I didn't let go in the elevator, down his hall or even under the watchful eyes of Anton and Rafa as we walked to Leo's room.

We moved with a quiet understanding. He stretched out on the bed and pulled me on top. I nuzzled my cheek into his chest and the crisp scent of his soap eased my stress even more. It didn't seem real, especially when he stroked my hair. He made me feel safe, wanted.

But I had a debt to pay — and not to him. I should have been cozying up to his boss. I should have been finding ways to get to know the steel-eyed mountain of a man on the other side of the wall. And what was Leo thinking, holding my hand and bringing me into his room? He'd not just done it in front of Anton, but Rafa had seen it too. I didn't know much about their group dynamics, but I was pretty sure it was a no-no to flaunt taking the girl to bed who was supposed to be banging the boss.

The problem was that I didn't want to pay that debt, even after everything I'd seen. I wanted to be exactly where I was, being cherished by a man who I wasn't meant to be with. And I needed him to know that.

I whispered, "I don't think I'm ever going to want to have sex with Anton." There were a lot of secrets in my confession woven into the words — like I was pretty sure I wanted to be with Leo, that I understood that the night before he hadn't wanted to leave me with the boss. And, for whatever reason, that day was different, and he'd claimed me for his own. Whether or not he'd gotten permission didn't seem to matter.

"Then don't," he said, his simple words carrying their own hidden meanings.

We lay there for a long time, his slow heartbeat a gentle lullaby that carried me away. Eventually, his stomach rumbled and I had to giggle. He laughed too, and I sat up next to him.

"Thank God. I've had to pee for an hour." Leo winked and hopped up.

I scooted to the headboard and bent my knees into my chest. It had been ages since I'd had a free night, and the confines and stress of Covington were pecking at me from every angle.

When Leo came back in the room, I peered at him with caution. "Do you want to...I don't know...maybe do something?"

"What did you have in mind?" His flirtatious tone was so foreign that I almost laughed.

"I don't know, get tacos or a burger or…" I stood and twisted my hands. He was making it harder by being nice and open. Besides, I was asking him to do something ridiculously casual after he'd just saved a girl's life.

I shook my head. It had been a stupid idea. "Sorry. I just don't want to be in this building another fucking minute. It was selfish. You must be exhausted."

Leo scratched the back of his neck before sporting a wide grin. "I'm more confused. I'm pretty sure you just asked me out on a date."

There it was, the cocky, smug reliable side of him.

"It's not a date. It's two people eating a meal together after a long day. Besides, you are obviously hungry."

"I'm starving, actually." Leo twisted his lips before rubbing them together. "Come on. I haven't had decent Italian food in months."

In the living room, Anton and Rafa sat on the couch with beers in their hands and an empty pizza box between them. An older woman with short, strawberry-blonde hair and massive green eyes came down the hall from Anton's room.

"Leo," she said, her smile off, "any injuries?"

"Clean as a whistle, Doc. How's she doing?" Leo asked and Anton stood and joined us in the kitchen for the answer.

"She's in shock. She's not in much pain and I've set her nose. The wounds she's endured are far beyond my scope." The doctor turned to Anton and brushed the lapel of her gray jacket. "You're going to need to put a therapist on your payroll."

Anton closed his eyes, cursed under his breath and went back to the couch.

The doctor watched him then announced, "If there isn't anything else, I'll be on my way." Her judgmental gaze came to me. "What about you? Do you need a prescription for the pill? I'm not very fond of abortions."

"I..." Was there even a response for that? Number one, I wasn't having sex — not that she needed to know if I was. And number two — what kind of doctor just offered up prescriptions like a business card? Oh, right, the doctor of criminals. *Duh.* Maybe that was why she was a presumptuous slut-shamer, too. My nostrils flared while I debated laying into her pale ass.

Leo put his arm around me and tugged me close. "Don't you worry about us, Dr. MacAllister. I'm a big fan of wrapping my presents before I give them." He lifted his eyebrows and smirked, and his lie made me wonder why he didn't trust the doctor.

His crudeness had worked, though. She rolled her eyes and let herself out. Once the door was shut, Anton lifted a hand.

He glared at Leo. "Don't say it."

I was beginning to realize a small dynamic in Leo and Anton, and I wondered how many others were as well. Leo wasn't good at following orders. It was proof positive when he spoke.

"She was fishing."

Rafa and I exchanged curious glances before shifting our attention back to Leo and Anton. Yeah, he'd noticed that trait in Leo, too.

"You're paranoid," Anton said with a scoff.

"I have instincts."

There was a long moment of silence as their stare-down sucked all the air out of the room. But despite not using words, an entire conversation passed between them. Finally, Leo broke and said to me, "Let's go."

To our backs, Anton called out, "This isn't over."

Leo's familiar grumble leaked out in a long, slow exhale, and he grabbed my hand and led me down the hall. He punched the elevator button and I let him have his quiet. There was a long story behind him being in Covington, and if he wanted to share it with me, that would be up to him. All I needed was a meal and a change of scenery.

The orange setting sun warmed the car as we drove downtown. The escape, even if it was brief, was more than welcome. Leo found a parking spot on a side street and pulled in. His huff had disappeared and a twinkle I'd never seen flickered in his eyes.

"You are in for the best meal of your life."

I smiled back, preferring this odd version of him that I wasn't sure a lot of people had the luck of seeing. "You're practically giddy. Oh my God, are you going to be Skip again?"

We got out of the car and he took my hand. The gesture was gentler than in Covington. I liked it.

Leo whispered in my ear, "I seem to remember you kissing Skip."

We walked down a quiet street until we were in front of a small, casual restaurant with the name 'Chezzie's' painted red in the window.

He held the door open for me and heat flushed up my neck. Holy Shit, we *were* on a date. I smiled through my nerves and walked in.

"Well, well, well, the prodigal son returns." A pretty, older Italian lady in a tight but flattering burgundy wrap dress frowned at Leo before a wide grin spread across her face. She waved her hands in front of her. "Get over here, gorgeous. Give your Aunt Chezzie a kiss."

Leo not only obliged but he lifted the woman up, hugged her tight and spun her around.

"Easy, doll." When she was back on her own two feet she smacked his cheek a few times. "I've missed this face." Then she turned to me and sized me up. Her dark, appraising eyes were the exact same shade of scary as her nephew's. "Who's this?"

"Fiona, this is my Aunt Francesca."

She shooed away Leo's words with a brush of her hand and came over and hugged me. "Call me Chezzie."

I might have let out a little 'eeep'. Being hugged by a woman, a stranger no less, was not something I'd done on the regular. But the warmth in Chezzie seeped through her skin and I had a feeling I was privileged to see a glimpse of Leo's life before Covington.

Chezzie led us to a booth and we had sparkling water and red wine in our glasses before I'd had a chance to take in our cozy surroundings. The other patrons were older couples who sent occasional glances to our table. They must have known Leo was related to the owner.

Chapter Fourteen

Leo

The shy glances at our table meant that if my brother didn't already know I was at Chezzie's, he would in a matter of minutes. But I didn't care. The slow pull back to who I was meant to be had begun the moment I'd walked away. And my little stare-down with Anton was him reminding me that I'd once again stepped on his toes.

It was hard to find a part of me that gave a shit. I was going to eat up my slice of normal with Fiona and lick the plate clean. Hell, maybe she'd even kiss me again. Or maybe I would just go ahead, man up and kiss her. Christ, if she kept blushing like she had when I'd opened the door for her, I was going to lose my mind.

Fiona took a cautious sip of her wine.

"Not a fan of wine?" I asked.

She batted her eyelashes, but not in a fake way—more like reflection. It was one of those small things that added to her greater beauty. "I don't like to be out of control."

Everything she said seemed to have hidden meanings, half of them being unraveled by my brain and the other half wishing she was flirting. But there was no mystery about why she would never let go. She'd never had a safety net. In fact, she *was* the safety net—not just for Violet, but for herself, too.

Chezzie walked over carrying a huge plate of antipasto, and my stomach did a happy dance. Roasted red peppers, grilled eggplant and zucchini—all drizzled with oil and balsamic vinegar. *Real food.* I could have wept.

We thanked my aunt and I served Fiona before piling up my own small plate.

"So..." Fiona leaned in. "There are no menus? She just brings us food?"

"Yup." I cut the eggplant and shoved it in my mouth. As I chewed it, the tension that I'd been holding in my shoulders the entire day softened. A brief flash of a gun being pointed directly at me popped into my head. I hadn't flinched, nor had I hesitated. All my movements had been perfect. Dad would have been proud—or maybe not. I hadn't killed anyone.

"Hey," Fiona said in a soft voice and she placed her hand over mine, "where'd you go there?"

I shook my head, rattling away the memory. "Sorry. Long day."

Fiona brushed her thumb over my knuckle—it was a tender gesture that I shouldn't get used to. She glanced around before asking in a low voice, "How did you do it, anyway? How did you get her back?"

Telling her it was easy would have been pompous, and I didn't want to be that way around her anymore.

I raked my fingers through my hair then squeezed my shoulders. She waited with such patience, such concern, that it merited the truth, however tiny it might be.

"It's what I've trained for. Plus, most of Bradford is high half the time. It's not even a fair fight." I went back to my food and mopped up the remaining sauce with a piece of olive bread.

God, I've missed Chezzie's olive bread.

Our starters were cleared away by a busboy I hadn't seen before and Chezzie came out of the kitchen with two bowls of Spaghetti Vongole. When it was below my nose, I looked up to Chezzie, who had a knowing smile on her barely wrinkled face.

"I love you."

Chezzie rolled her eyes and turned to Fiona. "He loves my food."

I couldn't wait, and I pulled a clam out of its shell with my fork and twisted the oily long noodles into my spoon.

"I'm never going to have that problem." Fiona's eyes widened with her confession and Chezzie laughed and walked away.

After a cringe, Fiona brought her hands to her face and rubbed the base of her palms under her eyes. I chewed the blissful pasta, also enjoying the mortification show in front of me. Frazzled Fiona was a delightful sight.

"Ugh. This is insane. I wasn't implying that you would ever love me."

"Yes, you were," I said between bites and loved the fact that it made her more uncomfortable. I was still an ass, after all.

Fiona dropped her head back and banged it on the booth a few times. "This day has been a nightmare — and long. I'm pretty sure this is the longest day of my life." She stared at her plate then up to me, her lack of food knowledge apparent in her unsure frown.

"Trust me. It's amazing." I reached over the table for her fork and spoon. "You pull out the clam, stick it and wrap it in the most perfectly cooked pasta you will ever eat. Then repeat."

I motioned for her to take the silverware but she just stared at my hands. She looked up at me with her soft brown eyes. There was a hint of sadness and a touch of confusion, but mostly warmth.

"Twelve hours ago, I hated you. And now we're on a date." A weary frown spread on her lovely face. "And I like it. Jesus, Leo, we're being *kind* to each other. What has happened to us?"

"Eat." I insisted with the fork and spoon again. Gingerly, she took them out of my hands and did as I'd ordered. After a bit of silence and a confession that the pasta was indeed amazing, she wiped the corners of her mouth with the cream-colored cloth napkin.

Her confidence was back, perhaps fueled by Italian cooking at its finest. She asked, "Were you afraid this morning?"

"Yeah. When you ran off—"

"No, I mean when you went to get Callie."

"No."

Part of me hoped that showing her my strong side would comfort her. The other part hoped like hell it wouldn't scare her. Either way, I was tired of hiding it.

"Were there guns?"

"Yes." I sat back in the booth and our plates were cleared.

She watched the busboy walk away before asking, "There were guns, but you weren't scared?"

"Correct. It's one thing to have a gun and another to know how to use it."

"And you know how to use one?"

She was searching for something, but the intrusion didn't bother me. In fact, it might have been refreshing on some level.

"I do." There was nothing playful about my tone. It was a solid affirmation that I was sure she believed, maybe craved.

Fiona licked her lips and her chest rose and fell at a hypnotizing pace. She had on one of the dark tank tops she'd recently bought and it fit her like skin.

"Did you use a gun this morning?"

I loved that she stared me down, challenged me, so I told her what she wanted to hear, which also happened to be true. "Yes."

Fiona tapped her finger gently three times on the table where her plate had been. She closed her eyes for a long blink then asked, "Have you killed someone?"

"I'm not a murderer." But I was. I just hadn't taken a life.

She must have missed the lie because she said, "Okay," and nodded, as if she understood all the turmoil I went through on a daily basis—as if I had a chance at being normal, like there was a future with happiness waiting for me. There wasn't.

Because the truth, the real horrifying truth was that I'd *wanted* to shoot those Bradford fucks between the eyes even before I'd heard Callie's screams. I'd enjoyed flexing my muscles of knowledge and power. I'd cherished the fear in their eyes when they'd realized that they were fucked. And that taste I'd had... It was just as addicting as the drugs I sold to make Anton richer.

So while Fiona might have been justifying this date on some sort of level only she could wrestle with, deep down, I was still faking.

The problem was that she was becoming just as much of a delicious habit as the rest of it. I'd laid on the bed with her earlier telling myself lies — lies of a relationship that would not, could not work. No one was going to stay around and love a murderer. My mother had proven that point. And I could try to lie like Frankie did and lead a double life, but eventually, relationships based on fake foundations always crumbled — some even burned.

And yet, I needed to be with her, wanted to be with her — however that was possible.

The chicken Marsala came and cut the tension we'd created through our short game of twenty questions.

"There's more?" Fiona asked with big eyes once Chezzie had left. "God, and it smells amazing." Fiona deflated but took up her knife and fork and cut through the tender chicken breast. She popped in a bite at the same time as I did and our eyes met, each of us mirroring the other's emotions. Yeah, it was good.

About halfway through, she slowed down and eventually gave up. Her stomach hadn't grown up Italian, so I forgave her and finished her plate. We spoke of lighter subjects — the food, the neighborhood... Hell, we even talked about the weather.

Chezzie brought over my expresso and scooted in next to me. She brushed through the hair above my ear with her long nails. "This mean you're coming home?"

Her question was both a plea and a wish. I'd never asked her how much she'd known about her brother's life. I'd always just assumed it was enough by the way she looked at Frankie and me so knowingly.

"I don't know." I let out a long breath and offered a small smile. And I didn't know. What was sure was that Covington was becoming less and less of an option. I'd really thought I could lie low and be a simple, contented criminal. But that wasn't in my blood.

Maybe she sensed the shift, because Fiona perked up and said, "Chezzie, thank you so much. That was the best meal of my life. I loved it."

"Anytime." Chezzie stood and motioned for me to do the same. "Give me a hug. I never know when I'm going to see you again."

I obliged and she squeezed me tight. For my ears only, she said, "I don't know what brought you to me, but I know you'll be okay."

My chest tightened. I wanted to believe her.

Once Fi and I were outside, she pulled me in the opposite direction of the car. "I don't want to go back yet."

I held her hand and let her guide me to a small nearby park. We found an empty bench, where we sat under a streetlight.

"Do you know why I took off this morning?" she asked without looking at me.

"To piss me off?" It had worked. She could have easily been Callie.

"Nah. That was an added benefit. It was because I wanted to do something nice for myself. And whenever I do that, something goes wrong and proves that I shouldn't have."

I could relate. "So why bother, right?"

"Anton's not happy about us." Fiona bowed her head and fiddle with her fingers in her lap.

"He's probably going to ask me to leave." At least it would be civil.

"Not if you don't go back." Fiona swiveled toward me, a sad hope in her eyes. "You must have somewhere else to go. Chezzie—"

I lifted up a hand. "I'm going back."

"Why? Why would you live there when you have another option?"

Because you're there and you don't know the other option.

She danced her eyes around my face, trying to will an answer out of me. But I'd had my fill of truthful confessions. I wanted to keep our night going as much as she did. And she was right about something. I didn't have to go back, not right away.

"How long will your mom stay sober?"

Fiona narrowed her eyes then looked away, blinking several times. "Until she meets a guy. Then maximum one month. Why?"

"Ever been camping?" I had no plan, zero, but to get far, far away, and a complete change of scenery was exactly what we both needed.

"Leo, the farthest I've ever been from Covington was a boat ride on the river. You're not talking about sleeping outside, are you? Like on dirt?"

"Come on." I popped up but she stayed on the bench, shaking her head.

"I don't like bugs, Leo. I don't like…trees."

I couldn't help but laugh. "You don't like *trees*?"

She rolled her eyes, but I could tell she just needed a little convincing. The fresh air would do us both good.

"I'll do everything. I promise." *Anything and everything.* "Come." I held out my hand.

Fiona peered at me. I'd already convinced her. "Let me guess. Skip was a Boy Scout?"

"Sorta." I was pretty sure the kids in little uniforms and scarfs had duller knives.

We stopped at a deli for another coffee and I grabbed some supplies. There was a crappy motel a couple of hours north where we could spend the night, then I could get us organized for the next day. Fiona's flip-flops and cut-offs would never do for the wild.

At the counter, Fiona cleared her throat and pushed a box of condoms into our pile. There was no point in lying. My heart skipped a beat and I was pretty sure my eyes bugged out of my head.

She shrugged. "I like presents."

I had a present. I absolutely, positively had a present for her. And there was no doubt in my mind that I wanted to give it to her, but I didn't want her to feel obligated to give it to me. So I paid, and when we got to the car, I turned to her.

"I don't want you to think you have to pay me for your safety. I'm not Anton."

She studied me, and for the first time in a long time I had no idea what to think, how to read the person in front of me. Fiona stretched and yawned.

In a matter-of-fact tone she said, "Leo, we went on a date—you and me. I got turned on about you knowing how to use a gun."

Okay, I probably didn't need to know that. It gave flight to those little birds of hope that I'd been trying to cage.

With more volume, she continued, "You blend dangerous and safe in a way that fucks with my head and my hormones. If I'm going to be in a tent with you—cuz there is no way I am sleeping alone in the woods. I've seen too many movies for that — something *might* happen between consenting adults. I just want to be safe."

"I just don't want you to feel like it's some sort of obligation." *God help me, I'm cock-blocking myself.* Fiona was right. There was something wrong with us.

She crossed her arms, plumping her breasts — breasts that would be next to me in a tent, breasts that I'd been dreaming about for months. She was a genius. We would absolutely need those condoms — *if* she gave the green light.

"Eyes up. And do you honestly think I would do anything I didn't want to?"

"No."

"I'm not saying it's going to happen. I'm saying it could. Now stop thinking about my boobs and drive us out of this fucking city."

Fiona nodded off with her face smashed against the window. It didn't bother me to not have that conversation while I drove. She'd given me a lot to think about — and not just in the sexy, dirty, can't-wait-to-get-my-hands-on-her department.

Something she'd said casually played over and over in my mind. She just wanted to be safe. It was why she wanted out of Covington Heights. She'd confused location with safety. But threats were everywhere we went. It was why my father had taught us self-defense before he'd ever shown us an offensive attack. *Assess the greatest threat.*

Part of me wondered if my greatest threat wasn't gently snoring next to me.

Chapter Fifteen

Fiona

I woke to Leo's quick exhales and a vague memory of checking into a motel. With my eyes still closed, I reached for his pillow and pulled it over my head. The luxury of sleeping in was lost in his noisy huffs.

"Ahh-h! What are you doing?" I asked with a muffled voice.

"Pushups. A thousand."

I bet there was a smile on his face. He couldn't be serious.

"Do them quieter," I complained but slowly rolled to the side of the bed where his grunts were coming from and opened an eye.

Holy shit. Leo was shirtless and somehow the pants he had been wearing the day before had mercifully been lost as well. When he'd done the pushups in my living room with Violet on his back, his baggy jeans had failed at displaying his harder-than-should-be-allowed ass. That thing was tight — bounce-a-quarter-off-it tight. Up and down the glorious olive-skinned man went, his back muscles glimmering with perspiration and that ass solid as a brick.

I had to stop my hand from reaching out of its own accord and grabbing or smacking the damn thing to make sure it was real. And it got worse. His thighs were like trunks on a thousand-year-old tree. He had more defined muscles than I even knew our legs had. His calves were equally carved out. It was like his skin was being stretched to its limits.

How had I missed all of it before? Maybe all those muscles had to be flexed to intoxicate me with their raw power. I had no idea. But drunk I was. Why was I sweating when he was the one doing all the work? Also, why did I have the urge to crawl under him and make him kiss me every time he bent the elbows of those... Sweet Baby Jesus, his arms in action were sinful.

"I can feel you staring at me."

I should have been embarrassed. That was what he was trying to do. And truthfully, a part of me was. But there was a hungrier part of me — the part that had confessed to being turned on by his confidence.

"And?" I dared.

Instead of another smart-ass remark, he let my challenge hang in the air, taunting me to follow through. *Fine.* I could do that. Hell, I wanted to do it. I stretched out like a lazy cat then dug through my little backpack for the bath bomb I'd bought the day before. I stepped over the human muscle machine and headed for the bathroom.

The tub wasn't as big as Anton's, but it was cleaner than mine. I pulled the stopper and flipped the water on. While the bath filled, I brushed my teeth and washed my knickers in the sink. I chuckled to myself at the thought of me camping. I was the least outdoorsy person I knew.

When the tub was half full, I dropped the pink bomb in and it fizzled into nothing. I slid into the warm, tinted water. I closed my eyes and went to that safe place deep inside me. But instead of the solitude I usually found there, I went back to the moment on Leo's bed at the apartment—the minute in my life where he and I had shifted.

There was something happening between the two of us that deserved to be explored. It was why, when he'd offered to take me away—even fucking camping—I couldn't say no. We were different when we were out of Covington. And while Leo was holding something back, I was pretty sure there was a mutual underlying acceptance growing between us that couldn't be nurtured with my mom or Anton around. For the first time in a long time, I was grateful. It warmed me more than the steamy water around me.

Tap. Tap. Tap.

"You okay in there?" Leo called from the other side of the door. Why did he knock? He was a barge-in kinda guy.

"Never better." I weighed the truth of my statement. Out of Covington, out of danger, hot man in a motel room… It might have been true.

"We need to get going. We have to get supplies and we have a long hike."

Blerk. Had he not heard the part about me and bugs?

"You're not coming in to ogle me naked?"

Even through the door I could hear his airy grumble, and it made me smile.

"Hurry up."

I drained the tub. After a shimmy and a bit of a dry, I wrapped myself in a towel and used the hairdryer on myself and my underwear. I was dressed and about as ready for camping as I'd ever be.

Or so I thought.

I'd known there were stores for people who liked to do things outside. I had just never been in one. Two hours after checking out of the motel, we had a portable tent, I was wearing hiking boots and we had all sorts of shit I'd never imagined existed in my life — like tick spray. Just the idea that I had to put something on my body in hopes a little bug wouldn't crawl up my leg and suck my blood was disturbing.

We grabbed some sandwiches for lunch and some food for dinner and breakfast, and drove north for another hour. Leo exited the highway for a town I'd never heard of and the winding, rural roads had me transfixed.

Green grass and darker trees sprawled over hills. We drove through actual small towns where houses had mailboxes at the end of their driveways that were disguised as smaller matching houses. My goal to get out of Covington had always been limited to another part of the city. Maybe it was time to think about a whole new kind of escape.

"You're quiet." Leo glanced over to me before turning down a tree-lined dirt road. It was like we were in a tunnel of forest.

"It's beautiful up here."

His response was a small smile. He was peaceful, serene. I would have never imagined how much it suited him. We came to a stop in a gravel parking lot.

"We walk from here."

With our packs loaded, we followed a small path uphill. Leo would stop every now and again, pick off a wild blackberry or tiny bright red strawberry then offer it to me. Their juicy flavor was sweeter than any candy I'd ever eaten.

At one point, on a particularly steep and rocky bit, Leo offered me his hand for stability and I was sure I swooned. I was also becoming more and more certain that the Leo I'd met in black jeans and a muscle tank was all an act. This gentle side of him was who he really was, and it was mesmerizing.

My legs were sore, my feet ached and I'd swatted away my fair share of flying bugs, but I didn't complain. In fact, I couldn't lie to myself. I loved it. The steady gushing of a river not too far off and the calling of various birds mixed with the sun peeking through the foliage, and I was sure I never wanted to step foot into the city again.

After what must have been three hours and with my back at its complete limit of exhaustion from carrying the heavy load, Leo held back a tree branch and motioned for me to go first.

A small lake glimmered in front of me with a large, deep green hill on the opposite side. My heart skipped a beat. The dirt and grass below my feet led to a rocky beach where a long wooden dock reached out a quarter of the width of the deep blue water. It was a secluded paradise.

"It's beautiful." The grin on my face hurt, it was so big.

Leo studied me as if a compliment was on the tip of his tongue. Instead he dipped his shoulder and let his much larger pack slide to the ground. "You can drop your bag and chill. I said I would do everything, and I will."

The weight off my back was a massive relief and it was true that three hours of walking uphill wasn't exactly something I'd trained for, but I didn't want to be an ungrateful ass. "I can help. Just tell me what to do."

"Go sit on the dock and put your feet in the water. They must be killing you." He winked and my throbbing feet screamed that he was right. "I got this."

"You sure?" I bit my lip but prayed he would insist.

"Go." He shooed me away.

On the little dock, I unlaced my boots and took off the thick socks Leo had also insisted upon. The cool water tickled my toes and the clean air purified my lungs. The warm sun lulled me into a lovely, tranquil state. I had always been right. Life outside of Covington Heights was better.

The crackling of wood woke me from my meditative bliss and the smell of smoke hit my nose at the same time. The tent was up and a fire was burning in front of it. While I'd sat on my rear and daydreamed of never going home, he'd made a campsite.

I dried my feet on the warm skin of my bare legs, put my shoes and socks back on and found a big rock next to the fire pit opposite Leo. He stirred the flaming wood with a long, pointed stick.

"You've been here before."

His gaze shifted around the landscape before it met mine. "My dad used to bring my brother Frankie and me here to train."

He hadn't needed to add the last detail and I took it to mean that he was letting me in, and even if the opening was small, I decided to take it.

"Train for what?"

"Survival." Leo grabbed the backpack I'd carried and unzipped it. "Hungry?"

The change of subject was duly noted, and I decided not to push.

"Starving. I've never walked that much in my life."

He chuckled and pulled out the thick hot dogs. "I was sure you were going to bitch and moan." Leo dug out a Swiss Army knife and flipped it open to the blade. He sliced the ends of the sausage in a cross, impaled it on a stick and handed it to me. As I held my dinner above the fire, he repeated the same process for himself.

"I think I might like camping," I said, barely believing my own words.

We ate our char-burned hotdogs as the sun set behind me. A chill blew off the lake and I rubbed my arms. I could have reached for the sleeping bag or the hoodie that was somewhere buried in one of the bags, but the perfect day needed a perfect night.

I stood and Leo's dark eyes followed me around the fire. The energy shifted between us as he recognized the intention I was sending. I lowered myself onto his lap.

"Thank you — for this, for everything." I brushed my cheek against his stubble and kissed his neck — my pressure as gentle as my words had been. He was only docile for a minute before his little grumble steamed out of him.

He held me at arm's length. "You can't do this. You can't give yourself to a version of me that's not real."

A pain in his eyes reached into my heart and took hold.

"I think this version of you is a hell of a lot more real than you in black jeans." I lifted my eyebrows, daring him to object.

He looked away, confirming I was right. I laid my head on his shoulder and threaded my arms under his. His heart beat fast and his breath was shallow. But he'd wrapped his arms around me, a sign that I could stay where I was.

I swallowed past the nerves. "Why are you hiding in Covington?"

He let out a slow hum. "Anton is going to ask me to leave."

"What will you do?"

The darker it got, the braver I became, and the crackling of the fire filled the space between the long pauses of our exchange.

"I'll turn into the man I grew up hating." The honesty of his words, the most revealing thus far, broke my fragile heart. Their weight hovered in the air above us and I struggled to fill my lungs.

For the first time since we'd met, I understood that Leo needed me more than I needed him — that he was sharing a part of himself that was not just secret but exposed everything about him.

My next question was the most daring and I asked it with care. "And what was that man?"

"A killer."

I let his confession sink in. His deepest fear was essentially my own — turning into the bit of a parent that lived inside us. It was why I wanted out of Covington and, ironically, why he wanted to stay. I needed to run, and he needed to hide. And there we were, perfectly aligned in our own crosshairs.

"You don't have to be that. You can choose—"

Leo shook his head. In a desperate whisper he said, "Every single day of my life says you're wrong."

My soul ached for him. A tear fell down my cheek. It was much easier to cry for someone else's pain. He'd convinced himself of his destiny, and maybe on some level he was right. Being a criminal was a slippery slope. He'd said the day before that he'd used a gun. How long until he shot to kill? I didn't know why he didn't just disappear, but then again, it would have been incredibly lonely.

The need to show him he was good, that he could be cherished as he was, overtook everything else buzzing in my brain. Sex wasn't going to solve any of our problems, but it was the only thing I could give him to prove that what he'd shared hadn't changed the way I saw him.

It was also about me. I wanted to get lost for one more night. I wanted to remember the way that Leo looked at me like I was worth fighting for, that he put me first. I needed our brief glimpse of a different life to have more meaning than a quick vacation.

I sat up and searched his eyes. There was so much sadness that I had to fight more tears. But this wasn't about pity. This was us showing each other that all the moments we'd shared were real, that our connection was deeper than we would have otherwise admitted.

I kissed him, once…twice. "Don't say no."

Leo closed his eyes for a long blink but didn't move.

"I need to get lost, Leo. And you're the perfect maze."

He couldn't deny wanting the same thing. "We have no future."

Regret mixed with honesty and wove between us.

"Then let's steal the present."

Chapter Sixteen

Leo

To be fair, Fiona was incredibly convincing. Her lovely lips brushing against mine, her intoxicating gentle voice, the vulnerable side to her spirit... It was more tenderness than I'd ever been shown. And she was right. The next day would change us. I wouldn't be welcome in Anton's crew after taking Fiona. Hell, I'd already been on thin ice for challenging him on other occasions.

So as the beautiful brunette continued to pepper sweet kisses down my jawline, any guard I'd had left melted away. No one would look at me the way she did once I went back to life with Frankie. They would either fear me or never see who I wanted to be.

"Please, Leo," Fiona half whispered, half begged. "I need this. I need you."

It was too soon, not soon enough and would never be enough. But I relented. How could I not? I was drunk on her grace. I'd never wanted anyone or anything the way I wanted her. It was like she not only understood me, she also accepted what she saw. And she was helping me forget who I really was.

Once I'd flipped the switch to complaisance, my body commanded my brain, not unlike when I was fighting. But instead of the quick moves, everything slowed down. The flames from the campfire danced behind her, giving her face a divine glow.

She interlaced her fingers into mine and kissed back up to my mouth. Done with being the good boy from before, I deepened the kiss. Her small moans only fueled my desire and she rubbed her chest into mine. *Vixen.* She knew I was a sucker for her rack.

The mischief that flickered in her eyes as she stood and pulled me up was the celebration party of my defeat—not that I'd put up that much of a fight. Thirty seconds of me pretending I wasn't enjoying having her in my lap was hardly a protest.

I followed her into the tent, where I'd laid out the sleeping bags. On our knees, we kissed again. This time her hands snuck up my T-shirt and crept to my pecs.

Her small, confident smile was by far the sexiest smirk on the planet. And who was I to argue? A woman who went after what she wanted? *Yes, please.*

She feathered her fingers down my stomach and lifted my shirt. The chill up my spine had nothing to do with the cool air outside the tent. Our little triangle canvas hut was all forms of steam.

"Stay put," she said and held up a finger. Fiona rustled around in the bag until she found the box of condoms.

Oh, she was serious.

"We don't—"

Her mouth was on mine before I could finish. I didn't want her to feel obligated to do anything, especially after Anton's stupid rule of paying for protection. *Jesus. Will he keep it up when I'm gone? Will he still want her?*

I yanked away and held her at arm's length. "I can't. Shit, I've totally failed you. If I'm not in Covington, how are you going to be safe?" I pushed the base of my palms into my brow. "Fuck."

Fiona closed her light-brown eyes tight then opened them. "I'm *not* your responsibility, Leo. And you know what? I'm going to find a way to get Violet and me out of there. I'll get another job. Hell, maybe I'll move up here. They'll forget about me."

I laid down on my back and banged my head into the earth. How could I have been so stupid? So selfish? By wanting Fiona, I had ensured my demise and her own. I would be gone, and the best-case scenario was that she would end up with someone else. I'd confused wanting her with wanting to keep her safe.

And it wasn't like I could take her home. The minute I went back to Frankie, he would put me to work. My father had always wanted a double legacy. Plus, it was rather presumptuous to think that Fiona would want to come anywhere with me, especially since she didn't know the truth about what she would be coming home to. That shit ate at people.

All my options sucked.

"Hey." Fiona crawled over to me and stroked my cheek.

That look. That innocent expression. That damn docile side to her reminding me that I'd only ever lied to her. She didn't know me, not truly. And she deserved to know that she wasn't the reason I wouldn't be chasing her down and begging for a life with her.

It was time to roll the dice and pay the up. A funny thing, fear… It wasn't something that I was used to. But in that moment, it snaked up my stomach and tied a tight knot. I stared into her pretty eyes for a few more seconds. It was how I wanted to remember her — the slice of caring before she found out I was a man-made monster.

"I wasn't exactly honest before when I 'd said we'd come up here for survival."

A hint of a frown pulled at her lips. "You don't owe me any explanations."

I did. I owed her the truth. "My dad was a hitman." Yeah, that got her attention. And, Christ, it was oddly refreshing to say it out loud. "My brother *is* a hitman."

"And you don't want to be."

I darted my gaze away from her. Honesty was easier that way. "I will be, Fiona. It's in my blood. My father trained my brother and me every day. *Every. Day.* I've been fighting since I could walk. Hell, before. I can shoot a gun with both hands and not miss."

As my explanation went on about how my hitman father had trained his two boys to not just follow in his own footsteps but also to be better than he ever was, her face fell and curiosity was exchanged for pity. But she had to know why I wasn't going to fight for her, that someone like me could not be loved by someone as selfless as her. That the deeds of my past and future would assure our demise. I had to nail my own coffin.

"I could have killed those guys and not even blinked. I wanted to."

"But you didn't." Fiona chewed her bottom lip.

I appreciated that she was trying to find the good in me — like I'd had some empathy — but she was wrong. "The time will come and I won't be able to resist. I'll be a killer, just like them." The emotion was gone in my voice. I was stating facts — facts I knew, facts I couldn't hide from in Covington Heights, as much as I'd tried.

It was possible that, on some level, me swiping Fiona from Anton was a way of hurrying my fate. There was too much wrong with me and not nearly enough right.

So it was a surprise when Fiona nudged my arm and placed her head on my chest. "I feel the same way about drugs. It would be easy to follow my mom's path, to escape how she does. That's why I hate Anton and his crew, hated you. You guys made it easy for her and harder for me."

"I'm sorry." It wouldn't change her struggle, but at least I could acknowledge I'd played a part in it.

She hummed her exhale into my chest. "My worst fear is getting high, because I'm sure I'll like it."

My worst fear was taking a life and not giving a shit.

"But you resist, Fi. You are not your mom."

"And you're not your father or brother."

That was where she was wrong. But it was nice that she believed it.

We fell asleep like that, somehow knowing it was a stolen moment, and we didn't wake up until a sliver of sun cut through the tent. My confessions from the night before lingered in the air and brought occasional little smiles from Fiona as we packed up. The soundtrack to our walk down the mountain was the cracking of branches beneath our feet and the calls of hawks above our heads.

When I closed the hatch of the car, Fiona had her arms crossed and peered up at me with big, sad eyes.

"If it wasn't for Violet, I would have tried to convince you to run off with me."

I reached out for her and pulled her in. She was just short enough to fit perfectly under my chin. There, in each other's arms, I let the connection between us swirl around me. I savored its existence and already grieved its soon-to-be absence.

I kissed the top of her head. "If it wasn't for Violet, we'd be in another country by now."

Fiona hugged me tighter. "Why does it all have to change?"

Because I'd fucked up. I'd gotten selfish and proud. I'd convinced myself I could be something that I wasn't. And I'd lost sight of what mattered. But I didn't want to remind her of my faults. I wanted her to remember my strengths.

"I wish it didn't have to. But you are the toughest woman I've ever met. You're going to be fine."

"I don't want to go home." Her words were quiet, as if she were admitting a horrible truth.

"Neither do I."

But we had to. Maybe if I played my cards right with Anton, he would still look after Fi and she could continue to work the games. Then again, that would only ensure that she stayed under his control. Maybe I could pay for her freedom. After all, Anton was in it for the money.

I kissed the top of her head. "Come on. Time to go."

I'd left my phone in the car and the sun had overheated it. I plugged it into the charger and as I pulled down the tree-lined road, a plan formulated in my brain. I could get Fiona and Violet out of Covington. I could use my money to give her a fresh start and a chance at a new life. It would require me paying my debt to Frankie, but hadn't I already sealed my own fate by messing things up with Anton? The more I thought about it, the more I convinced myself I was right. And once Fiona would realize that it was a chance for Violet, she wouldn't be able to say no.

My phone buzzed and I thought it was just the fact that it had cooled down. But it kept buzzing and when I glanced at it, the masked number made my gut clench.

"Where the fuck have you been?" Anton shouted in my ear.

"We're on our way back. Why?"

"BTs want revenge. Rafa got a tip. We need all hands on deck. Get the fuck back here."

On the one hand, Anton wanting me back in Covington should have been a good sign that he wasn't too pissed. On the other, he was a selfish prick most of the time, so him wanting me was probably more for my skills than friendship. He'd still ask me to leave once it all blew over. I was no fool.

"What's your ETA?" he asked.

"Two hours if I speed." I was sure that wasn't the answer he wanted.

"Jesus... Then fucking speed. I don't need a courtyard full of blood." He hung up.

Chapter Seventeen

Fiona

Leo zipped down the highway, his phone lighting up with texts all the way to the city. I tried not to stare at him, but I was worried — worried that Anton was going to use him to be exactly the thing he'd been fighting against. Telling him that he didn't have to go back would have been useless. As messed up as it was, Leo was loyal. He would never have left his friends to fight without him, especially if everything he'd told me was true. Skill and ego could make the muscle of pride flex to its fullest.

When we pulled up to the complex, Leo hesitated for a brief second as he took in the scene in front of us. There were about twenty guys from Bradford beating the shit out of Anton's crew with pipes. Only Jackson and Anton seemed to be giving it back as much as they were getting it. It was a full-out brawl. Even from the car I could see the blood splattering on the pavement. I recognized Scooter in a ball on the ground and one of the assholes who'd chased me down the block was kicking him repeatedly in the kidneys.

"Sneak around the back. Go upstairs to your place, lock the door and stay fucking put." Leo reached around my seat and grabbed a baseball bat.

I didn't answer. I slipped out of the car and jogged around to the broken emergency exit. With more energy than I'd had in months, I climbed the seven flights of stairs and was surprised to find the door to our apartment unlocked.

Deep green eyes and a wicked grin sat on my couch. My mother was curled up at the opposite end, her sedated state so familiar but nonetheless shocking. Bile rose from my stomach and sat painfully in my throat as Violet smiled at our visitor, offering him her dinosaur.

"Ah, Fiona"—the intruder licked his lips—"right on time."

Every muscle in my body tensed and the air was sucked out of my lungs. Mac—fucking Mac—tousled my sister's dark hair as my mother lay out of her mind next to him. Only my eyes were able to move, and I shifted them around the apartment, trying to make sense of what I was seeing, but it was all a horrible blur. The only thing I was capable of focusing on was his wicked hand on my baby sister's thin, dark hair.

With a satisfied smile on his pale face, Mac stood and rubbed his palms together. "I knew there was something off about Leo parading you in public. That's so desperately out of character for him..."

The vulgar and haunting exchange we'd shared at the poker game weeks prior flashed in my mind. Mac took slow strides until we were face-to-face. His spicy cologne almost made me gag and the flakes on his skin reminded me of scales on a venomous snake. I had no doubt that his metaphorical fangs were about to latch on to me and release their toxic blow. He'd been waiting for me, expecting me.

With breath that stunk of warmed-over death and a rotten gut, he said, "My sister tells me they're all quite fond of you."

I studied his eyes, his deep green, forest-like eyes. They were emerald pools I'd only seen on one other person in my life—the fucking doctor. Mac ran a crooked finger down my cheek and I shuddered.

"Leo—"

Mac scoffed and shook his head. "Leo is busy, my darling."

Two bald men from Bradford came into my peripheral vision—one from the kitchen and the other from the hallway. I didn't need to look to verify Justin's presence as the one by the stove. Mac glanced in their directions then back to me, and he narrowed his eyes. My heart raced and my head spun. I was fucked.

"Here's my educated guess… You can tell me if I'm right—and I do so love to be right." A glib smile plastered his pitted cheeks. He walked back over to Violet and sat down in front of her.

I tried to breathe but my trembling chest didn't seem to want to expand.

Mac continued, "You ran down that street and Leo saved you. But, since Leo belongs to Anton, so does your protection." Mac spread open his hands like an offering on both sides, and they pointed to both of the assholes staring directly at me with disgust. "This makes you valuable to both them *and* me."

I was sure the walls of the apartment were tightening around me—restricting like a trash compactor from all sides. I had no defense, no escape. The ease with which Violet accepted his smile and touch reminded me of how starved she had been for attention. I was a fool to have left her.

Violet climbed up on the couch and Mac opened a book. He complimented her on identifying the picture of a yellow candle. A new fear iced my veins. What would Mac do if I didn't comply with whatever the fuck he was conjuring up for me in his obscene head? Worse, my new back-up plan was Justin.

My mother was probably ounces away from an overdose, if not on the other side of it. Mac didn't look like the type who was afraid to pull that trigger. Justin definitely wasn't. If they did so, even in the best-case scenario—which was horrible to think about, my mother dying and finding anything good about it—I would most likely lose Violet to a social worker, at least for a while.

But worse, so much worse, was the impression I had that Mac, who continued to stroke Violet's soft dark hair, would take her, a fucking child—the sweet little soul I'd fought to shield from her mother's disease for over two years, the reason I got up in the morning and the only purpose in my shitty life.

Christ, I'd been horribly selfish going away with Leo. I'd created the gap in Violet's safety and let Mac creep right in. A lonely tear ran down my cheek and I wiped it away before another could think it needed company. Somehow, I managed to swallow over the baseball of fear in my throat.

"It's going to be nice, finally making some money off your ass." Justin moved in front of me and his sour breath flipped my stomach.

I was going to leave with them. That was painfully obvious. My only hope would be not to abandon Violet completely.

"Let me take the baby to a friend's and I'll go peacefully. No tricks. I promise."

The same nefarious grin I'd seen on Mac's face when I'd walked in appeared on his disgusting cheeks.

"So sensible. So smart. I knew I liked you."

Trying hard to fight the shaking that was commandeering my body, I managed to walk over to the couch and signal for Violet that I would pick her up. She pointed to a brown bear in the book and I was thankful for her young age and that she couldn't smell my fear.

But as soon as her warm body was pressed into mine, the floodgates opened with a stark realization that if it wasn't the last time I would hold her, it was definitely the last time I would hold her before a chunk of my soul would be ripped out of my body.

All of Leo's warnings had been spot on. I was going to be raped, either by Justin or worse…whatever it was that Mac had planned for me.

As I held Violet tight and tried not to sob, I looked at my mother. The disease had devoured her, sucked out every capability, possibility and ounce of potential happiness from her body. She was nothing more than a shell of herself, no help to me or Violet.

Justin said, "We need to go. That asshole Ricci is helping their odds." He slid a phone into his back pocket.

My heart stopped. There had still been a foolish piece of me who'd thought I'd had a bit of time, a moment to figure out how to wake up from the nightmare.

Mac rose and grabbed my elbow. "You heard him."

The Bradford prick from the hallway moved toward us, dug a small plastic bag out of his pocket and waved it in front of my face. I pushed Violet's head into my shoulder and shot my eyes to Mac.

"That's just a little bit of insurance to make sure you don't fuck this up. He'll stay here. If you scream or blink in Morse code on our way out, your mother will magically overdose. I'm letting you leave Violet with someone in exchange for your composure. Don't make me regret it." Mac motioned for me to leave.

Every step was a death sentence. Justin, Mac, Violet and I proceeded down the hall and tiny threads of hope tried to weave themselves into my heart. I silently pleaded to any energetic power to send help—to dispatch anyone in Anton's crew my way. I pictured Leo and his disappointed eyes after Callie. I'd done this. I'd set these lurid wheels in motion.

With Violet still tightly wrapped in my arms, I entered the elevator and my body shook as I reached to push the button for the third floor.

Mac cut in front of me as I drew back my hand. "Pull yourself together or I take you both."

I nodded, wiped my cheeks, and let out a stuttered exhale before kissing Violet's sweet head. The doors closed and the ride was over too soon.

The third floor was empty, all of the crew probably still battling their foes in the courtyard.

"We'll wait in the stairs, but don't think for one second I'm not watching your every flinch, Fiona. Do this the easy way and no one gets hurt—not your friend, not your mother and not that little girl in your arms."

The paradox in his words almost made me laugh. We would all be hurt. It was only a matter of perspective and time. They slipped into the stairwell and left the door open a crack. Mac's green eyes glowed like cursed jewels in the dark shadows next to the evil dark slits of Justin's. There was no doubt in my mind that the threats were real.

When I got to Lisa's door, I desperately wanted to take one last loving look at Violet. I longed to hang on to every detail of her innocent face, give her an explanation that would somehow justify my absence from before and after. But if I did any of that, if I caved to my heart, I would break. I would melt down into a puddle of tears and hold that baby until she was ripped from my arms. I would wail and fight and kick and scream.

And all that would risk her. The exchange Mac had offered left me no choice but to play along. That was why instead of doing any of those things, instead of toying with my little sister's future, I straightened myself and knocked on Lisa's door.

When there was no answer, a new panic took hold of me. What would I do if she wasn't there? I knocked again, hoping my previous one had been too soft.

"Lisa?" I called out. "It's Fiona."

The door cracked open and Lisa peered at me from behind the chain.

"Hey. Can we come in?" I asked, my plan formulating with each word.

Lisa darted her eyes around me. "Scooter said not to let anybody in."

"Yeah, I know. Leo said the same. It's just that my mom is on a bender and I don't want Violet to see her like that. Can we stay here? Please?"

After a long exhale and nibble of her bottom lip, Lisa said, "Yeah. Sure. I can't see anything from my window, so it will be nice to freak out with someone else." She closed the door and released the chain before opening again.

"Oh shit," I faked, "I forgot her bunny. She'll never go down without it." I transferred Violet into Lisa's arms. "I'll be right back."

Lisa fumbled a little, then went right into caregiver mode with sweet words to Violet. A glance more would have ruined everything, so I didn't look back as Lisa closed and locked the door behind me, my sister perched on her hip.

My strides down the hall were my last taste of freedom before Mac pulled me into the stairwell and gripped my upper arm. Justin spoke into his phone as we descended but I couldn't understand his words. There was a deep buzz between my ears and I was sure the only thing keeping me grounded on the earth was the pinch above my elbow from Mac's sweaty hand. Somehow, when we arrived at the emergency exit, the trio from my apartment had reunited.

We walked at a swift pace down the dirty alley and to the street. Through the narrow gaps between brick buildings, I caught a glimpse of Leo swinging a bat at a tattooed, bald head. Anton's arms were being held behind him and another one of his rivals came at him with a metal pipe. Before the bloodied asshole could land a blow, Anton kicked both legs up and twisted the pipe between his booted feet. He headbutted backward and the quick distraction was all it took for Leo to whack the guy struggling with the pipe.

"Come on," Justin urged. "Time to take you to your destiny."

A beep of the alarm unlocked the doors of a white SUV. The dude holding the keys climbed into the driver's seat as Justin jogged around to the passenger side. Mac opened the back door and slid in, tugging me with him. As the ignition cranked, Mac's spicy scent floated under my nostrils while he bent over me and slammed the door.

The tires screeched and the speed forced me backward. From the seat pocket in front of him, Mac retrieved a vial containing a clear liquid, and he bit the plastic top of a hypodermic, holding it between his teeth.

My skin crawled like a million baby spiders searching for their refuge.

Mac spat the top on the floor and charged the needle. "This will keep you nice and docile until we get you to your final destination."

I stared out of the tinted window. The prick and sting hit my bare thigh and chocolate eyes widened in horror from the passing courtyard.

Chapter Eighteen

Leo

A white SUV tore up the street and the fuckers from Bradford Towers around us dropped their pipes and ran in its direction. They piled into matching white trucks, some flipping us off and laughing as they retreated from the carnage that was our crew.

I dropped the bat to the bloodstained ground. Both Jackson and Anton were leaning over and catching their breath. Rafa moaned to my left. He slowly sat and spat onto the pavement. Scooter was the worst — a whimpering ball and the farthest away from us. The rest of the crew hadn't gotten it that bad. Bradford had known who to target.

The odd thing was, they'd picked the fight but left before they'd finished it. And yet, that first SUV had come from somewhere else. I wiped my face with the bottom of my tank and walked over to Anton.

"It was a fucking trap," I said for his ears only.

"Raf!" Anton surveyed the crew. "Call the doctor. Jax, get everybody inside at our place *stat*."

The groans and moans followed the crew into the building. Jackson signaled for help with Scooter, and they carried him by his hands and legs past the bench while Rafa held the door with one hand, his phone at his ear in the other.

"You okay?" I asked Anton, once the place had cleared.

"Yeah." He sniffed. "Those skinny fuckers aren't that scary if they don't have a weapon."

The white SUV flashed in my head and landed a blow to my gut much more painful than anything I'd sustained during the brawl. "Something else went down. I can feel it. They'd planned it. We'd known they were coming. They could have showed up with guns, but they wanted a fight. At least two of them weren't fighting when they took off and everybody else followed."

"You're right." Anton spread his fingers. His hands were covered in scratches and blood. He flipped them over and flexed them in and out. "I need a fucking shower and probably some antibiotics. Dirty fucks."

The sight of the courtyard would scare the shit out of the people we were trying to protect and put a crack in any kind of confidence they had in our crew, not to mention that it was bad for business. We'd taken a blow, not just to our bodies but also as a collective. If Anton's clients and community couldn't trust him or believed that they were safer without his crew, we were as good as dead. There would already be rumors and gossip. Anton needed to show that he was still solid, in control of the turf. All the rest of our personal bullshit could wait.

"I'll rinse this shit down and be back in a minute."

Anton nodded and clapped me on the back. "Thank fucking God you got here when you did." With his head hung low, he walked away in brooding silence. I found the hose on the side of our building in the narrow pathway that led to the alley.

I was missing something. I was sure of it. With a twist of the faucet, the hose stiffened and shot out freezing water. I rinsed my hands first then sprayed the blood, teeth and patches of skin into the grates that led to the park.

When I stored the hose back twenty minutes later, it hit me. They'd been inside. The SUV had come from the direction of the alley. Which meant *something*—like all our fucking cash—or *someone* was gone. *Fucking fuck, fuck.*

I broke into a sprint and blasted through the front doors. The elevator would never be fast enough for the answer I needed. I took the seven flights of stairs two at a time and the metal door to the stairwell bounced on its hinges as I slammed it open.

Fiona's door was unlocked, and as I turned the knob and pushed it open, my heart beat stronger and faster than when I'd raced up the steps. Vicki was passed out in the corner of the sofa, her dark hair spread across her face. I crept over while darting my eyes around the room.

"Fi?" Calling out was foolish. My gut had confirmed her absence when I'd seen the fucking SUV peel out.

"Violet?" *Fuck. Where is her sister?* With my index and middle finger, I checked Fiona's mother for a pulse. It was there, but her breathing was shallow. I made my way around the apartment, again my eyes and brain playing catch-up to my instincts. Violet wasn't under the bed, in the closet, in her crib or in the damn oven.

They were gone. *She* was gone.

I dragged my feet out of the door and closed it behind me. When I got to the stairwell, I sat on the first step leading down. Our stupid idea of compensation for protection was bullshit. It had put a fucking target on her head. *I'd* put a target on her head. I'd flaunted her as my own, kissed her in public, been possessive. Any enemy would know that plucking Fiona from under our noses wouldn't be just an emotional blow. It would be a physical gash in our armor. By keeping her close, I'd managed to make her a billboard advertising revenge.

I rested my elbows on my knees and scrubbed the stubble on my cheeks. Heavy boots made a low, scuffing echo as the only person brave enough to face me climbed the stairs.

"Let me guess… She's fucking gone." Anton stood in front of me. He'd showered and had put on fresh clothes. His steel eyes flashed to the doorway and back.

"It was organized. Deliberate."

Assess the greatest threat. My dad's words rang in my head.

I shook my head in self-disgust. I'd let this happen, *caused* this to happen. "It was Mac."

He joined me on the step and took a long breath in as we both stared forward. "Maybe."

Jackson, still filthy from the fight and with a gash under his eye, climbed the stairs. Anton shot me a look of warning. Apparently we weren't sharing the Mac theory. When Jackson's tall frame was just a few steps lower he said to Anton, "The doctor's not answering.

We need to take Scoots to the ER. I think he's got some internal shit going on."

After Anton nodded his approval, Jackson fixed his gaze on me. "You should go see Lisa. She's freaking out."

"Why?" Anton asked before I could.

Jackson glanced to the bossman but looked back to me. "She has Violet, but says Fiona dropped her then promised to be right back but never came."

His dark brown eyes said more. They asked what the fuck was up with my girl. They wanted to know why I'd been away with her and why half our crew had just taken a massive beating the minute she'd come back with me. There was accusation, curiosity and a big dose of disdain in his stare.

But all of that had to wait.

"Violet is at Lisa's?" I asked and wondered how relief and terror could blend so well in my heart. "You saw her?"

"Yeah," Jackson answered. "She's playing with Junior." He brushed off the question like I was an idiot. "I'm taking Scooter. Everybody else will be okay."

Anton jutted his chin in Jackson's direction and we watched him disappear down the stairs.

Even though we were alone, Anton kept his voice to a whisper. "I'll call my mom. She'll know where Mac took her."

Both of us stood at the same time and jogged down the stairs. When we got to the third floor, all I wanted to do was to go see Violet, but I was a scary, bloody mess.

I pushed open our door. Scooter and Jackson were gone, but Rafa and the rest of the crew were scattered between the sectional and the kitchen. Anton found a minion—the same guy I'd noted had been absent in the fight. He stuck out like a sore thumb because he was the only one of us besides Anton who was clean.

The bossman stared him down, knowing damn well the same thing I did. "Go get Scooter's girl, wherever the fuck she is, and bring her here."

The minion nodded quickly, his hands behind his back.

"Fucking *now!*" Anton shook his head then looked to me. "Shower."

As I walked toward my room, Anton barked another direction to the crew. "Everybody get cleaned up and be back here in fifteen minutes. They stole my girl and we're going to make those bald fuckers wish they'd never heard of Covington Heights."

His girl?

My blood boiled under the hot spray of the shower. She wasn't *his girl*. She was fucking *mine*. My soul could hear hers screaming at me to find her—desperate. Did Anton have those pleas echoing in his head? Did he have the connection of more than just attraction? *No.* Which made the situation worse. I was emotionally attached to her. It was a bad sign, something my father had warned me about. If I wasn't careful—tightrope careful—I risked making everything worse.

We had a window of a few hours before Mac would ship her off, because that was what he did. He was a human trafficker. Anton's father had ruined his trade years prior, but contacts in the seedy underworld don't just disappear. They might evolve, but the ebb and flow of the dark underbelly of society was always there.

I knew the drill. Mac would drug her—Fiona's worst fear realized. The BTs would probably rape her, first dibs going to the guy she'd mentioned she had a history with—creating an entirely new horror. Then they'd take some pictures and get her to the highest bidder before midnight. That shit moved fast. I would need to be quicker.

I scrubbed the bloody grime at a pace that would make a sprinter jealous. When I found Fiona, I promised myself one thing. Whatever it took, I would give her all her freedom back.

In my closet, I found the black cargo pants I'd sworn to never wear again and pulled them on. I laced up my combat boots, pulled on a tank and grabbed my sleek black hooded jacket. *Death clothes*, as Frankie would say when our father was still around and made us train in the middle of the night.

There was one small issue... I needed my gun and my favorite knife. Slicing Mac's throat would be messy but worth it. It didn't even matter the depths of his sick cruelty to Fiona. Step one of taking her had been his death sentence. I didn't even need confirmation that it had been him. The BTs planning a brawl then leaving before they'd finished? That was not their style. They'd fallen like flies when we'd gotten Callie back. Bravery in Bradford Towers only came with the promise of money.

The good news was that I knew exactly where both of my weapons were, and I could grab some cash for Fiona while I was there. I would owe Frankie—the money at Nanna's was both of ours—and unfortunately, me paying a debt to him would give him exactly what he wanted. *Me.*

I would also need to lie low for a bit. The police let us run our drug game, but multiple homicides would need a little attention. After a few months, the cops would chalk it up to gang violence and move on to the next headline. Plus, it wasn't like they would have a bounty of witnesses. No one talked in the projects.

A deliberate double knock came from my door. Without waiting for my permission, Anton entered. He closed the door behind him and leaned into it. His frown deepened as he crossed his arms.

"You're done in Covington."

"I know." A part of me had known since the day I'd shown up.

The tension he'd brought in with him faded as he blinked a few times.

"What's your plan? I mean..." Anton pushed off the door and uncrossed his arms. He motioned to my clothes. He understood what they represented. "You're very much in reaction mode here. Let's take a minute to think this through."

We didn't have a minute. Every second Fiona was with Mac—I was convinced it was him—she would be losing a piece of her delicate soul. Her potential for happiness was being chipped at with every tick of the clock.

"I'm going to kill them." I shrugged, because that was how easy it would be if I could focus on the task and not her. "Then we all win. She's alive and Covington comes out on top. I'll go to Frankie's and none of you will ever see me again."

Anton stared at me for a beat. "Great overall plan, Ricci. Really. But we need to work out the details. We need to get her out of the building calm. She needs to come back here in better shape than Callie did."

Jesus, Callie had been a mess. And her high-pitched screams had pierced through every fiber of my being.

"What are you saying?" I might have been a touch offended. I was pretty sure killing his enemies and disappearing was one stone to his two-birds problem.

Anton tapped me on the back. "I'm saying your father taught you how to be a killer. My mother taught me how to be a leader."

I opened my mouth but he held up a hand.

"It's not an insult. But we need to be smarter than them."

I scoffed. "That shouldn't be hard."

A wry grin spread across Anton's face and a twinkle came to his light eyes. "How do you get a criminal to lower their guard?"

"Get them cocky." I let out a long breath. It wasn't the plan I would have preferred, mostly because it involved time I didn't want to waste, but with every slow breath I took, I came to terms with the fact that he was right. Not only were we more skilled than Bradford, we were smarter.

Use every advantage to guarantee success. My father's younger face was stern in the memory. I must have been about eight, Frankie around eleven. My brother had taken me down again on the wrestling mat that we'd had in our basement. I'd turned around and studied Frankie. He was vain, hadn't wanted to get his hair cut short like mine because a girl had liked his curls. I'd nodded to my father, and on the next go, I'd pulled so hard on Frankie's locks that I'd yanked out a patch. It had put him on the defensive and my takedown after that had been swift.

I remembered looking between them — my father's eyes glowing with a fever and Frankie's shock at what I'd done to win. Pride and shame. They were emotions that had fed me my entire childhood.

"Fine," I said to Anton, "we do it your way. But when she gets back, you're done with her. I'm going to leave her money for a new life. You'll give it to her and whatever you think she owed you is erased. You'll only see me again if it's not."

He studied me, maybe wondering what the hell Fiona had done to get me to care about her so much. Hell, part of me was asking the same question.

Finally, he gave me a curt nod. It sealed our pact and our silence.

Chapter Nineteen

Fiona

One time in high school, I'd gotten drunk. I'd puked my guts out at a party and hated the feeling of losing control, not to mention the bed spins and hangover. Since that time, I rarely drank, and if I did, it was just to the point of a buzz, never getting wasted like some of my friends. And after Violet? Barely a sip. In fact, the couple of drinks I'd shared with Leo had been the most I'd had in years.

There was something in me that needed to prove that being responsible for a child could be sobering. And with my mother's addiction? Well, I'd never really wanted to fall down that slippery slope. I'd avoided situations that put me at risk, dodged people and places that would tempt me. It was probably why I hadn't had a real boyfriend. I hadn't gone out looking for one.

So as the warm release from Mac's needle spread over me, I was terrified – not that he was going to take me somewhere and sell me, not that within hours I would be raped and not that I would never see my family again. The real, true horror was how much I welcomed his escape. I had no idea what his drug was, but my shoulders relaxed and my brain fogged.

My eyelids grew heavy and I had to focus through long blinks as the turns of the car swayed my body back and forth. The artificial serenity was the best thing to happen to me in months. But while the body can be fooled, the soul holds on to the truth. There was a fraction of me at the surface who was sure that, given the chance, I would ask for more of the high.

That sliver of brutal honesty was more piercing than the needle he'd jabbed into my bare leg. I tried to store it away in the back of my hazed mind, but it kept poking me in the skull, reminding me that there was no such thing as happiness — only escape.

I rolled my head into the seat and Mac's blabbering echoed between my ears. It was odd that he was in charge. I'd always imagined my fall to be at Justin's hands. But the greedy excitement of Mac's phone call was easy enough to understand. Jesus, he was practically bouncing up and down. Spit flew from his mouth and a tiny drop landed above my knee. I stared at the miniscule, transparent puddle on my ivory skin, all the horror of the moment glimmering back at me. Mac had planned this, maybe since the first time he'd seen me. *Why?* Probably the same reason I'd met him in the first place — money. I was a commodity.

My stomach clenched and I retched once…twice. On the third time, the bile came and before I could bring my hand to my mouth, I vomited all over the back of the driver's seat.

"Oh fuck!" Justin cringed. "Jesus Christ, Mac. How much did you give her?"

"She puked?" The driver asked with disgust.

Mac hung up from his call and said, "Give me some tissues or something."

"I'm not your fucking grandma with Kleenex in my purse. Jesus Christ. What the fuck did she eat? That smells fucking horrible." Justin pulled his white T-shirt over his nose and shot me a dirty look.

I wiped the spittle from my chin on the back of my hand. The sour taste in my mouth didn't leave when I swallowed. I may have even smiled that I'd pissed them all off.

Without turning around to check on my handiwork, the driver said, "You're paying to have this car cleaned. Fucking bitch fucking pukes."

It probably should have embarrassed me, but in an odd way it was satisfying. The only act of rebellion I could have offered and my body had managed to find a way to object where my mind could not. I was almost hopeful for the future. If I could just keep throwing up, surely no one would want to rape me.

In a neighborhood along the river that I didn't recognize, we pulled in to an underground parking garage. The men got out and the driver opened my door then muttered a slew of curses under his breath before snarling in my direction. Yeah, the bile hadn't just hit the back of the seat. I was covered in it.

"It's a pity I can't smack you." He dragged me out of the car by the arm then spat at my feet. *Better than the face.*

"No fucking bruises," Mac said and pointed to a door.

My head must have been made of iron. It swayed back and forth as my neck muscles fought to keep it atop my shoulders. It wanted to hang heavy with all the dark thoughts dragging it down to hell. When Justin pushed me from behind, I stumbled forward.

I was sure I'd told him to fuck off, but my tongue was so thick that it came out as more of *'the the'* than its true intention. Behind a steel door was a freight elevator and they shoved me in. As it closed and we rode up, the driver scanned me then turned to Mac.

"You'd better hope she sobers up. Ain't nobody gunna bid on her if they think she's a junkie."

"Yeah" — Justin's glare raked over me — "we learned that lesson."

Mac frowned and narrowed his brow. "Here's another lesson. Don't touch the merchandise."

The driver scoffed. "She needs a shower and some fucking toothpaste before I'd fuck her."

I didn't know whether to be relieved or still horrified.

Justin clicked his tongue. "I don't need no mouth. And clothes can come off pretty quick with a blade."

A shot of sobriety bolted up my spine.

The elevator rattled to its stop and opened up to an almost-empty floor of a warehouse. There was a beat-up white leather couch to my right, where both Bradford fucks went to sit and proceeded to get out phones and text into them.

Mac ushered me in the other direction, past a long, dirty kitchen and behind a dividing wall. I hadn't given much thought to what I would find, but a metal table with stirrups and straps hadn't even entered into my world of possibilities. In the corner stood a rack of women's clothes.

I wobbled a little, trying to take it all in and none of it at the same time.

"When my sister gets here…" Mac said as he ran a slimy finger down my jaw line then forced my chin up, his green eyes gleam, "we can do this the easy way or the hard way." He shoved me into the corner of the room, near a filthy single mattress.

How any of this would be easy was beyond my understanding. This asshole and his bitch of a sister were going to violate me, of that I was certain. Then, I didn't know what would happen next. I wasn't sure I wanted to. The only thing I could think of was to remind myself that it was better me than Violet — that it could have been her.

But Mac's push had made my head spin. Combined with the death sentence of my future and the beating in my gut that I wanted more of the drugs to forget about where I was, I vomited again, this time on the mattress.

"I told you that you gave her too much. We should have never trusted you." Justin's voice was farther away than Mac's own breathy swearing.

"My sister is on her way. She'll sober her up." Mac pushed me to the floor and I broke my fall with my hands, only to throw up yet again.

"What else have you got in that bag?" The question was the last real thing I heard and it echoed like a warped loop in my head as I tried to remain conscious. I couldn't think of Violet, certainly not Leo. One was too painful and the other brought hope. No. I focused on one spot, throwing up when I had to — my pride as distant as my former life.

The next voice I heard was that of a familiar judgmental woman. "She's wasted."

I glanced over my shoulder and tried to focus. Dr. McAllister — well, several doctor McAllisters, all equally foggy — stared at me with big green eyes.

Many Macs lifted their hands into the surrender position and cringed. "I may have given her too much of the benzo."

"I fucking told you how much. Can you not follow simple orders? *Christ*." As the doctor approached me, she came into focus. From the front pocket of her blue blazer, she took out a tiny light and flashed it in my eye while holding it open. "We can't take pictures like this. Her pupils are dilated."

I blinked away. The harsh light had stung. I prayed that Mac's fuck-up had bought me time. Time for what, I didn't know. They'd found Callie, but the damage had been done. And hadn't mine, too? I was high and never wanted to be anything else.

"Give her something. Pep her up. She needs a shower and we need to get her picture online."

The doctor shot one last disdainful look at her brother before a wicked grin, very similar to Mac's, spread across her pale face. "As punishment for the drugs, you don't get to touch."

Mac laughed. "You can't do that."

She shrugged him off. "Covington has been blowing up my phone. You didn't see how Leo protected her. One little pin drop and I bet I could get more from them than the cut you're giving me."

I'd never had a sibling to be a rival with, but it was obvious from this exchange that the McAllisters loved fucking with each other. I guessed that being a corrupt member of society started at home.

Mac stepped closer to his sister. "No fucking way is that happening. I had to let her junkie of a mother put her filthy hands all over me. I've been working this fucking thing since I laid eyes on her and knew Leo was lying. Get her functional and dressed, then get the fuck out."

The doctor rolled her eyes, but Mac left us alone. He stomped into the other room and a wave of relief rippled over me, even though I didn't think it would last.

Dr. McAllister rummaged through a bag until she found a vial and popped another needle. Once loaded, she held it in her teeth as she tied off my arm.

I'd had a mantra. I was sure I had. But words were pointless. A tear streamed down my left cheek. The needle punctured my vein and spirit at the same time. Everything I'd ever hoped to be, gone — more by the idea of drugs pumping through my veins than being abducted in plain sight.

She studied me as my eyes fluttered. A sharp focus took in all of my surroundings — the sour sick next to me, the cold, hard concrete floor below and the deep green eyes in front of me.

"Good. You're back. Stand up and take off your clothes."

I stared at her.

"Now, Fiona — unless you prefer I call for help."

Even with my groggy mind, I understood. She would make things somewhat bearable, as long as I complied. It went against every fiber of my being, every ounce of pride and fight I had in me. But postponing the inevitable was my best option, not that time would help. A sliver of hope came to me and I quickly closed the door of my mind that had brought it. Callie had been different. I wasn't in Bradford Towers. Mac was more devious. I wasn't going to be raped for sport. I was going to be sold *and* raped for sport.

My feet were heavy. No part of me wanted to stand and do as she said. And yet, it was my best option. *Fuck,* I was partially grateful that I wasn't fully conscious while witnessing the scene in front of me. And this was just the introduction.

"Stop stalling. Get up and get undressed. Option B is in the other room if you prefer." She leaned back and looked into the other room. But instead of calling them in, she furrowed her brow then glared back to me. "*Now.*"

I reached for the buttons of my shorts and closed my eyes as I undid them. My luxury of choice had been ripped from me the minute I'd asked Leo for help. What fools we had all been for thinking my fate could be better than that of my mother's.

I risked a glance at the doctor, who was pulling out items from a drawer and placing them on a high metal tray with wheels. I bet she couldn't imagine that I was more than a body. Maybe that was what I needed to do, too. Just-a-body dropped my jeans to the cold cement floor and pulled off my tank top and undergarments.

Despite that fact that I was burning with embarrassment, I shivered.

"Shower." The doctor pointed to the door next to the rack of clothes.

Just-a-body walked through the door and turned on the water in the small stall. It was just-a-body that scrubbed my skin raw and washed my hair with a bar of soap. It wasn't me who rinsed my mouth several times and spat into the rusty drain below.

And I wasn't there when the strawberry-blonde doctor came in without asking and handed me a flimsy towel. Me, Fiona? I was gone, replaced by a shell. The funny thing was that when I looked in the fogged-up, spotted mirror, I recognized the reflection.

It was my mother.

Chapter Twenty

Leo

Anton paced behind the couch while our broken crew dared glances in his direction. I'd gone down the hall to see Violet with my own eyes and get any and all the info that I could from Lisa, but it hadn't been very fruitful. Fiona had dropped off the baby and not come back. I couldn't imagine what she'd had to promise to get that small amount of mercy from Mac.

Rafa tapped the keyboard of his computer at a frantic pace. He snarled at the screen. "Fuck you, Jefferson Manors."

"What?" Anton stopped his back and forth and frowned at Rafa.

"I can follow the SUV until they get to Jefferson. After that, all the traffic cameras are impossible to break into." Rafa flipped the double bird to his computer. "They've hacked the city's system, put their own shit up, fed it back to the city, then hidden the true feed in a jungle of code. It's fucking brilliant."

"Don't worry. We're working another angle," I said to Rafa, then tapped my wrist to Anton. He wanted to let Mac get comfortable and cocky. *Tick-fucking-tock, man.*

The minion and Callie came through the door and she scanned the room for Scooter. She was smart enough to take cautious steps in our direction and wait.

When she stood in front of me, I knew my job as mouthpiece. "Jackson took Scooter to the hospital. We'll update you when we know anything."

She nodded and flicked her eyes to the floor. I exchanged a glance with Anton.

I stepped closer to her and tilted my head so she could see me. "We didn't push you before because it was all fresh and we were just happy you were okay." That was a small amount of bullshit. Anton didn't really *care* about the girls we were protecting. He had too much criminal blood in him. Image and money were more motivating than being a good guy.

In a soft voice, I said, "But now we need to know every single detail of what happened between the time they took you and when we got you back."

Callie blinked several times and her chin trembled. She grazed her bottom lip with slightly crooked teeth. "They laughed a lot — at my fear, my looks, my clothes. I kept thinking that if they hated me so much, why did they bother to take me?"

She rubbed her shoulder, perhaps an injury from the ordeal. In the brief break of her story, Anton and I exchanged glances.

"Did they drug you?" I asked, still trying to stay calm.

She shook her head.

Anton's phone buzzed from his back pocket. When he saw the number, he motioned for me to follow him into his room.

"Hey, Ma. Leo's here. Lemme put you on speaker."

I closed the door to his bedroom then followed Anton into the bathroom, where I also shut us in. No one could know we were talking to his mother. Word on the street was that she was pissed at him for not being her heir-apparent. The truth was that she wanted him to have his own crew and grow a territory before she would give him the keys to their Cadillac crime family. They'd both agreed it was best to make a fake feud out of it, insuring his independence. So him calling her for help had to be hidden, even from his top-level crew.

In her icy calm voice, Anton's mom said, "All signs lead to her being trafficked. Communication went out this morning. Things have changed a lot since the last time Mac sold a girl, but remember, *he* hasn't. He's most likely taken her to his loft on the East side, which is both stupid and sloppy. Typical."

"Callie was a decoy to make us think they'd take Fi there," I said, more to myself than them.

Anton's mother continued, "The good news is that she won't be raped. Buyers of girls don't like damaged goods. The sick fucks like to do that themselves. So she'll only be drugged. I can get eyes on the warehouse if you want."

"No." Anton stared at me. "My crew, my problem. Send me the address."

"Are you — ?"

"Ma, I got this." Anton rolled his eyes. If my stomach hadn't been flipping at the thought that Fiona might have preferred to be raped than shot up with drugs, I would have taken that moment to give him a little shit for being a closeted Mama's boy.

"You owe me dinner, at the very least." Her tone made me shiver. I may have had a murderous hitman for a parental figure, but Anton? His mom could rip the soul out of a body with one cold, understated glance.

"Bye, Ma." Anton hung up before she could say anything else. I admired his balls.

"As soon as we get the address, I'm going. I just need to run down to Nanna's and get my gun." *And knife.* I'd been craving my knife since the minute I'd seen Fiona's mom on the couch. *Fuck.* Someone should probably deal with that.

Anton shook his head. "Then you're the fucking hero again. It can't go down like that. You fucking owe me. I gave you a place to stay, a fucking alternative to your brother. We had a deal."

He was right. We'd absolutely had a deal. I would lie low by lying low, which I had not done. I'd shown my true colors to the upper crew by demonstrating how easy it would be for me to kick all of their asses. Then I'd offered up Fiona and snagged her right away. I'd made him look weak.

"What's your plan then? We let him fucking sell her? She's going to lose her fucking mind, thinking we're not coming."

"You heard my ma. She won't get raped. We have time."

I didn't know what his plan was, but it sucked. I could be in and out of that fucking warehouse — wherever the fuck it was — in thirty seconds flat. All would be dead and I could carry Fiona to safety. Hell, I could maybe even light a match and toss it behind me like in a movie.

Then…then nothing. There would be no way I could leave her, no matter how I would find her. I hated Anton for having the big-picture view. But considering how many emotions I'd already attached to this — my fingers twitched for my knife again — it was safer to hear him out.

"What's your plan, then?" I flared my nostrils. It was the only way for all the grumbling in my throat to escape.

"We buy her. Well, not us, *exactly*."

Before I could object or hear more, Anton pushed past me. He slammed both his bathroom and bedroom doors open and called down the hall. "Rafa! Call the Hirotas. We need a middleman."

I followed and, when I got to the kitchen, the minions were already buzzing about how happy they were that their leader had taken charge. Next to the counter, I stood silent. I wasn't like any of them. I didn't like to take orders or give them. I was a lone agent, by design and desire. Seeing Fiona again would only confuse the truth once more. Anton was right to have taken charge. Hell, he thrived on it.

The bossman walked over to me and patted me on the chest. "Have someone drop you off in midtown, then go get what you need. I'll send you the time and location."

His instructions went down like a jagged pill, but I swallowed it nonetheless. There was no point in taking anything from my room. I wouldn't be wearing black, baggy jeans and a muscle tank with Frankie. My feet ached at the thought of dress shoes, and I was sure I could feel the noose of a necktie already strangling me.

But it didn't matter. We would save Fiona and, with a little boost from my savings, she could have a fresh start.

"Who has keys and can drive?" I shouted to the crew.

A chubby kid stood and raised his hand. He looked to Anton for approval, and when he got the nod, we were out of the door.

I probably should have glanced back and taken in the last few seconds of my life in Covington Heights before manifesting my destiny. But that would have meant that I cared about any of the guys in that room. And the stark, honest-to-God truth was that I didn't. The only thing that squeezed my heart was when I was waiting for the elevator and I thought about Violet behind Lisa's door.

Saving Fiona meant saving that sweet little girl as well. *Eyes on the prize, Ricci.*

Chapter Twenty-One

Fiona

"Out." The doctor pointed to the room I'd come from and the sour vomit wafted back as a reminder of my previous state. Worse, Mac stood next to the metal table with his arms crossed.

"We need to get her up on the site soon." He propped his hands on his hips. "Every minute she's here is one too long. Anton—"

"You're focusing on the wrong one. I told you that before. Leo is more invested in her than Anton. His switch is going to flip. As soon as she's sold, I'm getting the hell out of town. I haven't—"

Mac stared at his sister. "What?"

She looked down at her pocket and pulled out her phone. "They've stopped calling. They know I'm here, which means they know it was you."

The siblings shared a long stare before Mac said, "Well, it's lucky for me that Anton and his mom are in some kind of Oedipean war. And if she was Leo's, then chances are Anton won't waste his time trying to find us. Get a dress on her. The bidding starts in seventy-five minutes." He walked out and barked indecipherable orders to the BTs.

Dr. McAllister stalked toward me. "You heard him. Get dressed."

My heart thumped in my throat. They were going to sell me. In less than two hours I would be the property of a stranger—and said stranger would abuse me, maybe murder me. I shook my head. And Violet... What would happen to Violet? "Please. I have a sister. I need to take care of her. You—"

"I," she said, taking a step and leveling me with her horrible eyes, "don't give a shit about you, your sister or your boyfriend. The more trash like you is off our streets, the better."

I'd clawed my way through poverty only to come to the surface of a darker future. Even in my buzzed state, I understood that I was the only chance I had. I wanted to believe that Leo would find me, but the window of time for that was shrinking. The only person I could rely on was me.

I spat in her face.

The doctor wiped it off and slung it to the ground. "That? That was a mistake. Mac!"

I lunged toward the bathroom, but Dr. McAllister grabbed my wrist and twisted it behind my back. Pain shot up my arm and burst at my shoulder. I cried out and did my best to hold the flimsy towel with my free hand.

Mac ran into the room flanked by Justin, and he had a wicked grin on his face. He assessed the doctor and me, then said, "I do love it when they're feisty."

The driver appeared over Justin's shoulder and licked his lips.

"Get her on the table and hold her down." The doctor shoved me toward the men. I was defeated. There were four of them and I was one naked, shaking mess with tears streaking down my cheeks.

"No!" I screamed over and over.

The doctor let go of me as Justin took her place and pushed me to the table. I tried to fight, squirm and kick, but he had me in a bear hug, and before I could gain any sort of advantage, my face was being smashed into cold metal. Hands gripped my ankles and pushed against my kicking legs while Justin sat on my back, with his knees putting pressure on my arms behind me.

Cool air on my ass told me it was exposed, but being naked was the least of my concerns. I continued to scream, but my cries were only met with wicked amusement. A sharp prick in the meat of my butt preceded a warm inner calm that began to spread throughout my body.

I continued to fight, but my screams switched to sobs, and once the pacifying heat hit the base of my brain, I forgot to cry. Someone flipped me over and lewd comments rang in my ears. The hard metal below me was a stark contrast to my soft body and blurred mind.

I could see why my mom liked to get high. It deadened all feelings. I floated above my body in a state where I didn't have to think, because I couldn't. There was no need to understand the reality I was living because hovering in a lost void wouldn't allow me to witness truth.

Because truth was a nightmare. And if that truth seeped into my consciousness, I would be forced to face the fact that my life as I'd known it was over. So, much as I imagined my mother did, I bathed in the glow of the chemicals stirring their way through my blood. I welcomed the escape, cherished its deliverance and embraced its liberation.

If I was lucky, I could spend the rest of my life in the same state.

I drifted away and down a dark well of veiled relief. I told myself that it was okay to like where I was…what I was…who I had become.

It was the only gift I could give myself. A white lie for a dark future.

Chapter Twenty-Two

Leo

A light was on at Nanna's brownstone, but it was just a security measure. No one had officially lived in her building for years and the city's residents didn't ask questions. I lifted up the flip-top of the security panel, typed in the code and the door clicked open.

Nanna's house smelled like rosemary and lavender — one her perfume and the other her favorite herb. Frankie hadn't changed her furniture, but someone had come in and cleaned. There wasn't a speck of dust on her mantel and the soil was moist in her live plants.

I walked up to the first floor. Even in the bathroom at the top of the stairs, the tile shimmered and fluffy towels were hung in perfect lines. In the guest room, I flipped on the light and opened the closet. Sure enough, an empty duffel bag sat on the floor and was the perfect size. I slid my hand between the mattress and box spring until I touched the familiar and soothing wooden handle of my knife. A calm washed over me, and I couldn't resist giving the weapon a small kiss.

My next moves were deliberate and filled with purpose. I'd speculated that Fiona would go for a maximum of one hundred thousand. Once a bidding war started, no one liked to lose. Proving they had money to throw around made the sick shits who were buying women and children feel even more important. *Warped fucks.*

I started in Nanna's closet. Hat boxes lined the top shelf. One by one I opened them and took out ten thousand in tightly wrapped bills. I was already at half of what I needed by the time I'd returned the boxes to their place. Next were her shoes, and I was almost to my goal from just her accessories. I closed it all with care and stored it back where I'd found it. I grabbed the bag, switched off the lights and jogged down the stairs.

In the kitchen, I opened the freezer and unwrapped the tin foil packets. Another ten grand into my Fiona fund. What had Nanna always said? *Can't go wrong with the classics.* I grinned and made my way to the living room and her books. Dante and Mary Shelley provided the rest of the money.

Nanna's cloth sewing bag lay perfectly plopped next to her reading chair by the back window. I reached in, found the gun and silencer, then sat and pulled out my phone.

Patience. My father had always said patience and a cool head were the keys to killing. I thought about how easy it had been just to shoot the guys from Bradford in their knees. Taking lives would be a fraction of an inch of difference. Although I should probably make it look less professional than I was. *Pity...* I would have loved to put a bullet between all of their eyes. I tapped the side of my phone then sat back.

Damn it. Mac had played us well. He'd inched into our lives little by little, just waiting for the right opportunity to strike. My father had been right about patience. I just needed to cool my head, because the thought of what Fiona was going through was making every drop of blood in my body burn with rage.

I stood and paced. I was in the wrong state of mind for murder. There was no room in my head for Leo and his frivolous thoughts. That boy and his feelings were officially evicted from my being. Leonardo Ricci had his official first victim…himself.

My phone finally vibrated, and I swiped the blocked number. Anton's sigh crackled in my ear. He wasn't nervous. He was pissed, which meant he knew something I didn't.

"They're live," he said and I could practically see him working his jaw.

"And?" Did he really think after years of friendship I didn't understand his every breath?

"Bidding is low, so we're waiting."

I stood and looked out to the back garden, as if the darkness would bring clarity. "Send me the pictures."

Seeing she was alive would help my composure. If they'd beaten her, marked up her face because she'd fought back, her price would be affected. Buyers wanted to make their own scars, inside and out.

"I don't think…"

He couldn't be serious. The days of him deciding anything on my behalf were over, if there'd ever been a day like that to begin with.

"Did you see the pics?" I spat.

"Yeah. She doesn't look good." Anton's voice lacked the confidence I needed from him.

Those bald fucks would rough her up. Maybe she'd put up a fight. They wouldn't have raped her, thank

God. Mac wouldn't want to have spoiled his goods. So why the fuck would they have beaten her up?

The heat in my chest needed to simmer. "Send them. *Now*."

"She's high."

My heart stopped before it slammed into my throat, preventing me from speaking. I'd known they would drug her, but I'd held out hope that we wouldn't have to see her like that. With a junkie mother, Fiona had taken every step in life not to follow that path. Hell, she barely drank. She feared her mom's addiction would be as genetic as their dark hair. Kids with parents like hers went down one of two paths — the same or the straight and narrow. Fiona's worst nightmare was being like her mother.

My question was stupid. I'd known there was something wrong the second he'd called, but I asked anyway. "Are you sure?"

"I get people high for a living, Leo. She's fucked up and the bidders are accusing Mac of finding a junkie on the street. No one believes she's clean."

I reached for the gun and tucked it into the back of my pants. "The plan stays the same. How far are you from midtown?"

"Ten minutes."

I did a quick calculation as I grabbed the bag of money and headed to the back door. "I'll be where the kid dropped me. Don't fuck this up."

Once I'd left the side streets, the theater crowds and their expensive attire allowed me to blend right in. I lagged behind two older women who were trying to hail a cab without much success.

The black SUV stopped at the light and I slid into the back. One of Hirota's men sat shotgun and Anton was driving. Rafa was next to me, his laptop closed. "We got her. Fifty K."

That was low — too low — but it didn't matter. Mac wasn't going to keep any of my money.

"Give me your bag." I tapped Hirota's man on the upper arm and he handed over a designer satchel.

"Where are they?" I asked as I opened my bag and counted out the money.

"They're still at Mac's, but I assume they're beefing up security." Rafa said and flashed me a map from his phone.

Anton said over his shoulder, "Fifth floor on the side of the river. I'll take out anyone on the ground. You know what you're doing."

His instructions were vague on purpose. He still wanted to be the leader in Rafa's eyes.

We drove along the river and headed north to the seedier parts of the city. There was no chance of Mac hosting the transaction downtown. There were too many cops. Doing it on neutral territory made sense. I was sure he wasn't planning on Anton bowing out so easily for his girl.

The problem was that she was *my* girl, and they had no idea who they'd fucked with. To Mac and his sister, I was just a thug who'd grown up with Anton. They'd never seen me with my father or brother. Hell, only a handful of people had known what my father did for a living and only one of those people — my brother — knew the extent to which I'd been trained.

When we got five blocks away from our destination, I asked Anton to stop the car. I tossed the remaining money into the back of the SUV.

"You know what to do with that, right?" I asked as I reached for the handle.

Anton nodded and we shared a long look that we both knew was goodbye. I shot my gaze to Rafa. "You never fucking knew me." Then to Hirota's man. "And you never fucking saw me."

Hirota's man was more solemn than Rafa, who was still trying to figure shit out. I climbed out of the car, walked down a dark alley and waited. A silver SUV raced by not ten minutes after. They'd switched cars somewhere.

I waited, because patience was what I had been taught. In that brief moment, I wondered if I could go through with it, take another life. What would it matter? Anton would get Fiona back, she would be safe and Covington Heights would keep their reputation for protecting girls. And yet a slap on the wrist to Mac and Bradford would not be enough. I knew it and Anton was counting on it. And what about Fiona? What kind of justice did she deserve?

No. The part of me that wanted to kill them out of vengeance needed to stay silent. That was the part that could fuck it all up. Instincts and training… There was no room for anything else.

I moved silently down the alley then through another to the back door of the building from the map. *Ah, the beautiful irony that I'm going to slip into their home the same way they invaded ours…*

When there was a big move as a crew, the fewest possible people were informed. That saved any loose lips. The problem with that was, even though we were on neutral ground and their crew could be called in a flash, they didn't know shit. That was why there wasn't anyone on the other side of the door.

I climbed the stairs and peeked at each floor until I heard them on five. It wasn't that I didn't trust Anton.

It was that I couldn't risk error. I cracked the door and spied down the dark hallway.

With my eyes closed, I could hear my surroundings and caught the cogs of the elevator grinding on its rise. There were only male voices, which meant that the doctor was gone. *Coward.* Hirota's man exited the elevator and carried his bag to an already-open door.

I slipped through the threshold, careful not to make a peep, then waited at the opposite end of the hall. Hirota's man was playing it perfectly, disgusted with Fiona's state and telling Mac he was lucky that his boss was taking the girl off his hands. She'd be on a plane for overseas before sunrise.

The drugs must have made Fiona groggy, because she wasn't fighting at all. As they counted the money, I ducked down the hall. She stood, wrists bound and head hung in a white dress, and despite her state, she struck me as beautiful. But she'd been damaged. She was not herself—definitely not the woman who'd flipped me off or dug her nails into me when we'd kissed, making me wonder if she wanted more or was trying to hurt me.

Cool serenity coiled up my spine and I was sure I would kill them all, but not in front of her. Fi had seen enough.

I glanced over the room. They hadn't heard me. The two Bradfords and slimy Mac were too busy thinking it was all over. The idiots were cocky.

Movies and books had fight scenes all wrong. They forced the hero to wait for the dramatic battle, confronting his most worthy adversary at the end.

'You're not a hero.' My father's voice echoed in my head. *'Get the biggest threat before anyone else, then the others always fall.'*

One of the Bradford boys was slightly bigger than the other, so he would die first. I wouldn't falter or bother to give some speech to Mac about fucking with the wrong man. One, two, three… I would kill them before they even realized I was there. It meant I couldn't use my knife, but so be it. My thirst for blood was trumped by my instincts. They would die quickly, then I would walk down the stairs, out of the back to the alley and never think of them again.

Because fate had knocked on my door and asked me to pay up… I was a killer and it was time to assume what I'd always known was coming for me.

Chapter Twenty-Three

Fiona

From the corner of my eye, I watched Mac count the money. He'd been pissed that he hadn't gotten more for me and his bitch of a sister had thrown his initial mistake in his face several times before she'd left. The happy buzz was fading and I missed its comfort and cloud.

The man buying me seemed oddly familiar. Perhaps the criminals in the city were a tight-knit group. But he'd insulted me — my state, my age, too. He'd also said I'd be on a plane within hours, confirming my worst fears.

"Do you want help getting her down to the car?" Justin asked my new owner. Maybe he was planning to take me and the money. He would be stupid enough to do that.

"I can manage just fine, especially since you've ruined the merchandise. Hirota will remember this."

The man in the shiny suit yanked at the zip cord around my wrists and I stumbled in his direction.

It was an unnerving thing, resolve. There was no more fight in me, no more tears or sobs. Coming down from the high had left me more numb than the drug itself. I had nothing—nothing to give and nothing to feel. I couldn't even muster up the hate for Mac that should have been brewing in me. There was no point. Even my heartbeat had given up. It was so erratic that it didn't know whether to settle or race.

My owner—or middleman or whatever the hell he was—tugged at my bindings again. "We done here?" He jutted his chin to Mac while the bald goons drooled over the amount of cash in front of them. Maybe they would kill Mac and take the money. I didn't hate that idea. *Jesus, my first happy thought in hours is murder.*

But the forward motion of the stranger meant more. It was official. I'd been sold. Whatever the price, wherever I was going. I was property. An odd thought popped into my head and drew a tear. Would I ever hear my name again? Even the stupid nickname Leo had given me? My future held nothing of my past, nothing of me. Abuse, that could be my new name. But more likely I'd be called 'slut' or 'whore'—unsuitable for the moment then probably too, too fitting.

Mac walked closer and tipped my chin up. I stared over his shoulder and out of the door, still silently praying Anton or Leo—fucking anyone—would barge in and save me. Anything besides those devilish eyes.

"Bye bye, Fiona."

Not him... Not fucking Mac saying my name... He'd already stolen so much. The tears I didn't think I had ran down my cheeks. Maybe I should have told him to burn in hell or spat on his smug face like I'd done to his bitch sister. Something… But that fucking resolve was so strong that it had beaten all the will out of me.

Mac turned to my new owner. "A pleasure doing business with you." His lips turned up in a wicked grin.

"Fuck you," The man said to Mac then frowned at me. He spun behind me and pushed me out of the door.

The hallway was dark, and as I entered the elevator with a shove from behind, a tiny movement caught my eye. A dark shadow who looked a hell of a lot like Leo emerged from the side of the door I'd just exited and rolled on his shoulder into the frame.

Clank.

Clank.

A gasp.

Clank.

The doors closed and my heart raced. I searched the man next to me and his blank face for a clue. Whatever figure I'd seen could not have been Leo. I'd manifested something in my head, some shred of wanting. The impending reality of not seeing Violet ever again was too much to bear. Leo was not a hero. And if it had been him, it meant he'd forsaken his future and become the one thing he'd hated. The irony was that I had, too. I was already craving more drugs.

In an even, if not haunting tone, the man next to me said, "When we get outside, you'll get into the first car. They'll take you where you're going."

I shook my head quickly, trying to rid myself of the fragments of hope that had landed on my shoulders.

No. It was the drugs. They were fucking with me. My lips quivered and my muscles twitched as we rode farther down, the floors passing with small, happy dings that had no place in my consciousness.

The final chime echoed and the doors rumbled open. A single bulb lit the filthy lobby and out of the glass doors two silver SUVs with tinted windows waited — not black, not white.

Fucking hope, she'd made a fool out of me once more.

Shiny Suit opened the door and reminded me, "First car." Then he gave me a final shove before turning in the direction of the second SUV and hopping into the back.

The back door of the first car opened. "Move your ass, Fiona!"

Steel eyes met mine and I froze — incapable of allowing the information to penetrate. But I could feel my frown and the tears start to pool. More dreaming. It had to be more of my imagination.

The screech of tires peeling out pulled my gaze away as the realization hit me. I ran to Anton, who helped me get in, and Rafa slammed the gas before the door was even shut.

It *had* been Leo. And he'd killed those fuckers…for me. But where was he?

A new sob built in my chest. It was a thick soup of relief, shock, gratitude and disbelief, and it couldn't be held back. I convulsed into Anton's lap. The previous hours of my life could not be erased, but I was free. The ugly wails didn't stop as Anton rubbed my back and we sped through the city.

When I finally caught my breath, Anton shifted a little and pulled out a switchblade from his back pocket.

"Give me your wrists." His voice was the softest I'd ever heard it.

I sat up, wiped my blubbery face on my shoulder and obeyed. He cut the tie and I massaged over the imprints it had left.

"You okay?" He brushed his thumb over my cheekbone.

No. Somehow I'd managed not to get raped, but the trauma in my soul made me wonder if I would ever feel safe again. I shook my head.

Anton beckoned me closer with a quick flex of his hands. My body went limp and I melted into him. His hard chest and strong arms welcomed me, and he stroked my hair.

In my ear he whispered, "I've got you now."

I should have been grateful. I should have just let the words sit and not question them. But there was something odd. It was how *he* had me *now*. Asking for Leo rang horribly selfish, so I let it slide.

I needed to recover, however I could, and make Violet a priority again. I had to get my head clear. I nestled into Anton and let out several long, slow breaths.

Rafa drove us to the East side, where he parked in a lot next to a Covington SUV.

"Car switch, then we'll get you home." Anton offered a tight smile. He clasped my hand and led me out of the back seat.

Home should have been a comfort. Home should have been welcoming. Mine wasn't. I didn't want to go 'home'. I wanted to get the fuck out of my living nightmare.

But I couldn't let go of Anton's hand, his warmth. His kindness, whatever the intention, was getting me through the motions — that and the idea of seeing Violet again once I'd cleaned up.

The courtyard of Covington Heights was empty and dark. I walked with Anton and Rafa to our building. We rode the elevator up to their floor. In Anton's apartment, a few members of the crew were scattered on the couch and at the bar in the kitchen.

"Everybody out. Goldilocks, you move in tomorrow." Anton raised his eyebrows for anyone to dare ask why, and no one did. Instead, they filed out in an understanding silence.

Leo was gone. *But why?* A shiver rose up my spine. Anton hadn't only saved me, he'd reclaimed me as his own. I was in the exact same spot that had started this nightmare. Now everybody knew it.

The empty room mirrored my blank emotional slate. Survival. If I wanted to see Violet again, my selfish wonderful dark place that was calling me with every fiber of my being would need to be fought.

When the door shut, he said, "Bath and bed for you. We'll get your sister and deal with your mom tomorrow. Come on."

He walked down the hall to his bedroom and the water turned on in the tub not long after.

Too dutifully, I made my way down the hall.

Anton sat on the edge of the filling tub, the whoosh of the water as comforting as the relaxation it promised. "Do you want me to leave?"

Yes. No. Maybe. The lesser of two evils. That fucking resolve crept back in. He'd just saved my life. How could I deny him anything?

"No." I reached for the zipper on my dress and tugged it down. It fell around my ankles, exposing my breasts and white underwear.

Anton didn't ogle. In fact, he glanced away. God, he was really trying to show me some compassion — and it was working. I slipped out of the white cotton and tossed it next to the dress. "Burn that." I held out my hand and he took it, steadying me as I lowered into the steaming bath.

A small smile brushed over his lips before he rubbed them together and furrowed his brow. "I'm sorry."

I interlaced my fingers into his and closed my eyes. "Thank you for saving me."

When I dunked my head under the water to wet my hair, I wondered if I'd sounded as fake as I'd felt?

* * * *

After a final glance over my shoulder to check that Anton hadn't stirred, I padded cautiously down the hall, wearing his oversized T-shirt. As exhausted as I was, sleep hadn't come. There were too many questions ricocheting through my head, the biggest one being, *Where the fuck is Leo?*

Anton had said that Rafa was moving in the next day. Had that meant that Leo had gone underground after killing Mac?

I passed the kitchen and headed for Leo's room. The door was open a crack and I pushed it the rest of the way. Thankfully the hinges didn't make a noise and give away my late night hunt for answers.

The bed was unmade and dirty clothes were scattered on the floor. In the bathroom, all the toiletries were still in place. Even his toothbrush was in a cup by the double sink. His towel was damp. I stepped into the shower and smelled his half-used bar of soap. The clean, simple scent filled me with comfort and longing for the only person I was sure was patient enough to allow me to put my shattered pieces back together before asking me for anything more.

The moisture under my feet was unfair. He'd just been there, hours before. Why wasn't he back in the bed stroking my hair while his silent strength seeped into my skin? I wiped my feet on the rug and exited the bathroom.

All his clothes — all of them — remained in the closet. He'd left his entire life. He'd left me. He'd left Violet.

I let my hand drag over his row of black jeans like a slow farewell. An ache in my chest climbed up my neck and clasped the base of my brain. My imagination had gotten the best of me, seduced me while I'd been in survival mode. The spark or connection I'd convinced myself I'd shared with Leo was fiction.

But it was a story I still needed for at least one more night. As if in a dream, I walked over to his bed on the side where he'd slept. I climbed in and hugged his pillow tight. I could smell his hair, him — the transfixing energy that was quintessentially Leo Ricci.

I wove a tale about his arms around me, hugging me into the brightest part of his soul, a sleepy illusion of safety. Dream Leo was just that...not real. Maybe the other one had never existed either.

Did it matter? In that moment, the bed, the fantasy, it was all I needed.

Chapter Twenty-Four

Leo

The guest room at Nanna's was a far cry from my suite in Covington Heights. But it hadn't been the stiff pillows and short bed that had kept me awake. It hadn't even been the undeniable fact that I had taken three lives. I'd foolishly hoped it wouldn't matter. I'd foolishly thought I could be cold, but I'd killed out of passion—broken the number one hitman rule. And it was that passion that had me staring at a blank ceiling for most of the night—tossing and turning, searching for any form of comfort.

Those cloudy brown eyes streaked with tears had appeared each time I'd closed my own. She'd been broken. All the fucking night, my chest had ached for her. And my overly healthy ego was convinced I could help mend the damage that I'd caused.

Because I'd done this. It had been me who had seen her from afar and had started asking around. *I'd* run to help her then brought her to Anton's attention. *Stupid fucking payback.*

I tapped the headboard several times. I fucking needed to see how she was, talk to her about what happened, let her cry in my arms, hold her. And maybe just a little splinter of me needed her to hold me back. *What a bitter pill.* The sacrifice I'd made would keep me away from her.

A small creak was all I needed to know that Frankie was on his way up. I'd been sure he would come, and in fairness, he'd let me sleep in—or so he probably thought.

And so it begins...

He opened the door with a huge smile that somehow made me want to both flip him off and pull him in for a hug. "I am so looking forward to kicking the shit out of you."

I smirked. The buzz from us sparring with each other was unmatchable. Even Anton was not at the same level as Frankie and me. "Aww. You miss me, big brother?"

Frankie tossed a gym bag on the end of the bed and shrugged. The years and stress were showing as a hint of salt-and-pepper just over his temples. But he was still cut. Even behind his black designer track suit, his muscles were obvious. I hadn't trained on his level for a while. He would probably beat me to a pulp.

I stood and scratched my hair with a groan.

"That tattoo is hideous and potentially dangerous." Frankie pointed to my arm. "No distinguishing markings."

He'd always been a bit of a kiss-ass to our father. Throwing out the rules from my dad's killing handbook was just another pucker on the cheeks to the dead man who'd made us what we were.

I rolled my eyes. "Really? Before coffee?"

He ignored me. "Shower and change. I have a lunch meeting, so I need to bruise your body and ego before noon."

I swiped up the gym bag. As predicted, we were going to start immediately.

"Oh," he said, and I turned back. "It's nice to see you."

Anyone could say what they wanted about our fucked-up childhood, but it was a secret that only we shared. Nanna and Chezzie knew our father had been a criminal, but both had stopped short of asking more. Sometimes I'd wondered if they hadn't been oddly proud of him. So being in a room with the one person on the planet who understood every ounce of me was comforting, despite the past.

"Yeah, you too." My words were sincere and I offered a small smile as proof. I shuffled down the hall, found a new bar of soap in the linen closet and got ready.

Showered and clean, I caught the smell of fresh-brewed coffee when I exited the bathroom. I jogged down the stairs to find Frankie at the kitchen table, the metal Italian pot on a hot plate to his left, the gun I'd used the night before on the right.

"You owe me three bullets." He crossed his arms and leaned into the teak chair.

I found a mug and opened the fridge. It was spotless and bare, so I closed with a little annoyance of no milk — not that Frankie had known I was coming. I put back the mug with regret. I couldn't drink coffee black. It was maybe the least Italian thing about me.

"Well?" Frankie did a thing with his face that was so typically my father that it almost made me laugh. It was a combination of a frown and snarl as he raised his bushy eyebrows.

I leaned into the counter and stretched out my legs before crossing them at the ankles. "Target practice."

"Were those targets the reason you came back?" Frankie knew damn well three bullets meant three lives. We weren't wasteful.

I looked away.

"Leo..." Frankie's tone haunted me. I knew what was coming. "Killing for your own reasons and killing for hire are not the same."

Killing was killing as far as I was concerned. Who knew what Mac had done to Fiona? Not to mention the bald fucks he'd looped into his plans. And what? I was just going to let them walk away with my money? *No fucking way.*

I looked back at Frankie, whose eyes were wide.

I didn't want to share the details, but I had to give him a nugget of truth. I decided on something that I'd wondered if he could relate to. "It's true. Everything he said would happen did. I was patient. I was calm. Ice ran through my veins. My instincts were flawless."

Frankie rolled his head on the back of the chair. "Yeah. Same." His stiff body softened, the connection between us stronger.

"Come on. No one knows my fighting habits like you do. Anyway, it will be good to work out what you did last night." He stood and pushed the chair back in place. "Just not the face."

A grin I couldn't hold back tugged at my cheeks.

"No." Frankie shook his head in a slow warning then motioned to the coffee. "You're not going to drink that?"

"I need milk."

He wove his head around. "You go to live in the fucking projects and you come back a diva?"

The familiar banter that had kept us sane in our youth blanketed my warped soul.

I walked over to Frankie and put my arm around his shoulder. "You gonna start name calling, Old Man?"

Frankie's jaw dropped and I squeezed him closer then planted a kiss on his cheek. Shit, I had to admit that I'd missed my big brother.

"You have gray hair. That's hideous and potentially dangerous. No distinguishing markings."

As we made our way to the front door, he groaned. "Ugh. I forgot how annoying you are."

"Ugh. I forgot how annoying *you* are." I delivered my sass in a high-pitched voice and followed him down to the curb where he'd parked in front of a hydrant.

In Frankie's baby blue Porsche, we headed downtown. He told me how business had changed since the days of our father, when someone handed over a name on a piece of paper in the back of a restaurant.

The times of clients seeing our faces were over, but that didn't mean that we still didn't need to be careful. A poorly planned murder was sure to have witnesses. And the money was laundered in and out of foreign bank accounts, then filtered through Frankie's 'investment' firm. He paid all of his taxes like a good boy, never over-complicating his finances to draw attention.

Clients themselves were researched back to when they had baby teeth, then the potential victims were surveilled for months. Cold feet and last-minute cancellations still paid full price — after all, the pulling of a trigger or pushing off a cliff was the easy part for us.

"You'll need to come into the office. I'll tell people you were getting your Master's degree abroad. People never know how to check that shit and don't give a fuck. But if they do, they'll find you in a private school in Ireland. I'll send you the link so you can drop random details, but trust me... No one cares."

We pulled into an underground garage and Frankie zipped the sports car into a private spot. He killed the engine. "You'll need to look the part. My tailor is expecting you this afternoon."

Frankie reached behind my seat and presented me with a phone.

Damn, Big Brother has thought of everything. "How long have you been expecting me?" I tried to mask the hurt of him knowing that I'd be back, understanding that the day would come for the inevitable.

"Since the day you left. It was just a matter of hitting Send on an email."

I let out a long gravely exhale. "Now I have to kick *your* ass."

We got out of the car and Frankie lifted out another gym bag from under the storage space in the front of the Porsche.

I followed him to the elevator and we entered alone. He turned to me and little wrinkles around his dark eyes folded into place. I hadn't seen them before. "If you need to talk about last night, you come to me...only me. You have no more friends. You only have family — and that's me."

Chapter Twenty-Five

Fiona

Coffee. The unmistakable smell of coffee brought the first smile to my face since I could remember. He'd come back for me after all. A warm relief brushed over me. I scrunched my shoulders up like a giddy girl at the candy store and, on an inhale, opened my eyes. My face fell and I swallowed.

Anton sat next to me on the bed, fully dressed in black jeans and a black tank. He cradled a cup of coffee in his lap and his strong legs were stretched out and crossed at the ankles. He studied me through narrowed eyes and his little frown made me understand that he'd caught my disappointment.

"Coffee?" he asked, still keeping his lips turned down.

I pushed myself up to sitting and shook my head. "I don't—"

"Right." Anton set the cup on the nightstand then crossed his arms. He stared ahead. "I'm not going to lie. This stings a little, Fiona."

"I…" *Shit.* I was an ungrateful bitch. Anton had saved me and I couldn't even extend him the favor of sleeping next to him. It wasn't like he was going to make a move on me. He'd been gentle, practically sweet.

"You couldn't sleep so you came in here?" He turned his head and his crystal eyes bored into me. Behind the accusation was something else. It took me a second to find it, but when I did, it hit me hard. *Hurt.* He'd been wounded that I'd left him.

He has me now.

I bowed my head and rubbed my temples. What had I been thinking, sleeping in Leo's bed?

I met Anton's gaze and he lifted both eyebrows.

"That wasn't a rhetorical question." Any pain he'd showed had shifted to annoyance with a tiny bit of anger.

Great.

"I'm sorry. It won't happen again. I was just…" *What?* I was just what? A fool on all fronts, it seemed.

Anton dropped his head back and closed his powerful eyes. I was happy to be rid of his scrutiny but didn't dare move. I thought about climbing into his lap and trying to make it better, but he would smell my lie, so I saved us both the embarrassment.

After a torturous silence, he finally said, "Let me ask you a question." He let out a long exhale through his mouth. "If you could choose between him and me, who would it be?"

It was an impossible question to answer. My free will had been silenced the first day they'd noticed me.

And, quite frankly, even though I literally owed them my life, I was still a little salty about the fact that they'd taken that choice away from me.

Leo was out of the picture, by either Anton's design or some other reason. Choosing the tall, dark, gorgeous mound of Italian muscle was pointless. And yet it was rather obvious that I already had. My heart raced. If I were honest, maybe any protection for me or Violet would be gone. Maybe that anger bubbling below Anton's surface would pop and be directed at me.

I pressed my lips together and bit down on the inside.

"Whatever you do, don't lie. I'll know."

His steel eyes hammered into me. There was only one thing to say.

With the last drop of strength I had, I said, "I would choose me."

Anton let out a quick, airy chuckle and shook his head. "Funny. I think he knew you'd say that." He swung his legs over the side of the bed and stood. His anger was gone, replaced with a tight, forced smile. "Rafa's gonna be here soon. Grab some shorts and go back to your place. Your mom's still a bit out of it, but your sister is asking for you."

I didn't understand. "Are you—?"

Anton's grumble and fake scowl brought a smile to my face. "Letting you go? Yeah. I don't want someone who doesn't want me. I told you that."

"But—" I rose from the bed, unable to believe what I was hearing. I walked over until I was just inches away from Anton. His strong chest beckoned for my hand to confirm the reality.

I stared into his eyes, eyes that had hurt me, lusted after me, fucked with my entire being. They glimmered back at me, exposing a flicker of hope that I would still change my answer.

The curiosity got the best of me. "What changed?"

Anton wet his pouty lips and I had to stop myself from being dragged into his luring haze. "Everything." His gentle word said more than he knew. It revealed that he, too, had lost Leo. That sometimes the respect of a memory was stronger than the need in the present.

Without thinking too much about it, I wrapped my arms around his waist and pressed my cheek into his chest. The embrace was more than gratitude. It was understanding and closure. The tension I'd been carrying for weeks melted out of me.

"Okay, okay." He pushed me away and held me at arm's length. "There's something else I need to tell you." His tone was playful, so I met it with my favorite response of sarcasm.

"If you're going to tell me I'm Rafa's or Jackson's now, you're gonna get a knee in your balls."

Anton stepped back with a smirk. "You're crazy if you think you could get one on me, but no. You have a nest egg." He pointed to a bag I hadn't noticed next to the bed.

"What?"

"A parting gift from your boyfriend." There was a tease in his words that brought back my sass.

"He was never my boyfriend." I rolled my eyes, enjoying what seemed like friendly fire with the man I'd once vowed to hate for life.

"You sure about that?" Anton walked out of the room.

I went over to the side of the bed and knelt down in front of the bag. When I opened it, more money than I'd ever seen, in tight, perfect packs, stared back. I leaped back like I'd been burned and looked around the empty room. With caution, I was half afraid something would pop out and say 'boo', because it had to be a fucking joke, I leaned back over for another peek.

Nothing darted out, but that didn't mean I still wasn't scared shitless. There was a fucking lot of money in that bag and, according the Anton-From-Another-Universe, it was mine — from Leo.

I tentatively reached for a bundle and examined it in disbelief. The bills were so crisp. They had to be counterfeit. I thumbed through the tight stack. My eyes probably looked like giant saucers and may have been bugging out of my head like a damn cartoon. I checked over my shoulders again. Where were the hidden cameras to prank me?

A new and previously unknown type of tear pooled in my eyes, making all that damn money blurry. A happy sob poured out of me and I grabbed the bag and pulled it to my chest. I rocked back and forth on the floor next to Leo's bed, trying to let go of all the terror I'd seen in the previous twenty-four hours, ridding myself of my insipid and unremarkable life. Attempting to erase a past that should not have been so ugly.

I stilled. With money, I could do anything. It was absolute freedom — a liberty provided by Leo with the added and precious gift of my life. I could move down to one of those better neighborhoods, get a damn job and put Violet into real daycare.

My daydream came to a screeching halt. What had this cost Leo? If he'd had this kind of money, why the hell had he been in Covington Heights? What, exactly, had he traded, sacrificed for me?

I darted my gaze around the room, but the answer didn't come. With the bag still pressed into my stomach, I stood and examined the bathroom and closet again. Perhaps the daylight would provide an opening for a clue of where Leo had gone.

But, just as I'd found nothing the night before, I came up empty. I stopped before exiting the walk-in. I turned around, swiped a jersey and shoved it into my bag then found a pair of his shorts and cinched them at the waist.

I was certain I looked like the epitome of a walk of shame, but I didn't care.

Anton was on the phone in the kitchen and I waited for him to finish.

"Can I, uh, leave this with you?" I pointed to the ceiling. "Mom junkie and all."

A warm, knowing smile spread across Anton's face. It made me regret not being able to choose him. There were layers under his stone-cold surface that were worth discovering.

"Yeah, sure. Did you count it?"

"No. I don't even understand what one of the bundles is worth." I shivered and sat the bag gently on the counter.

"Fifty thousand."

My mouth fell open. "How...? Why?"

Anton grabbed the bag and swung it over his shoulder. "Thought you should know, so I don't take any." He headed down the hall and said, "It's safe here. I promise."

I jogged to catch up with him and pushed around so we faced each other and I was blocking his path. "Will I ever see him again?"

"No—and that's the way he wanted it." Anton's eyes narrowed slightly, probably detecting the rebel in me who refused to accept that answer. He tilted his head in a warning. "Get your shit together and move on, Fiona. Forget him."

"Right." *Wrong.* Well, halfway. I would get my shit together, but forgetting Leo would be impossible. Plus, if he'd really never wanted to see me again, he wouldn't have shown me so much of his real life. I smiled to myself and went to get my little sister.

Chapter Twenty-Six

Leo

Frankie had handed me my ass on a paper plate. My hopes of messing up his handsome face had died pretty quickly once we'd stepped into the ring. He'd dropped me back off at Nanna's and I'd crashed on the bed, where I'd been staring at the ceiling for an hour.

Not knowing about Fiona was eating at me like a painful virus. The curiosity and concern had spread from my brain to my heart and was making my skin itch. If I could just see her with my own eyes, I was sure I would feel better.

Had I known it would be so hard to stay away, maybe I would have never left to begin with. I let out a loud battle cry. The internal war I was fighting only had defeats. I'd lost her, lost my friends, lost money, lost my free will. I belonged to Frankie, at least for a while.

I put on my only suit and went out to shop for food and some extra clothes that fit my new lifestyle. I went to Frankie's tailor and spent the afternoon getting measured.

But I came back to Nanna's alone. After months of constantly being with a crew and at Anton's side, I'd forgotten how lonely solitude was. I sat down in Nanna's chair and tapped my fingers on the arm.

I was a good sneaker. My father had taught me to be more discreet than a shadow. It wasn't like I had anything else to do. I couldn't even start 'working' for Frankie until I had my new suits. I could go uptown, just look at her and see that she was okay, come back then sleep through the night.

No one would see me, I was sure.

But what if she wasn't okay? What if the drugs they'd given her had flipped an addiction switch in her brain? What if she was using the money I'd left to get high with her mom and her fucking life was over? What if she'd fallen into a depression? What if she was on fucking Anton's arm?

Fucking fuck fuck.

I could hear my father and Frankie in my head, lecturing me on my stupidity. They were right. I should *not* go back to Covington. It was a rookie move fueled with passion. But had either one of them ever had a magnetic pull from a woman?

Besides, it was just to see her. I wouldn't talk to her. I'd just assess her wellbeing for a good night's sleep. *Fuck.* I sounded like a stalker, although 'stalker' sounded better than 'dude crushing on a chick he'd killed three people for'.

Yeah. Nothing good would come from me laying eyes on her. And that was exactly why the rebel in me stood, marched out of the door and hailed a cab.

I had him drop me all the way East and zigzagged my way until I was in the alley behind our building. Correction...my former building. I snuck down the narrow path and stopped next to the hose.

At the bench, Jackson and a few of the crew held court. *No Anton, no Fiona.* I couldn't hear what they were saying, but they were dealing and had a couple of groupies watching them from the park. Less than twenty-four hours had passed since the fight, and other than some bruises and scabs, there was no sign anything had changed.

Business as usual.

I crept back to the alley and hesitated. Going into the building was risky. I might get seen, although deflecting questions wouldn't be a problem. The issue would be more *why* I'd come back after I'd made it clear that I was gone for good.

But Fiona was too close, her pull too strong. That was why I slipped into the still-broken emergency exit and climbed seven flights of stairs. I peeked through the doorway and down her hallway. It was as abandoned and as run-down as it always had been.

But the muffled voices perked my curiosity, and I left the stairwell and pressed my ear against the door to her apartment.

Fiona's mom screamed, "You can't just take her! She's not yours!" Her high-pitched shrill reminded me of the insults that junkies yelled at us when they were itching for a fix. I should probably have been thankful that Vicki was alive, but I couldn't help wondering if Fiona would have been better off without her — not that *I* was going to make that happen.

"Violet deserves better. She's just a baby." The strength in Fiona's voice brought a small smile to my face. She wasn't as broken as I'd thought she might be.

"No. It's out of the question. If I lose her, I lose part of my benefits."

Fiona groaned. "Fucking fine. You make this easy for me and I'll pay you the difference."

"Double."

I could practically see Vicki's evil smirk through the door. It would have been easy to call her a selfish bitch. But she was an addict, something Anton and I had counted on in others just like her. Drug dealers didn't get to judge their customers. Their cravings paid our bills.

"I'm going to the deli to get dinner."

Shit.

As the knob turned, I darted down the hall and flattened myself against the wall in a dark corner.

The door to Fiona's apartment didn't slam. Instead, she closed and locked it quietly then tucked her keys into the back pocket of her cut-off shorts. She scrubbed her face and whimpered. Fiona leaned into the doorframe and spun slowly so that her back was to the wall. After a deep sigh, she slid down the wall and held her head in her hands, knees supporting her elbows.

The shaking of her shoulders and quiet sobs were a far cry from the tone she'd had with her mother. The fortitude I'd thought I'd registered in her voice had been an act. Once again, Fiona was putting her sister first. And, once again, no one had her back.

The list of my mistakes grew exponentially as I took a cautious step toward her. Fiona lifted her head and her mouth went agape before turning into a deep frown. Tears streamed down her lovely cheeks and she sniffed.

It was what I'd been afraid of, that she wasn't okay at all. And it ripped my heart out right then and there.

She wiped her nose with the back of her sleeve and sucked in a stuttered breath. Her sweet eyes looked up to me before more tears pooled in their corners.

"Are you real?"

I sat down next to her and did the one thing I'd been aching to do since I'd known she'd been taken. I pulled her into my lap and wrapped my arms around her. Docile Fiona was somehow smaller than her normal self and she fit like a tiny ball with her head on my chest. I smoothed her hair and her breathing slowed.

Holding her was instantly addictive. Her tiny wiggles, soft scent and normally well-hidden vulnerability were a gift she didn't share with many. I'd seen them briefly the night we'd camped and I knew I was privileged to witness something that she wouldn't show again any time soon.

Our quiet moment whispered a beautiful lie that we would be okay, that we had each other.

Fiona slipped her hand inside my jacket and in a quiet voice she said, "I saw you. You killed them. I didn't want you to do that, not for me."

If she thought I would confess or confirm, she would be mistaken. In the years of training, my father had said, *'Never, ever, admit to anything.'*

She seemed to understand there wouldn't be an answer, and her free hand fiddled with a button on my shirt.

"They said you were gone."

I closed my eyes. I should have been gone — definitely not where I was, holding the most precious piece of my life.

Fiona swiveled quickly and stared me in the eyes, a small fire behind her own. "Can you fucking say something? They shot me up with drugs and I'm worried I'm fucking hallucinating here."

I grinned. "There she is."

A little smirk crossed her lips and she maneuvered again so we were face-to-face and she straddled me. "Why are you here? In a fucking suit? Why did you give me all that money and where the fuck did you get it?"

"That's a lot of questions. Pick one and I'll be honest. I promise."

Her gaze fell and she scrutinized my face. When our eyes met again, the innocence looking back at me shattered my soul. But there was more — a hopeful plea and a quivering lip.

In a whisper, she asked, "Why are you here?"

The energy between us thickened and my mouth went dry. A brief glimpse of another life, where I would be free to love her, be there for her, hold her like I was whenever I wanted to, flashed behind my eyes and gripped my heart. But the choices I'd made to keep her alive meant the death of that pipe dream.

And with the possibility of a life with her in the grave, I was afforded the right to be fucking honest and true — something I'd hadn't done much of in my life. I started, "Do you think, deep, deep down inside, where you know what's real and not real, that I could have *not* come here?" The truth of my own words shocked even me and my chest tightened. "How could I not be here?"

Fiona's chest rose and fell. She snaked her hands from my stomach to my shoulders, wet her lips and swallowed. I wondered if the lump in her throat was a big as the one in my own.

"You saved my life...twice." She looked away. "I...I can't pay you back." Fiona slumped then shot me a look with raised eyebrows. "And the money... Leo..."

"Fi, the money is yours. You're saving Violet's life every fucking day, one push on a swing at a time. Don't act like your sacrifice is nothing."

Fiona closed her eyes tight and rested her head on my shoulder. "I was convinced that we had something. I don't know..."

"We did, Fi. We did. I don't think it was love, but there was a connection. I felt it, too."

She sat back up. "And now you're leaving me, just when we could be honest about all of this?"

I nodded. "I have to."

Fiona brushed my cheek, pushing my stubble in the opposite direction that it'd grown. "Can we kiss goodbye? 'Cause the idea of you not annoying the shit out of me ever again and smacking my ass is pretty fucking depressing. And that's saying a lot considering—"

I pulled her into me, my smile against her lips quickly morphing into the passion she'd created in my soul. I grabbed her ass—that delectable fucking ass—and dug in. I gave exactly zero fucks if she walked away with my handprints as proof that I wanted her. She trembled and rocked on my crotch, tempting and luring my cock to harden. The kiss was frantic, both of us hungry for our fill and knowing it was the last time we'd get a chance to share whatever the fuck it was we had. We couldn't kiss deep enough, fast enough, furious enough. There was no point in thinking about what it meant or where it would go. It was unabbreviated lust in its purest form, and the ability to be honest about it only fueled my need.

But it couldn't last. *We* couldn't last. I tempered the kiss, slowing with pecks of my swollen lips. "I have to go."

Fiona nuzzled into me. "I'm not moving."

I dropped my head back into the cement wall behind me. "Trust me. Staying away from you is going to be the hardest thing I've ever done." With more willpower than I thought myself capable of, I pushed her off my lap and stood. Looking at her again, taking her all in, would have been the final blow that I was sure would have kept me in Covington Heights. I was already pushing it.

I walked down the hall, and just as I opened the door, she said, "You're hot in a suit."

The grin on my face led me all the way down the steps, through the alley and back to the East Side, where I found a cab.

With a little pep in my step, I climbed the stoop of Nanna's brownstone and punched in the code. In her chair, with his fingers steepled, sat Frankie, a bored and disappointed frown on his olive-skinned face.

"That? That was a mistake, little brother."

Chapter Twenty-Seven

Fiona

The gate creaked and Jackson held out his arms for J.J., who barreled toward his daddy.

"Hey, big man." I tucked my new phone into my back pocket and smiled to Jackson as I walked over.

"Hey, Sis." He kissed his son's cheek then let him back down. J.J. blabbered something to Violet, who clapped her hands in excitement. "I hear you got that job. Nice."

I smiled and nodded. "I just have to work there for a month, then I can ask for temporary custody. Social services wants to see a paycheck."

We walked over to the swings and sat down, gently swaying back and forth. There had been a calm that had swept over Covington Heights after my nightmarish abduction. The crew had saved two of their girls and Bradford had taken a blow physically and reputation-wise. I'd even seen new customers in the courtyard. It seemed like Anton was winning the territorial war on drugs.

I studied Jackson. He had become a friend, as odd as it was. "Can I ask you something?"

He slowly turned to me with a knowing grin. "About your boy?"

I picked a cuticle and swiveled. "Yes."

That goodbye kiss had played on repeat in my brain for the better part of two weeks — two weeks where I'd started to get my shit together. Step One, gainful employment, was a box I'd officially ticked off. With the help of a few of Anton's family connections, I'd gotten a job as a hostess in a restaurant downtown. Luckily, the only requirements were a smile and manners.

My next step was to find an apartment out of the neighborhood.

Jackson rubbed his shiny bald head. "I don't know where he is. I don't think even Anton does." He let out a small sigh.

I continued, "Do you know anything from that night?" It was the first time I'd asked anyone. The aftershocks of emotional trauma hadn't let me think too much about what had happened, what *could* have happened. But I was sure of what Leo had done...for me.

After a little hesitation Jackson said, "Rafa told me they dropped him and picked him up in midtown, then dropped him again a few blocks away from the building where they found you. That's all I got." Jackson opened his hands then stuffed them in the front pockets of his jeans. "We're gonna stay in touch, right? These two little monkeys would be sad to leave each other."

There would be nothing mournful about my departure from Covington Heights. Leaving the poverty and filth behind would be just fine by me. Violet and I would start a new Chapter. Hell, a whole new story. I had changed too much to stay within the blocks where I'd grown up. And when the social worker had suggested I see a counselor for emotional support, I'd taken the business card and seriously contemplated it.

Jackson stood, still waiting for my answer. I rose as well and snaked my arms around his giant, strong body. "We are absolutely going to stay in touch. I want to hear more about you and Lisa."

He hugged me tight then held me at arm's length. "You noticed that, huh?"

I tried to hide my smirk. "You mean you, in your underwear scratching your ass when I dropped off Violet yesterday? That was pretty hard to miss."

Jackson lifted his eyebrows and bit his plump bottom lip. He jutted his chin in my direction. "You check me out?"

"Oh, yeah." I exaggerated. "You are one fine piece of man meat." I did a little dance with my shoulders and allowed an honest, playful grin to spread on my face. Damn, having a light conversation with a friend was nice — fucking normal even. It gave me hope for the future. Maybe I could become one of those easy breezy girls who batted eyelashes and men took to dinner. I just needed to survive one month of work, getting a new place and organizing childcare for Violet. I was sure I could find a rhythm, chase down an average life and kiss its boring-ass face.

"I gotta take J.J. to his mom's." Jackson scrunched his nose. It wasn't the first time he'd hinted at baby-mama drama. "You good?"

Anton's crew had been doing a decent job of checking in with me, almost babysitting. Somehow I was off-limits but still their concern. I didn't know how Anton had explained to them how I'd gone from Leo's to his to no one's in a matter of hours, and to be honest, I didn't care. I'd gotten my freedom. That was all that mattered.

And the bossman himself had kept his distance. The only time I saw him was if I needed money. It was almost as if he'd shut the door on any further thoughts of me, which was fine by me. His stupid debt repayment had only caused me pain and heartache. But it was odd, the walking around and receiving tight smiles from the crew, like I was precious and respected.

"I'm good. Just gonna take her out for pizza. You know…the one where they let the kids make their own." I smiled up to Jackson. Giving Violet a childhood was my number one priority. And with the money Leo had left, it was making it a hell of a lot easier. I fantasized about repaying him, but even if our paths crossed again, he would never take a dime from me. That was how he was.

Jackson swung J.J. over his head and positioned him on his shoulders. The already-lanky Jackson towered over me with his son atop him. "You call me if you need anything. Got it?"

I signaled for Violet to come and take my hand. "Thanks, Jackson. We're gonna be fine. I can feel it."

Violet and I swung our hands all the way down the street to the same pizza joint we'd gone to with Leo. The employees fixed her up with a paper hat and apron, and they didn't seem to be worried about the massive cloud of flour she was going to create. As my little sister sang some version of what she thought was an Italian song, I walked over to a booth in the corner and pulled out my phone.

The thought of starting from total scratch was overwhelming. Photos of empty lofts and studios only reminded me that my worldly possessions were a pair of heels and some hoodies. And the city was huge. The listings were sorted by neighborhood and I hadn't known where I'd wanted to live...until Jackson had said midtown.

It was stupid to think I would one day just magically bump into Leo. But he'd come back and been that quiet version of himself that had a way of soothing my soul. He'd ruined me for other men, I was sure — which was fine. I needed to focus on Violet and me for a while.

I swiped through the listings in my new decided-upon radius and found a furnished sublet on one of those side streets I'd dreamed about. It was the perfect blend of next-to-everything but quaint and private. It was expensive, but so was everything else.

Violet giggled. Her life would be forever changed, thanks to Leo — not just his generosity with the money, but also the sacrifice he'd made that I could sense in my bones. There had to have been some sort of trade-off. It was obvious by the suit he'd worn and what had been hidden behind his dark, tortured and beautiful eyes.

Eyes that could see deep inside of me. Eyes that I vowed to get lost in again someday.

I stared at the phone number for the listing.

Fuck it.

After a shaky breath, I hit dial. Three rings later, a man with a thick accent answered.

"Hi. I saw your apartment online." I bit my thumbnail and eyed Violet, who was sprinkling a serious amount of cheese over her pie. She had a smudge of tomato sauce on her cheek.

"Oh." The man said, drawing out the short word and making my heart palpitate. "I'm about to show it. You might be too late."

There was no room to hesitate. My brand new normal was to grab life by the balls and use every resource I had to get what I wanted.

And the happy, carefree kiddo was all the inspiration I needed. "I can pay a year in advance. Cash."

"It's all yours."

After exchanging a few details and setting up a meeting, I hung up with a nervous smile. We had a new home. Fucking hell, maybe I would finally learn how to cook. There were so many possibilities, and I would never underestimate financial freedom again.

Not that I could live forever with what Leo had left us. But a fresh start? That was exactly what we needed.

Chapter Twenty-Eight

Leo

For someone who claimed to be happy to have me back, Frankie's decision to send me to Turkey for three months seemed a hell of a lot more like him getting rid of me.

Yes, I'd done a bad thing in going to see Fiona. Did that really merit exile to a European country to spy on a local politician who wanted us to take out the businessman supporting his opponent? I sipped my beer and pretended to read my book. I'd picked it up at the airport, but, since it was in Italian, it was as good as gibberish. I could speak enough to get by, but read? Not so much. The verb tenses constantly confused me. I'd been trying to hide my American-ness and blend in as an Italian grad student. I even had glasses.

The overweight rich crook on the other side of the restaurant let out a boisterous laugh. He was obviously impressed with himself. Flanked with escorts, his evening smelled more like pleasure than business. Frankie's mission was research and I noted the lustful weakness, paid for my drink and walked down the narrow, colorful street to the small apartment I was renting.

Alone.

My new life was that of an isolated hitman — not that I was going to kill the guy on this trip. Frankie had sent me to check out the man and the lay of the land. The politician had only paid half the fee and was trying to negotiate with Frankie on the terms of the other part of the payment. Frankie had doubts that the client could pay the rest, so the price of my plane ticket and stipend were worth the extra confidence that we wouldn't get fucked over. It wasn't like we could file a civil lawsuit for unpaid services rendered.

But the solitude was eating at me. I'd gone to museums, concerts and open-air markets. Women in coffee shops had flirted with me, but I couldn't stomach the thought of anyone but Fiona. It was ridiculous to think she was pining away for me somewhere at home. And it was utterly pathetic the way I was doing just that thousands of miles away from her.

The thing was, I couldn't help it. Somehow, distance was not just making my heart grow fonder, it was fucking aching for her. I wanted to know how she was doing, what she was doing, everything. Had she gotten Violet away from their mom? Did she have a job? Did she like the job? Hell, I'd invented a story in my head that she'd come home from work and I'd rubbed her damn feet.

And while all the missing her was comforting, it was scaring the shit out of me at the same time. One, because 'mental stalker' wasn't something I'd strived to be. And two, because what would it mean if it was all in my lonely head?

To complicate things, I was pretty sure she would be long gone from Covington. Any snooping around would require help from Frankie. That door wasn't just firmly closed. He'd put a padlock and an alarm on it the night he'd busted me. He'd been very clear — 'No ties to Covington.'

I'd tried not to make the murders look too professional, but in my hateful passion and need for revenge, I'd been too eager to be sleek. I could have used two different guns, for example, leading investigators to believe there'd been more than one of me.

Making matters a hell of a lot worse and unbearably frustrating was the fact that I hadn't sparred since I'd last seen Frankie. I was so in need of a fight that my skin itched at the thought. Work-outs were me, endless push-ups and any abdominal work I could dream up on the rug in my small apartment.

So it was with a huge smile on my face that I packed my bag for my flight the next day. I was ready to get back to the city, back to trying to kick Frankie's ass, back to finding a way to be with Fiona.

The next day, I slid the key to the apartment into the mailbox and hailed a cab to the airport. My forged passport didn't even get a blink and I was on the plane and sprawled out in business class without so much as a second look.

For the eleven-hour flight, I dreamed of ways to convince Frankie to let me have a girlfriend. Over Ireland, I realized that 'convincing' was the wrong verb. *Force.* I would force him. The flight attendant must have thought my beaming smile was for her or some kind of gratitude for the meal she'd served me but nope. It was me ticking off every little habit in Frankie's game. Each weakness in his armor would bring me one step closer to Fiona. That was, if she'd have me.

Chapter Twenty-Nine

Fiona

There was one thing I'd learned in my months away from Covington. I was a truly shitty cook. I'd also learned that because I worked at a restaurant, it didn't really matter. My new job, daytime hostess for a modern chic eatery downtown, allowed me to drop Violet off at her new preschool, work, have some alone time, then pick up my sister without too much guilt.

The social worker who I reported to had helped me find the preschool for Violet, and since on paper I wasn't making much money, the fees were being helped by the State. I didn't like taking the handout, but the money Leo had given us wouldn't last forever.

My sister was almost three, so I'd ditched the stroller, bought her a ladybug backpack that held everything she needed and we walked through midtown on our daily routine. She'd settled into life with just me in our new surroundings, perhaps somehow conscious of everything we'd gotten away from.

I swung her little hand as we walked down the avenue toward her school. With every step I took, I was grateful for my new life, thankful for second chances. And with each one of those steps, I still thought about him.

About what Leo had sacrificed for me. He'd become what he never wanted to be, in order to give me what I had. Why had I been so special? But more importantly, why hadn't Leo been back? I'd avoided going down and stalking him at Chezzie's, but that hadn't stopped me from wandering the streets, hoping to bump into him.

Which was silly. With eight million people in the city, the chances were pretty damn slim that it would ever happen. But hope lived on a prayer.

I gave Violet a hug and a kiss and watched her from the doorway as she changed out of her shoes into her slippers then gave me a final wave before heading into her class. She'd silently understood the need to be independent, much as I had at her age. The more a person could do on their own, the less disappointed they would be when no one offered to do what they needed.

I strolled down the crowded streets, the fellow residents of the city busying their way to whatever job or date awaited them. It was odd, the overwhelming sense of loneliness while being surrounded by thousands of people. I made my way to the train and found a seat. I always looked at the people, that tiny thread of hope pulling at my heart that Leo was watching over me.

But, just like all the other days since I'd started working at the restaurant, he wasn't there. I had plenty of time before I needed to be at work, so I walked to the river and sat at my favorite bench. The cool breeze off the water was a refreshing replacement for the city odors of exhaust and trash.

I rubbed the crisp cotton of my white shirt into my upper arms and closed my eyes. Cool, fall days were rare and taking them in was a simple luxury.

"Is this seat taken?"

There was something in the male voice that gave me pause, and I opened my eyes.

Leo!

I blinked, once, twice, thrice. *Not Leo.* But it could have been his twin in a few years. The same dangerous eyes looked down on me from the same strong nose and perfectly matched olive skin. Other than a dimple in the clean-shaven chin and a kiss of gray above the ears, it could have been him. And the suit… Leo's older doppelganger wore a sleek, perfectly fitted dark blue suit with a light blue shirt opened one button at the neck.

I must have been staring. I was pretty sure my mouth was agape.

The stranger chuckled. "We look alike, huh?" He motioned to the bench. "Mind if I sit?"

All the street smarts I'd gathered over the years had built an invisible wall around me, and inside, sirens sounded. This was no coincidence and I was almost certain of the identity of the man who unbuttoned his jacket, sat next to me and propped a foot on the opposite knee.

He spread out, his elbows on the back of the bench and forearms dangling. The reflection from a gold watch that glimmered in the sun bounced off his perfectly shined dark-brown loafers. Any other woman might have been excited by his almost-silver-fox flawlessness. Any other woman who had no idea that she was seated next to a killer.

"I really need to get to work." I stood but he caught my wrist and guided me back down.

"That's actually not true. Your shift doesn't officially start for another thirty minutes." His coy smile didn't do much to reassure me of my safety and it was a smoking layer of shit on the cake of information he'd just dropped. He knew exactly who I was, where I worked and *when* I worked.

He released my hand and shifted his gaze to the ferry passing by on the water. I glued my eyes on him, and my heart beat fast. The man next to me knew where Leo was, how Leo was. If I played my cards right, maybe I could get some kind of news and the reason why he hadn't checked in on me and Violet.

"You can stop pretending you don't know who I am, Fiona. But let's make it official." He extended his right hand. "I'm Frankie, your boyfriend's big, bad brother."

I shook his hand then withdrew my own back to my lap, where I was trying desperately not to fiddle with my fingers.

"I don't have a boyfriend, so I'm sorry. You must have me confused with someone else, Frankie." I moved to stand, but Frankie planted a hand on my shoulder.

"I admire your willpower. I'd thought you would have hit up Chezzie's ages ago. Although I can't help but wonder if all that aimless walking isn't an accident. Pointless, but intentional, in my opinion."

Okay... So, Frankie Dearest had all kinds of eyes on me. But I was still alive. That had to count for something.

"It's funny. I thought you'd be more talkative. A rare judgment error on my part." Frankie's cool tone sent a shiver up my spine.

I glanced around. The streets had emptied, the former pedestrians all behind desks or having coffee and gossiping with friends. He clocked my eye movement and winked. He'd known exactly when to approach me, and worse, where.

"You can relax. I'm not out to hurt you. Jesus, any more pent-up rage from him and he'd knock me into next week." Frankie rubbed his shoulder and winced.

"I'm sorry. I don't follow."

"Your boyfriend and I had a little bet."

I opened my mouth to object, but he raised his hand. "Spare me. Anyway, he won, so I have to tell him where you are."

I'd always heard of butterflies going *pitter patter* in people's chests and thought it was a load of romantic bullshit...until that moment, because my heart was absolutely flittering at the thought of seeing Leo. I sat up a little straighter and bit my lips inward.

Frankie narrowed his eyes. "The problem was that I wasn't sure I could trust you. But I've watched you. I see what you're doing with your sister. I don't think you would do anything to risk that."

There might have been a bit of a threat to his words. It was hard to tell. But he should know that they were truthful. "I wouldn't."

"You haven't gone to the police."

The laugh that popped out of me was brief and a borderline scoff.

Frankie shifted on the bench to face me. "You were abducted, drugged and sold on the black market. Don't you think someone should pay for that?"

His dark eyes dared me to say it, to admit that they *had* paid for it, with their lives, to confess to Leo's crime, but he wouldn't get me to betray Leo. No one could.

I let out a long breath, the confidence I'd lacked finally filling me up like a warm bath. "My mother's a drug addict. Justice isn't a comfort I'm used to."

Frankie sat back and rubbed under his chin with the back of his hand. Seconds ticked by before he said, "How about chicken Marsala for dinner tonight? I think you know the address."

Chapter Thirty

Leo

I dressed in a black suit that Frankie's tailor had made for me. I had to admit, nice clothes weren't the worst part of working for my brother. Besides, Chezzie loved it when we 'classed up her joint'. I yanked the cuff of my white shirt out of the jacket and couldn't help but admire the cut of the soft fabric. After one final glance in the mirror and a rake through my hair, I was out of the door.

Frankie waited for me in his baby-blue Porsche. He owed me some information, and by the smug look on his face, I was sure he'd found her. I hid my smile and waited.

He edged into traffic then said, "You should know that the Turkey contract is canceled. That guy was never going to pay us." Frankie looked over his shoulder and changed lanes to turn downtown.

I didn't bitch or moan about three months and a waste of my time, nor did I offer my apologies for the loss of income. I did hope my relief was masked with my silence.

He continued, "After you left for Covington, I did a lot of thinking about Pop."

That didn't surprise me. We always did a lot of thinking about our father. Some of his words were camouflaged as my own thoughts, since they'd run through my head so much.

"Do you remember what you said to me before you left?" It must have been a rhetorical question, because he didn't wait for me to answer. "You said, '*I don't want to take a life*'."

I didn't remember the exact words, but from his sincere tone, Frankie sounded like those were it.

"It made me think a lot. You know, like, I didn't either. I didn't *want* to do this. I just always assumed I had to. Then you opted out."

"I still don't want to, but I get it. What else are we going to do? It's not like we went to school. Shit, what am I going to put on a résumé? Knows where to bury bodies?" It had been something that I'd struggled with for years. Everything I was good at was violent and illegal. Making a living pouring drinks seemed like a depressing waste of my talents. Frankie had probably had the same struggle.

We stopped at a red light and Frankie tapped the steering wheel with his thumb. "The thing is, I've been looking for a way to get legit for a while now."

I cranked my neck. *Say what?*

"Don't look so surprised. Every relationship I have fails. You know why?"

Another rhetorical question. I let it hang in the air.

"Because I am a liar. I pick smart, beautiful women and they can smell my fucking lies. They never get the real truth, and the dishonesty always bubbles to the surface. It's why Mom left."

There were more reasons why our mother had left us with a killer. The untruths that had passed between her and my father were only part of the reason, but I wasn't going to contradict my brother in his big-boy sharing circle. He had a point he was getting to, and he could take as long as he needed to get there. Our relationship wasn't something I was going to play with. I needed Frankie—not for a job or money, but for the understanding of who I was and what I struggled with. Maybe this was his way of telling me the same thing.

"Anyway, I want a family. I want to teach a kid how to fish like Dad did for us. As fucked up as it all was, there were great times between us three."

That was another thing I wrestled with—how to love a man who'd taught me everything, when 'everything' meant I was a skilled assassin.

I finally spoke. "I get it."

"I know you do. So here's the thing… I don't want to take lives either." Frankie dared a glance in my direction and smirked. "Don't look so shocked. It's not as fun as Pop made it sound."

That, I wouldn't know. I'd killed Mac and those two Bradford fucks without a second thought. After what they'd done to Fiona and faceless other women, I wasn't sorry I'd seen them draw their last breath. I hadn't been constricted with guilt.

"So what are you going to do? Just stop? Turn your life around?" I asked.

"Funny you should say that. Yes, basically. I want to go from taking lives to saving them."

I laughed. It was probably rude, but it was so unlike Frankie that it had come out of me before I could control it. "You gonna put on a badge and protect and serve? Pop just rolled over in his grave, wherever the fuck that is."

Frankie scoffed and pulled next to a massive truck that hovered over his sports car. "I'm not going to become a cop. I'm going to start a security detail company for the rich and stupid. All those loaded brokers downtown do so many drugs that they've convinced themselves they're going to get robbed at gunpoint. But their liberal tendencies won't allow them to own a gun and few of them have the discipline to become actual fighters. Their gym routines would make you giggle like a schoolgirl."

"You're serious." If a fortune teller would have told me Frankie would be the one to give up on dad's business, I would have asked for my money back.

"The lies are eating me up, Leo." There was a sadness in his eyes that I'd never seen before but had recognized from my own. "Not to mention the body count. Fuck. See? My moral compass is shattered. If I don't stop now, I don't think I ever will."

We rode the rest of the way in silence, the weight of our conversation a heavy block in our stomachs and a lot to digest. It didn't feel right asking about Fiona after all he'd just shared. But when we got to Chezzie's, instead of pulling into the lot down the street, he double parked in front of the restaurant.

Frankie put the gear shift in neutral and pulled the hand brake. "The other thing I thought about when you were away, in Covington and Turkey, was that I didn't want to lose you again. Yeah, we have Chez, but it's not the same. I was selfish to keep you from your girl. I'm

sorry. I thought it had to be one or the other, because —
"

"Because Pop said we were all we ever had."

"Probably. But I need more. And you might already have more." Frankie thumbed to Chezzie's front window.

"What?" My heart skipped three beats. I'd expected a piece of paper with Fiona's address or where she was working, not a fucking date. I was in a suit. I was not prepared for our reunion. I hadn't even thought of what to say. 'Hello' seemed completely insufficient.

"She's inside?" My voice cracked. Holy hell, what was I, a fifteen-year-old boy?

Frankie laughed. "Oh my God... You are in a full-on panic." He wiped away a tear that was definitely not there. *He always has enjoyed my suffering.* "Pull yourself together and get in there."

I planted a kiss on Frankie's smooth cheek and checked the mirror of the car while I reached for the handle. Something poked at my heart. He hadn't wanted to lose me and deserved to know he wouldn't.

Over my shoulder and with my feet out of the door, I said, "I'll call you tomorrow. We'll work out the future together."

Frankie offered a tight smile as his goodbye and I tapped the top of the car as mine. Funny how much could change. I wondered if it would affect Fiona's and my connection. There was only one way to find out.

My heart thumped and I had to let out a powerful exhale before opening the door. The wonderful Italian aromas hit me in a mouth-watering breeze. But what slammed me in the heart was my Aunt Chezzie swinging Violet in her arms — Violet, whose dark hair had grown to her shoulders and whose bare legs were definitely longer.

"Leo!" Violet squealed. She'd remembered me, and from the excitement in her voice, they'd been happy memories. I could only hope her sister would be as enthusiastic. After all, I'd abandoned her for three months.

I kissed my aunt and Violet on the cheeks. "Hello, you gorgeous ladies."

"This little angel is my new helper." Chezzie smiled at Violet. She'd always wanted a daughter, especially after witnessing Frankie and me beat on each other for decades. My aunt pecked my cheek before tapping it. "Back booth."

Heat crawled up my neck.. The possibilities of how I would find Fiona ranged from broken to pissed off. Her brown eyes swept over me and she was chewing a nail. She was more beautiful than I had allowed myself to remember. She wore a simple dark-green dress and her hair was down. She'd put on makeup—a little mascara and a pink, glossy lipstick. The tight smile on her face couldn't hide the caution written all over her body language.

I slid into the booth. "Hi." I drew out the short word, inviting her to send back the low hum of energy that had already met her halfway.

Fiona stared at me and I realized that a reunion in real life was going to be a lot more difficult than the blissful jumping into my arms that I'd imagined. The panic from the car came back.

Her face twitched a couple of times before settling on a frown. "It's really nice to see you."

"Violet recognized me."

"I would hope so. She only reminds me that my spaghetti is nowhere near as good as yours every time I try to make it."

Mandolin music strummed in a quiet melody overhead. I recognized it from all the other nights I'd eaten at Chezzie's.

But the chemistry was well on its way to threading us back together. Her little smirk gave away the fact that it was breaking down whatever wall she'd put up to convince herself that she needed to be guarded with me.

"Why are you in a suit?"

"Why are you in a dress?"

Fiona rolled her eyes and I could have kissed her. That spunk... Christ, I'd missed that side of her.

"I have dresses now."

"Good," I said and meant it. But just to jab her back I added, "I have suits now."

"Fine." She shrugged a shoulder. "Glad we got that all cleared up." There was a little snip in her voice that both amused and reassured me. She needed to start with a little fight to prove that her showing up didn't mean we were going to pick up where we'd left off. Although, I wasn't sure that would have been a good idea anyway.

I narrowed my eyes and took the bait. "Are you mad at me?"

She looked away then back at me. "I didn't realize it until I laid eyes on you, but yes. Yes, I am. I needed you and you left me. Also, I plan on paying you back. I have a job and I haven't used all that money." Her volume rose with every word but I didn't care. A pissed-off Fiona was a much easier fix than a broken one. Besides, it was more an act of protection than true anger.

"What else?" I flapped my hand for her to give me more, then leaned back with my arms overhead.

"I'll tell you what else. You can't just mosey in here looking like a Dolce and Gabbana model, kiss my sister and think we're good. We have shit to talk about." She tapped the table with her index finger. It was adorable. *God, I love her mad.*

"Good point." I nodded. "Can we eat while we talk, or is smelling my aunt's cooking without tasting it some kind of penance I have to pay?"

"Oh, we're gonna eat." Her wide eyes may have read crazy to a stranger, but to me her loopy fuming was like going home. "Then you're gonna walk me home and kiss me goodnight."

"Is that so?" I motioned to Chezzie that she could bring the wine and starters.

"Yeah. Then you have to, like, properly date me." Her proud little tantrum ended with her eyebrows raised and arms crossed.

I faked fear with a cringe. "Sounds terrible."

"Oh, it's gonna be." This time her smile was real, and she kept it on while she scooted over to make room for Violet.

We filled ourselves with Chezzie's food and had one glass of wine each. I wanted to talk to her about her trauma and tell her about my plans for the future, but I had time for that. After many goodbyes and promises to be back soon, we left Chezzie and I hailed a taxi to drive us uptown. Her place was only four blocks from Nanna's and I escorted her and Violet through the entrance of the building and up two flights of stairs to her apartment. She told Violet to get changed for bed and I hovered in the doorway.

"I'm pretty sure your instructions involved a kiss."

Fiona stepped closer and brushed my cheek with the back of her hand. "You're real, right?"

"I am."

Instead of me kissing her, she leaned in and pressed her lips into mine for a long time, sealing our connection. All the starving, all the craving I'd had without her faded away. I interlaced our fingers, afraid my hands would shift into overdrive once they'd touched her.

"Fifi," Violet said from the hall, "teeth."

Fiona broke the kiss and looked up at me with a soft smile. "Be right there, baby girl." Then a whisper to me, "I missed you."

I kissed her forehead and she stepped away.

"Is it wrong to have our second date tomorrow?" I asked, then bit my bottom lip.

"Third. Technically it will be our third." Fiona walked backward and her cheeky smile woke up an entirely different side of me.

"Can I sleep on your couch?"

"Nope. But you can pick us up at six tomorrow." She scooped up Violet and made her wave at me. "Oh, and that's p.m., Mr. I-Have-Suits-Now."

"Copy that, Miss I-Have-Dresses-Now." I saluted her and closed the door.

She was right. There were things that we needed to talk about—probably work through. But damn it if just being normal for five minutes wasn't the best kind of medicine for our broken souls.

Chapter Thirty-One

Fiona

Chezzie and Violet waved from the curb in front of her restaurant. It was hard to tell which one of them was more excited for their sleepover. Over the last few months, Leo's aunt had become the fairy godmother Violet had never had. If they weren't in the kitchen together, they were getting matching manicures or cozied up reading stories of princesses and unicorns.

The presence of another strong, loving woman in Violet's little life had also given me some breathing room to work on healing wounds I hadn't had time to notice. According to my therapist, I had abandonment issues. Yeah, she'd really earned the diploma framed on her wall with that one. But I liked talking to her, and she was proud of me for taking things slow with Leo.

Leo. The man who winked his reassurance from the driver seat before reaching for my hand and kissing the back of it.

"She's gonna be fine, Fi."

"I know." And I did. I'd offered to pay Leo back many times for the nest egg that had allowed Violet and me to change our lives, our futures, but he always refused. While it hurt my pride, I also knew what it had provided for my sister. I didn't want to be a woman who took handouts, but I also couldn't let the opportunity for Violet's 'normal' life slip away due to my ego.

As we drove upstate, Leo filled me in on his and Frankie's first client. He was a former tennis-player-turned-reality-star who had a bad habit of sleeping with married women. All the drama was making Frankie irritable. And, according to Leo, it was made worse by the fact that Frankie wasn't getting laid. So our little weekend away was a much-needed break for both of us.

Leo turned off to the familiar tree-lined path and parked at the end. The crisp forest air was cooler than the previous time we'd hiked up the mountain to the little lake, but I was significantly more prepared. I even had a real pair of black mountain pants.

The hike seemed shorter, even though Leo had stopped several times and gathered wild mushrooms. The easy nature between us and around us was very much my happy place. All those months ago, when I'd teased Leo about being Skip, I would have never believed that he and I could have created a life after Covington. But there we were, doing just that.

When we got to the little clearing that led to the campsite, I was almost sad that the walk had ended. I loved the way he knew every bird call, every tree, which mushrooms were not okay to eat and which animal tracks belonged to what animal. The city boy I'd met on the street was a far, far cry from the soul that resided in my Leo.

Because he was mine, I was sure. We'd never formally professed our love, but I could feel it growing in me every second I was around him. And his past? As messed up as some of the bits and pieces he'd shared were, it had made him the man he was.

We dropped our packs next to the stone circle for the fire.

"I'll set up." Leo dropped to his knees and unzipped his bag.

"I can help." We both knew that was a lie. I was utterly useless in all things nature and cooking.

But he didn't laugh. "You're good. Maybe see if you can find any dry wood."

I nodded but wondered how one could tell the difference between dry and wet—and how damp was too damp. In the brush, there were a few sticks and I wandered a bit deeper into the trees before I found a couple of dead logs. I lugged them back and the tent was already up.

Leo sat on a small stump, dusted off his mushrooms and offered me a sweet smile.

"You spoil me. You know that, right?" I asked.

"I have to. You're the only woman who can deal with my massive ego." It was true. Leo Ricci had a healthy dose of self-confidence—but rightfully so. He could kill a man with his bare hands then turn around and sip imaginary tea with my little sister and make that hotter than any brutal force.

"I bet you could line a block with women willing to try."

There were times when I had to convince myself that I deserved someone like Leo. And almost every day I told myself it was okay to rely on him, that we needed to move with one foot in front of the other, not cheat our way to the finish line.

As if reading my thoughts—he had an eerie way of doing that—he said, "I'd pick you every time, Fi. Every time."

"Stop being dreamy. It's annoying."

Leo placed the mushroom to his left and crawled over to me. He kissed up my neck and I giggled. "You know what else is annoying?" He nudged me backward with his forehead and I fell gently onto my back. "How fucking beautiful you are."

We shared a long kiss, nothing forcing us to speed through it or hide its passion in front of a three-year-old's eyes. Leo hovered over me and pulled back with a growl.

"God, you are addicting." He shook his head. His hair had grown and the thick mop suited him. "But seriously, Fi, I need to tell you something."

"You can tell me anything," I whispered and brushed his cheek. Leo and I had no secrets. It made our bond that much stronger.

"That's the thing... I *can* tell you everything. So I need to let you know that I want more. I want everything with you, everything *from* you. I love you."

Leo's dark eyes still held danger, but I'd learned to understand that it would never be for me. In fact, I was thankful for it. It had saved my life and given me a new one.

"I love you, too."

"Good." Leo rolled off me and climbed into the tent. He came back with a shy grin and a sparkling ring.

Oh. My. God. I propped up on my elbows and my pulse raced.

"I was going to save this for later when I got you naked, but this seems better."

Yes. All I could think of was the word 'yes'. *A million yesses.*

"Fiona" — Leo tilted his head and smiled — "I meant what I said. I want everything. I want to adopt Violet. I want us to make our own babies. I want to get a damn dog and buy a stupid house. But most of all, I want you for the rest of my life. Will you marry me?"

Tears puddled in my eyes and my face grew hot. How Leo had integrated Violet into our life had been the first annoyingly wonderful side of him that I'd seen. And the fact that his plans had always included her was further proof of how much he cared for and understood who I was.

So much for one step at a time. Leo Ricci was the only person on the planet who truly knew me, and he loved me even then.

"I want everything, too. And for the first time in my life, I honestly believe I can have it. Yes. Yes. Yes. Yes!" The tears leaked down my cheeks and my hands trembled as he put the ring on. I wrapped my arms around his neck and kissed him.

After I climbed into Leo's lap, he nuzzled his head into my shoulder. In a quiet voice he said, "Please, never stop loving me." His tender words were a confession of the fear we both shared — that our pasts made us not good enough for certain things. It was the same reason I had to reassure myself. And if I could give him that proof that he had a right to be loved, I wasn't going to take that lightly.

"It would be impossible for me to ever stop." I kissed his temple and cherished the glimpse of vulnerability he'd shown me of his battered soul. For the first time in my life, I was privileged. I'd seen something no one else ever would.

Love Repaired
Deana Birch

Excerpt

I parked the loaner SUV in line next to the other shiny overpriced automobiles, did a final check for personal belongings in the seat next to me — no need to learn the same lesson twice, my cell phone had spent the day in my car — and headed into the office. With the sun set, the cool evening air hit my cheeks and I perked up as I walked. My Cayenne sat in front of the large metal garage doors, a sparkle reflecting its recent wash. At least luxury came with attention to detail.

When I reached the glass door, I tugged it toward me only to find it locked. *Jesus.* I'd even failed at picking up my car. I stood on my tiptoes and rapped my knuckles against the glass. On the other side, the room was dark and the half-circular reception desk was abandoned, a black office chair pushed into its place. But from the hall behind it, a light peeked out — my ray of hope.

I knocked again and pressed my lips together while readjusting my shoulder bag. I shifted my body weight from side to side and banged louder.

Florescent beams flooded the showroom and I blinked. My skin flushed, and my mouth went dry. A legal aide at the firm had once said something about man candy, but I thought that was like a unicorn—not real, a legend in a forest I would never visit. But Man Candy had a warm smile, combed-back dirty blond hair and a build that screamed heaven through a tight, black, untucked work shirt. The last few buttons were open and matching pants hung low on his waist. He was also headed right toward me, tapping a wrench in his hand.

With dimples in his smile, he slipped the tool into his back pocket and unlocked the door. His sea-blue eyes must have been designed for skinny dipping.

"Mrs. Benton, I presume." The low, scratchy voice matched the light stubble on his cheeks. His dimples deepened, and the warm showroom air hit my already-heated body.

"Ms." I couldn't resist the urge to brush against him, and as I did, the perfect blend of motor oil and earthy spice came with me.

Testosterone, how I've missed thee.

I walked over to reception and placed the key fob on the desk.

He followed and squinted down at the neat paper piles next to the flat computer screen and keyboard. He picked up my keys from the tail of the stuffed squirrel that held them and dangled it like a time piece.

"Nice keychain." After a quick arch of his eyebrow, the damn dimples reappeared with his tight-lipped smile.

"Thanks"—I glanced at his chest—"Ben." I took the stuffed animal from his grease-stained hands and slid the other key toward him.

"Did you fill it up?" he asked.

"Uh…no." Add one more failure to my day.

Ben shook his head and grabbed the fob before popping it into a drawer. "No one ever fills it up. You know it costs double, right?" He peered up with one eye closed.

"Well, it was either fill it up or make you wait longer."

"Either way, it's my time. I'll have to do it Monday." He rubbed his face with both hands and a tattoo poked out from the tight sleeve around his bicep. His very full bicep.

I cringed and lifted a shoulder. "Sorry. Anyway, I only drove it to my office and back."

Ben walked out from behind the desk and over to the door. Holding it open for me again, he motioned for me to leave.

I'm too young to suffer hot flashes, right? And I was not dreaming of ways to sabotage my brakes or engine. That would be silly—and a further inconvenience that my schedule would not allow.

"You had a failed fuel pump. It's a pretty common problem. That was what was causing the stalling."

Note to self— Get another failed fuel pump.

When we stood in front of my car, he pulled up on the handle, swung the door open, and I froze. A big white pastry box sat on the passenger seat.

"Fuck me."

"Pardon?" he asked with an airy chuckle.

I brought my hands to my face and pulled them down slowly, probably ruining the effects of the anti-aging cream I'd put on that morning. "Fuck. Fuck. Fuck."

"Are you okay?" Ben leaned in closer.

"I forgot the fucking cupcakes. Fuck me. Fuck." I let my bag fall off my shoulder and dragged my feet over to the steel garage. My back met the cool wall and I slid down to the rough concrete. I stomped my sensible beige heel before slumping into a ball and whimpering into my hands. My entire day, week, month… They had all been colossal fails.

The motor oil and musk were back, now touching my wrist and seated on the ground next to me.

"Shitty day?" He draped his defined forearms over his knees with his fingers interlaced.

"I wish I could say it was the shittiest, but it just seems to be par for the course. *Fuck*." I stomped again.

"You have quite the potty mouth for a lady."

"Did you just call me a lady? Oh my God, now I'm really going to cry." Forgetting Shae's cupcakes was the cherry on top of my botched-Mom sundae. But being one step away from a 'ma'am' was the rainbow sprinkles. Asshole-expensive face cream… It obviously wasn't working. And I wasn't even forty.

"You wanna talk about it? I'm a pretty good listener."

If that were true, then Man Candy truly was a unicorn and I was in an enchanted forest. But the words flew out before I could stop them.

"My client lied to me and made me look like a fool in a deposition. I forgot my phone in the car this morning, which means my older daughter has probably called it three hundred times. And because I was behind closed doors with said lying client, I couldn't call her.

"It was my little one's last day at dance camp and I was supposed to bring the cupcakes. Which, as you can see, I did not do. Oh, and their father is in prison for vehicular manslaughter. Sorry you asked?"

He frowned and shook his head. "Where are they now? Your girls?"

"My sister takes care of them so I can keep working." I wrapped the hem of my skirt around my legs.

"Who takes care of you?" The smile and dimples were gone, but the warmth stayed in his eyes.

"Me, I guess." I shrugged and tried to recall any moment my ex, Pete, had ever really taken care of me, and I drew a blank.

He narrowed his blue eyes. "Is that enough?"

The beautiful stranger next to me had gotten as far as my walls would let him. Although, I had to admit, someone being concerned about me might have made a tiny crack.

"That and the half-bottle of Chardonnay waiting in the door of my fridge."

"That's depressing," he said, getting up. He offered me his strong, rough hand and I clasped it. With a gentle yank, I was on my feet. "You ready for me to add insult to injury then?" He wet his lips and tilted his head.

"Oh, God. I don't even care about the bill. Just tell them to send it to me." I smoothed the front of my skirt and dusted off my rear.

"It's not that." Ben cleared his throat.

I scanned my car for a scratch or dent.

He continued, "I'm really sorry, but I ate one of the cupcakes."

I darted my eyes back to him and he hunched as if waiting to be smacked.

"You eat cupcakes?" I leaned back a little. Whatever moment sugar had spent on his lips, it was not spending a lifetime on his hips. Bastard.

"It's my cheat day. And those damn things were next to me in the car all day. Staring at me. Taunting me. Like, *'Ben, you know you want me.'*" He wiggled his fingers. "Then you were late, and, well…I made some kind of weird justification that I could have one. I'm really sorry."

"You ate one of my daughter's pink frosted cupcakes?" I planted my hands on my hips.

Ben nodded with a clenched jaw.

"You're a fucking unicorn." I picked up my bag, tossed it in the back and climbed into the car.

With the seat belt fastened, I reached for the door, but he held on to it stopping me from closing.

He blinked hard. "Did you and your potty mouth just call me a unicorn?"

"We did." I smiled at the mythical man candy creature, shut the door and drove out of the enchanted forest.

Home of Erotic Romance

Sign up for our newsletter and find out about all our romance book releases, eBook sales and promotions, sneak peeks and FREE romance books!

About the Author

Deana Birch was named after her father's first love, who just so happened not to be her mother. Born and raised in the Midwest, she made stops in Los Angeles and New York before settling in Europe, where she lives with her own blue-eyed Happily Ever After. Her days are spent teaching yoga, playing tennis, ruining her children's French homework, cleaning up dog vomit, writing her next book or reading someone else's.

Deana loves to hear from readers. You can find her contact information, website details and author profile page at https://www.totallybound.com